PLACE
OF
EXILE

Visit us at www.boldstrokesbooks.com

What Reviewers Say About The Author

"...her characters seem fully capable of walking away from the particulars of whodunit and engaging the reader in other aspects of their lives." – *Lambda Book Report*

"When Jennifer Fulton writes mysteries, she writes them as Rose Beecham. And since Jennifer Fulton is a very fine writer, you might expect that Rose Beecham is a fine writer too. You're right...On the way to a remarkable, and thoroughly convincing climax, Beecham creates believable characters in compelling situations, with enough humor to provide effective counterpoint to the work of detecting." – *Bay Area Reporter*

"A well-written blend of subplots and well developed characters...An intriguing mystery which introduces a competent and complex cop to the ever-growing lesbian detective genre." – *Washington Blade*

"...Rose Beecham certainly can write! *Grave Silence* is set in the remote Four Corners area of the Southwest, and Beecham's descriptions of the landscape rival Nevada Barr's. Detective Jude Devine, lesbian and ex-FBI agent, brings some secrets of her own to the Montezuma County Sheriff's Office. When the body of a teenage girl is discovered with a stake through her heart, Jude finds ties to a fundamentalist Mormon sect that practices polygamy. The story involves graphic, but not gratuitous, violence and abuse. With social consciousness, a believable plot and strong characters, *Grave Silence* is an exemplary thriller..." – Nan Cinnater, *Books To Watch Out For*

"[*Grave Silence*] is by far the most unique and intriguing murder mystery I have ever read. Why? Because of the backdrop. Sheriff's detective Jude Devine finds herself balancing two calls of duty as she investigates the murder of a teen. As the investigation deepens, the two duties begin to entwine resulting in a conclusion no reader can foresee. The entire story is set against a backdrop of Utah and religious zealots who believe in plural marriage. And, there's romance, too..." – Patricia Pair, publisher, *Family & Friends*

By the Author

ROMANCES as Jennifer Fulton

From BSB:

Dark Vista Series

Dark Dreamer
Dark Valentine

Standalones
More Than Paradise

Other:

Moon Island Series

Passion Bay
Saving Grace
The Sacred Shore
A Guarded Heart

Standalones
True Love
Greener Than Grass

CONTEMPORARY FICTION as Grace Lennox

From BSB:
Chance
Not Single Enough

MYSTERIES as Rose Beecham

From BSB:
Jude Devine Series
Grave Silence
Sleep of Reason
Place of Exile

Other:
Amanda Valentine Series
Introducing Amanda Valentine
Second Guess
Fair Play

PLACE
OF
EXILE

by

Rose Beecham

2007

PLACE OF EXILE

ISBN 10: 1-933110-98-8
ISBN 13: 978-1-933110-98-1

THIS TRADE PAPERBACK ORIGINAL IS PUBLISHED BY
BOLD STROKES BOOKS, INC.,
NEW YORK, USA

FIRST EDITION: DECEMBER, 2007

CREDITS
EDITOR: STACIA SEAMAN
PRODUCTION DESIGN: STACIA SEAMAN
COVER DESIGN BY SHERI (GRAPHICARTIST2020@HOTMAIL.COM)

Acknowledgments

I work with all the support an author could hope for, especially one who is perpetually late turning in her manuscripts. My family always steps up with love, practical help, and hot dinners. My daughter Sophie helped me this time with intelligent feedback and proofreading. My partner Fel kept me technically functional and stopped me from having a meltdown when my computer died.

Stacia Seaman copy edited with her usual precision and exhibits remarkable patience with my sometimes whimsical approach to style and syntax. Thanks to her, my flaws are not exposed to all. My publisher Radclyffe has allowed me to explore content that is not exactly typical for the LGBT mystery tradition, and for that, and her unconditional support, I thank her sincerely.

Dedication

For Kim, *lupus in fabula*

"We all carry within us our places of exile, our crimes, and our ravages. But our task is not to unleash them on the world; it is to fight them in ourselves and in others."
—Albert Camus

ACRONYMS

ADD	Aryan Defense Day(s) *(fictional)*
ASS	Aryan Sunrise Stormtroopers *(fictional)*
CIA	Central Intelligence Agency
CPA	Christian Patriots Alliance *(fictional)*
CPOC	Compartmented Planning & Operations Cell (U.S. Northern Command)
CRAP	Christian Republic of Aryan Patriots *(fictional)*
DEA	Drug Enforcement Administration
DIA	Defense Intelligence Agency
FBI	Federal Bureau of Investigation
MCSO	Montezuma County Sheriff's Office
NORTHCOM	U.S. Northern Command
NIC	National Intelligence Council
NSC	National Security Council
NSM	National Socialist Movement
P2OG	Proactive Preemptive Operations Group
PNAC	Project for the New American Century
SAC	Special Agent in Charge (FBI)
SSA	Supervisory Special Agent (FBI)

CHAPTER ONE

It's two weeks till these douchebags hit town, and we're on the front line," Sheriff Orwell Pratt said. He was visibly relieved to reach the end of his hour-long PowerPoint presentation.

Jude hauled herself up in her chair. Friday, mid-afternoon, midsummer, and they had to be crammed into an airless conference room listening to Pratt's assessment of the joint resource burden for this year's Telluride Film Festival. The Montezuma County Sheriff's Office wasn't really at the front line but they stepped up when their colleagues in adjoining counties needed extra manpower. This year, the festival coincided with the Four Corners Biker Rally, a national get-together that drew thousands of potential law-breakers. Today's briefing was a strategy session aimed at establishing communication protocols, cohesion, and calm as the twin-event "perfect storm" unfolded.

"They got those free screenings at Elks Park again?" some optimist asked.

Everyone wanted that gig in case there were foreign films with kinky sex.

"You bet," Pratt said. "They call that 'giving back to the community.'" Dourly, he added, "Needless to say, there's still not a single traffic signal anywhere in that goddamn town. Certain so-called celebrities throw their weight around, and here we are. You know what I'm saying."

Jude didn't, but from the snorts of laughter around her she concluded the traffic signal issue was another black mark against the Telluride council, a body that could pass an ordinance to impeach Bush and Cheney, yet balked at the idea of twenty-first-century traffic control. Pratt had a bug up his ass about Telluride, which he variously referred to as "that enclave of overprivileged pinkos" and "a bad joke looking for a bar mitzvah, no disrespect intended." In his opinion, the San Miguel sheriff had handed his balls in at the door to get elected in that county.

As for the staff of that emasculated colleague, Pratt liked to point out that you could hardly refer to them as a law enforcement detail. Most deputies were reserve volunteers, members of the public who wanted to swagger around wearing a badge on weekends. They spent their lives picking up dead birds as part of the avian flu precautionary campaign, real crime being scarce in Telluride. The place saw about seven violent incidents per year. The murder rate was zero, with only one significant blip on the radar.

Fifteen years earlier, the town's pristine record had been besmirched when a wealthy socialite was shot dead during a robbery at her fancy log cabin. Eva Shoen's family owned the U-Haul empire and was infamous for avarice, feuding, and shameful business practices. Eva possessed the class and kindness lacked by the clan she'd married into and seemed to have no enemies. The Shoens spent years blaming their patriarch and one another for having her hit, and the case remained unsolved. Finally a big reward brought in some tips and a drifter was convicted. Conspiracy theorists still believed his confession was phony and that another filthy rich family had gotten away with murder.

The residents of Telluride didn't appreciate the spotlight that came with the Shoen case. They saw their town an oasis of sanity in a world that had lost its way, and themselves as ordinary folk even though no ordinary person could afford to live there. The median house price in that Beverly Hills in the mountains was well over two million bucks.

It wasn't always so. Before the place began to crawl with celebrities and instant-money refugees from the dotcom boom, it was a ghost town taken over by hippies and dreamers who lived a counterculture fantasy. A few hold-outs from that wistful era still refused to sell their cottages to developers. There were rumors that they were bribed to stay put, their presence contributing to the town's carefully preserved aura of egalitarian rusticity.

The film festival crowd loved the idea that Telluride was "the real thing." Unfortunately for local law enforcement these visitors didn't just invade the town itself, which would have been a manageable proposition. No, they thought anyplace ten miles from the nearest low-fat latte was the wilderness and were in hog heaven at the prospect. On either side of the festival they set out to explore the entire Four Corners. Well-meaning flakes stumbled into the mountains in their three-hundred-dollar sandals, gaga over the wonders of nature. It was only a matter of time before they got themselves in a heap of trouble. A happy couple posing for the camera would fall down a ravine and get lost trying to walk out. Or some idiot swimming naked in a waterfall would drown himself. Or he'd do drugs and see Bigfoot. A couple of years ago a dispatcher made a tape of the wildest 911 calls from successive festivals. She sold downloads on the Internet and pulled in enough money to buy a car.

Then there were the sons and daughters of the wealthy, dabbling in filmmaking on daddy's dime and expecting the cognoscenti to be awestruck by their efforts. When their self-promotion gambits didn't pan out, they found ways to console themselves. They stole Anasazi artifacts or broke into a director's chalet so they could leave their screenplay next to his bed. Failing that, they got drunk and pushed to the head of the line so they could nab a gondola ride with Werner Herzog and his bimbo wife. When Herzog didn't talk to them, they left in a huff and assaulted a parking attendant who caught them tampering with Herzog's car. No festival was complete without some disgruntled wannabe in a holding cell, threatening, "Do you know who my father is?"

Jude couldn't believe it was that time of year again. They'd survived the sweet-corn festival, the annual Bear Dance and Pow Wow, the county fair, and the herpetologists' convention, and they would also survive a thousand bikers who were too old and successful to rape and pillage, and who poured money into local businesses. The Telluride crowd was another matter, not only lousy tippers but difficult to wrangle.

The sheriff checked his timepiece. "Devine. You're up next."

"Maybe we should take a break first, sir. It's pretty warm in here." She made a gesture to indicate that she needed to speak to him alone.

Pratt acted like he didn't notice her hand signals. "Let's just get on with it." He plunked himself down in a plastic chair.

Jude considered whispering in his ear but decided to rattle his cage instead. She strolled to the front of the room, picked up a fat red marker, and wrote two words on the whiteboard. As the silence got heavy, she read aloud, "Terrorist Threat."

Pratt gave her a *What the fuck?* stare.

Jude jotted a few words on a piece of paper and handed it to him. She'd been instructed to brief local law enforcement on what they could expect now that the FBI had confirmed the chatter they'd been hearing since last year. Originally, they'd expected the 2006 festival to be targeted but the subjects couldn't get themselves organized in time. This year, however, they'd advanced their plans beyond posturing on the Stormfront blog.

Jude had tried to give Pratt a heads up ever since she arrived in Cortez a few hours ago, but he was too busy eating lunch with Colorado's new governor, Bill Ritter. A Democrat, Ritter was reaching out to Republicans in the state's small towns, and Pratt was eager to be seen as reaching back. His sliding support since reelection had raised the scepter of the unthinkable: voters in the Four Corners might turn into wimpo liberals and elect the other guy next time.

Pratt thought global warming was the issue that could bridge the political divide. No one in the state of Colorado rejoiced over diminishing annual snowpack and water restrictions, and the Four Corners depended on the annual injection of money from ski-season visitors. No more snow would spell disaster, so Pratt was all about reducing the carbon footprint. He had just put out a declaration that the MCSO was going "green" and all lightbulbs were to be replaced by the CFL variety. With any luck the governor would inject money into local environmental initiatives and Pratt would take the credit.

Jude watched him read her brief mea culpa. He folded the note pensively and slipped it into his top pocket like he'd just received sensitive information. With the serene sang-froid of a man in the loop, he said, "Go ahead, Detective."

Pratt was the only person in the room who knew Jude hadn't left the FBI, as the official version went, but was working undercover in the Four Corners to keep tabs on domestic terrorist cells in the area. As far as everyone else was concerned, she'd left the Bureau under a cloud, swapping a prestigious career in the Crimes Against Children Unit for a slow-lane gig in Nowheresville. Speculation as to "the real story" behind her arrival in the Four Corners was still intense even after almost three years. It wasn't often that an FBI agent took the downward step of joining a sheriff's department but for some reason her masters thought this was an ingenious cover. Pratt was in on the deal and never stopped reminding her of the additional burden he carried as a consequence.

Jude swept a quick look around her audience. Senior personnel from the surrounding counties had gathered for the planning meeting. Pratt got competitive about combined operations and liked to host gatherings like this one so he could show off the impressive new MCSO headquarters and cell block.

"Let me emphasize that what I'm about to tell you has to stay in this room," Jude said, shaking up her sleepy audience once more.

"If this leaks out," Pratt interjected. "I promise you, heads will roll."

"Thank you, sir." Jude wrote on the whiteboard, "Telluride Film Festival."

"The film festival?" Virgil Tulley gasped from the back of the room. He covered his mouth like he'd just swallowed his own vomit.

Her only deputy at the Paradox substation, he was lurking near the rear exit, self-conscious of his junior rank and poised to make a quick escape. A fan of exactly the kind of movie they insisted on showing at the festival, he'd forked out almost seven hundred bucks for an all-events pass this year. He and Agatha Benham, the secretary at the substation, were supposed to be going together. They'd invited Jude but she told them she'd rather jump out of a plane. She'd brought Tulley to the briefing as a festival "expert."

When the noise level dropped, Jude said, "The FBI has confirmed a credible threat. They're sending a team to Cortez to establish a joint terrorism task force and discuss logistics. They'll hold their first briefing on Monday, next week. Meantime there's an ongoing investigation, and it's essential that the terrorists don't know they're under surveillance."

"Who are these knuckleheads?" Pratt demanded.

Jude wrote a few more words on the board. "The Aryan Sunrise Stormtroopers, also known as the ASS, are white supremacists who endorse an ideology of violence against Jews and other minorities. Three local men are involved, all with priors, and several others from out of state are thought to be co-conspirators. There may be more."

"Any names?" Pete Koertig asked.

Jude had partnered with Koertig on several investigations and also had dinner with him and his wife occasionally. They had bonded over the Corban Foley case, sharing each other's pain over the outcome of that memorable trial. Any cop hated watching a killer walk, and that particular killer had gotten under everyone's skin. Jude still had fantasies about slitting his throat.

She replied, "I'm not at liberty to identify the suspects today. We'll receive that information from the FBI."

"Harrison Hawke," a Montrose lieutenant said. "That freak with the compound in Black Dog Gulch. You can bet he's the mastermind."

Hawke was well known to Four Corners law enforcement. His organization, the Christian Republic of Aryan Patriots, hosted what he called "Aryan Defense Days." Every time one of those white power unity rallies was underway, protestors caused a traffic hazard, which pissed off the Colorado State Patrol. Troopers would then gripe to the county sheriffs and PD, who would step in to control the scene. Hawke would duly claim his freedom of speech was under assault by the forces of "Zionist Occupied Government" and his organization hadn't broken any laws.

Aryan Defense Days participants were careful to stay on the right side of the law. They were all legally licensed to own firearms and if they wanted to paint swastikas on their vehicles, that was their choice. To improve their public image they repaired the houses of old white ladies and military widows, and took time out from the shooting range to attend church on Sundays. Occasionally the local newspaper ran a feature on their good works as though they were visiting Rotarians. The words "Christian" and "Patriot" in the title of their organization seemed to induce a suspension of intelligence in reporters.

Jude needed to steer the discussion away from Hawke. She'd been nurturing a relationship of cautious trust with him for two years. Her handler thought if she couldn't recruit Hawke, she could at least seduce him into becoming an unwitting informant, "seduce" being the operative word. Hawke had been pissed when the ASS bozos broke away from the fold after trying to depose him. Already he'd let slip sensitive information, and the last thing Jude needed was to have her long-term operation blown by some overeager cops in the name of Homeland Security.

Cautiously, she said, "It's certainly possible that Hawke has relevant information, but we can't afford to sound the alert by confronting him. The FBI will determine how this is handled." To further dampen enthusiasm, she explained, "Last year the ASS broke away from Hawke's organization after attempting an internal coup. I don't think he's talking to them right now."

"So, what are we looking at here?" Pratt asked. "A car bomb?"

Jude had been of two minds about going into detail about the type of threat they were facing. It would only take one person in this room to leak the information and there could be a major panic. On the other hand, letting people have their reactions now instead of next week when they would need to be focused was probably a good move.

"The plot involves a biological agent known as ricin."

Noise erupted around her. Pratt leapt to his feet, his face the color of putty. "Ricin? Deadly-poison-no-antidote ricin?"

"Twice as deadly as cobra venom," Tulley said, abandoning the back of the room to claim a seat. "They make it out of castor beans."

A couple of female officers craned around. Jude figured she'd be talking to the backs of their heads for the next five minutes while they swooned over the man chosen as Mr. January for the next Southwestern law officers beefcake calendar.

She tried to quell the rising panic level. "Just so everyone knows, the U.S. Army has a vaccine for ricin." She didn't mention its limited effectiveness and the continuing lack of inhibitors to slow the effects of the bio-agent. "Let's not get ahead of ourselves. Biochemical agents are notoriously difficult to weaponize. Ricin dispersal has to be by aerosol, injection, or ingestion."

"Food contamination," Pete Koertig interpreted.

"That's the most likely possibility. Let's face it, this isn't the movies and these guys aren't Jason Bourne. They're not going to fire syringes at anyone, and for a credible attack they'd have to release gallons of aerosol. That's not going to happen. They'll run with the easiest method, poisoning hamburgers or something like that."

"My God, that's plain un-American." Sheriff Pratt shook his head in disappointment that a bunch of race-hate extremists might desecrate the national dish. "Does Cortez have anything to fear?"

"Sir, they're not coming after a whole town, not even Telluride. This is all about buying themselves publicity and hero status among their peers. I'm sure they expect a lot of Jewish people to attend the festival."

Sheriff Pratt looked to Tulley. "Deputy, you're the expert. Is that true?"

Tulley jumped to his feet, a response that elicited audible sighs from several areas of the room. "Sir, I'm guessing Noah Baumbach, Etgar Keret, and maybe Sacha Baron Cohen, the Borat guy." Tulley paused. "Sean Penn and Werner Herzog usually show up, but I don't think they're Jewish. I heard Huang Lu, the actress is coming. Those white power types don't like Asians either."

"All the minorities you can eat," Pratt noted sourly. "I don't suppose the organizers will step up with a list of names."

The Telluride lineup was always kept secret until opening day, a policy that burned those tasked with ensuring security for the celebrities who showed up. Jude wished she could be there to see the startled faces of the nerds who ran the festival when the FBI came calling. Their precious cultural event under siege by morons who'd never watched a movie with subtitles—oh, the horror.

She said, "I'm sure the FBI will secure their full cooperation. If not, they'll be arrested."

When the cheers and hoots died down, Tulley waved his hand. "There's a film." His speech danced up into the decibels Jude recognized as his anxious range. "*My Enemy's Enemy.* If it's on the program, the terrorists might want to target that screening."

"Why? Does it make fun of Hitler?" Jude asked.

"No, it's about Klaus Barbie." At the generally blank stares, Tulley explained, "He was a real Nazi who ended up working for the CIA. They protected him."

"Until he outlived his use-by date," Jude noted.

Barbie was routinely held up by counterintelligence boffins as an example of the moral dilemmas their community faced. Yes, he was a sadist sentenced to death for war crimes, but the "Butcher of Lyon," as he was colorfully known, wasn't the only Gestapo officer recruited by the West after World War II. Worried about the emerging threat of communism, the U.S. Counter Intelligence Corps had helped numerous high-ranking Nazis escape via their infamous rat line. These grateful former enemies became CIA assets in Latin America. Evidently this unsavory fact was what the Barbie film was about.

"Why would these skinhead creeps care if one of their heroes is starring in a movie?" Pratt asked with a puzzled frown.

Good question. "What do you know about this film?" Jude asked Tulley. "Was it made by a Jewish director or something?"

"No. Kevin Macdonald. That's the guy who did *The Last King of Scotland.*"

"Then what makes you think it could be a target?"

Jude would have expected opposition to an exposé movie about Barbie and the CIA to come from more illustrious quarters than the neo-Nazi movement. The Bush family would keep their distance for obvious reasons, but there were others who wouldn't welcome a spotlight on their roles. Lt. Governor David Dewhurst of Texas sprang to mind, but Jude had a hard time believing Dewhurst would be stupid enough to involve himself with amateurs like the ASS just to stop a movie being aired. The lieutenant governor had political ambitions and a carefully constructed public image to maintain. Besides, much bigger fish than he were responsible for the sleazy bloodbath that was Latin America under the military dictatorships of Operation Condor. The same official silence that protected them also provided cover for Dewhurst.

"I think it's a target because every Jew at the festival will go see it," Tulley said with a trace of embarrassment. He glanced at Jude as if he knew she was expecting a more Machiavellian rationale.

She almost laughed. Sometimes her job and her training made her overlook the obvious in favor of darker explanations. But very few felons were Mensa candidates. Most often their crimes and motivations were banal. The seven deadly sins pretty much covered all the bases. In this case her deputy had flagged those most often connected to hate crimes: wrath and envy.

"Good thinking, Tulley," she said. "I'll inform the FBI and they can check with the organizers to see if that film is on the program. Meantime, people, our job is to coordinate and assemble everything we know about this event. Venues. Access. Catering. Accommodations. You name it."

She glanced around the faces, reading a mix of excitement and stunned dismay. Apparently it was just sinking in that she wasn't kidding and the Four Corners really was at the epicenter of a domestic terrorism plot.

An officer new to the area suggested, "Maybe we could set up checkpoints. Pretend it's for drug prevention or something."

"Telluride PD tried that a few years ago," Sheriff Pratt said.

"Camouflaged officers along the road. Signs saying Narcotics Checkpoint and so forth. There was a lawsuit."

"Which we won," a San Miguel undersheriff pointed out. "We conducted the operation during the bluegrass festival. You should have seen what those bozos threw out their car windows. It was the littering that gave us probable cause to stop the vehicles."

Pratt shuffled his feet and looked at his wristwatch. "Problem was, you guys couldn't make anything stick. What it all boils down to is we can't make random checks. Although that might be different in this scenario. Devine, I take it the new Homeland Security regulations will apply."

"We'll know on Monday," Jude said. "In an antiterrorism operation, federal agents have extremely broad powers but state and local law enforcement still have to work within constraints. The FBI will explain everything. In the meantime, we have an intelligence-gathering operation to conduct. When the feds step in, we want to own a piece of the pie."

This sentiment, she knew, would strike a chord. If a plot to kill a bunch of celebrities was foiled, no one would want the FBI grabbing all the glory. She signaled Pratt, who rose and wrapped up the presentation, pointing out which undersheriffs would be in charge of leading teams from the various counties.

As soon as everyone filed out of the room, he dragged Jude aside. "How come I have to hear about this in a briefing?"

"Because I was only just told myself, and we have to move quickly."

"Are you sure Harrison Hawke's not in on this?"

"No, but don't worry, I'll find out."

Jude had been avoiding her increasingly ardent suitor for most of the summer, trying to cool things down. She'd broken her ankle in May, so she had a good excuse. But her ankle was back to normal now, and she could not longer avoid visiting Hawke's little corner of the Aryan nation.

CHAPTER TWO

B lack Dog Gulch wasn't a town, it was the site of a frontier camp on the banks of a creek that had dried up eons ago, in the middle of nowhere, in canyon country. Jude usually drove past it, missing the faded red arrow nailed to the stump of a long dead tree on the winding dirt road. The isolation suited its one inhabitant just fine. Harrison Hawke wasn't looking to be found except by true believers.

Recently a team from his organization had erected an impressive stone monument near the tree stump. This was adorned with a black Othala rune, a symbol especially favored by Hawke. A brass plaque above the rune was inscribed with:

IN MEMORIAM
DAVID LANE
2 NOVEMBER 1938–28 MAY 2007

We must secure the existence of our People
and a future for White children.

Below this quote, known by white supremacists as the 14 Words, were directions to Hawke's compound.

The place had expanded since the first Aryan Defense Days, with various outbuildings occupying the zone around a bunkerlike concrete dwelling. New eight-foot security fencing encompassed the compound perimeter. The razor wire along the top was a source of pride to Hawke, who cherished this echo of forgotten glory. His security fence served as a reminder of other such fences, like the ones surrounding Auschwitz and Dachau, those jewels in the crown of the Third Reich.

Hawke was not among the ranks of the Holocaust deniers, as were many in his movement. He was more of a Holocaust downsizer, quibbling over the final tally of the dead. Outright denials of the Final Solution struck him as offensive to the loyal Germans who'd taken pains to keep official records of their accomplishments. Auschwitz commandant Rudolf Höss had written his own firsthand account. Who were soft, modern-day Nazis to call him a liar?

Hawke saw no shame in the existence of concentration camps; in fact, he considered them a testament to the will of the master race. In the interests of the entire *Volk* a few individuals had been called upon to carry out distasteful tasks, and they had manfully stepped up to the plate. He teared up thinking about those race heroes.

Jude honked her horn and a member of Hawke's newly established personal security unit—named the Hakenkreuz Commando—rushed from an outbuilding to open the gates for her. With expressionless fervor, he raised his right arm in the Roman salute as she drove the MCSO Dodge Dakota into the "VIP" parking area in front of Hawke's house. She was now unofficially acknowledged as the CRAP commander's girlfriend, a fact greeted with rare emotion by her FBI handler. Arbiter viewed Hawke as the leader most likely to unite the fragmented white power movement, and the Bureau expected him to make his move soon.

So far, it had been a lousy year for American neo-Nazis. Reeling from deaths and imprisonments, they were ripe for muscular leadership. A lawsuit had bankrupted the Aryan Nations several years ago, and the movement was now punch-drunk from a fresh series of scandals. The National Vanguard was no more. Its leader was facing child pornography charges and the organization's powerful Boston unit collapsed when its head honcho was arrested for statutory rape. Another white power outfit, the National Socialist Movement, had been thrown into disarray when chairman Cliff Herrington was driven from the fold. Amazingly, he wasn't tossed out because of his notorious body odor, rages, or sexual harassment of Aryan women. He and his wife were discovered to be running a Web site called the Joy of Satan and having its mail sent to the NSM's address. Another demoralizing problem surfaced at the same time. Upon closer inspection, Herrington's wife turned out to be less than Aryan. They both had to go.

Since Satan-gate, the NSM had been controlled by Jeff Schoep, a reformed small-time criminal who beat out a rival, Bill White, for the top job. White subsequently resigned, taking his supporters with him. He showed up at white power events, sulking on the sidelines and exchanging insults with Schoep loyalists. The NSM had been on a membership drive lately. So had another notable, Billy Roper of White Revolution, a man attempting to present himself as a thinker and a face of reason within the movement. Hawke saw Roper and Schoep as his main rivals and frequently speculated on how he could obtain their fealty or, failing that, have them run out of the movement.

The Bureau had its money on a Hawke-driven unification, so Jude's femme fatale role wasn't going to end anytime soon. Her subject didn't like to be seen as a loser with women, so it suited him to have her around. Jude found him fairly easy to manage. Other than the occasional hint or lapse into innuendo after a couple of schnapps, he didn't hit on her. Hawke subscribed to the notion of white women as the bearers of racial honor, and Jude's refusal to move beyond the platonic only seemed to enhance her appeal. Instead of being depressed by her rejection, Hawke waxed on about the purity of Aryan womankind and how the desires of the individual had to be subordinated in the interests of race survival.

As Jude waited for her Wodanist suitor to emerge from his lair, she removed her sunglasses, touched up her lipstick, and fluffed her short hair. Hawke didn't seem to care that she was five foot ten and built more like a *bruder* than a cheerleader, but she made sure to behave as if there was an inner girl buried beneath the muscles, just clawing to get out.

The guard from the gate opened her door and said, "Good morning, *Fräulein*."

He looked spiffy in his Hakenkreuz Commando uniform of black shirt and pants, black boots, and emblem armband. Jude greeted him politely and stepped down from the Dakota. As he waited at stiff attention, she ran her hands slowly over her close-fitting MCSO uniform like she was overwhelmed with a girlish need to impress some hot guy. Her efforts weren't wasted on Hawke, who looked her up and down with pathetic gratification as he strode out to greet her. He had a fetish for women in uniform.

Jude extended her hand. "Good to see you, sir." In private she got to call him Harrison.

He drew her hand into the crook of his elbow so they could walk arm in arm. Baring his teeth in what, for him, was a tender smile, he said, "You could not have chosen a more auspicious day to visit, *Fräulein*."

Jude was afraid to ask.

"I'm preparing to make an announcement," he confided. "This comes at a critical moment in our struggle."

"You've changed your mind?" Jude allowed a convincing quiver of hope to infiltrate her voice.

Hawke had been vacillating over the idea of a presidential run, but since the NSM had put forward a candidate, he'd decided to wait until 2012. By then, he hoped, America would have woken up and the time would be ripe for a new order.

"No. There's another matter," he said. "I want you to be the first to know."

He ushered her into a living room that was the last word in neo-Nazi chic, the walls festooned with swastika flags, SS memorabilia, photographs, and posters. Jude unholstered her service weapon, a Glock 22C, and placed it on the modest sideboard below Hawke's favorite reproduction oil painting of Adolf Hitler. Hawke had never asked her to remove her sidearm, but her choice sent a signal. The gesture was more than just good manners, it was a sign of respect and womanly submission, and it worked. Hawke immediately regarded her with sappy indulgence.

Jude sat down in one of two matching leather club chairs opposite the fireplace. To her left a wall-mounted video surveillance monitor displayed the front entrance of the compound.

"I have some news for you, too, Harrison," she said.

He angled his shaved head attentively.

"No. Please," Jude insisted. "Your announcement first."

Hawke leaned against the stone fireplace surround, a thumb hooked in his belt. He'd been dieting and working out since his return from a vacation in Buenos Aires, a fact that intrigued Jude. He'd shown no previous concerns about being seen as a doughboy by CRAP recruits. His more streamlined physique wasn't the only change. Whatever had happened in Argentina, he suddenly had enough money to drill another well, build a small barracks and mess, put a few of Hakenkreuz Commando on his payroll for round-the-clock security, and set up a state-of-the-art Web site.

When Jude commented on these expensive advances, Hawke would only say that an old friend had done well in Miami property development and they'd made a few investments together. He claimed to have made out like a bandit on these and said he was now cashing in to fund his dream. Jude had passed the information to Arbiter, and the FBI had traced a few property sales that bore Hawke's name. Oddly, each property had been purchased via a Swiss funds transfer only a few months prior to resale. Arbiter thought cash was being laundered and wanted to know where it came from.

As Hawke's pale blue eyes devoured her, Jude fingered her shirt buttons, making sure nothing had popped. She didn't have much going on in the breast department so, on visits to the compound, she tried to maximize her questionable charms with a shirt that was a size too small.

Licking his lips appreciatively, Hawke said, "April twentieth, two thousand eight." He stroked his fingertips back and forth across his *Totenkopf* buckle as he waited for this significant date to register.

Jude glanced up at the portrait on the wall, knowing what was coming.

"Yes, the Führer's birthday." Hawke was instantly choked up and fell silent for a moment, collecting his thoughts as he always did when he was about to launch into a monologue.

"Shall I make coffee?" Jude inquired before he could wind himself up.

"Not for me." In a pensive tone, he said, "I've been waiting for the opportunity to present itself and I believe the moment has arrived." He cupped his head in his hands for a few seconds, then looked up with fiercely flashing eyes. "A leadership cadre must be established or our movement will fail. A *Kristallnacht* is called for."

"Killings?" Jude asked.

"No, the spilling of blood will be figurative. We can no longer saddle our movement with leaders who advertise their social incompetence on a daily basis. The very existence of the white race is in peril. It's time to act."

Jude nodded sympathetically. "Most people think neo-Nazis are crazy extremists and violent bullies."

"Precisely," Hawke conceded without expression. "And if we have any chance of winning the war against extinction, we must attract unawakened whites. More than ever we need a leader who can unify the white racialist movement politically and take the struggle forward."

No doubt he had the very man in mind. Prodding a sore spot, Jude said, "Isn't the political route the Knights Party strategy?"

Hawke narrowed his eyes. He thought the KKK had sold out when they reinvented themselves and adopted another version of their "invisible empire" shtick, instructing members to infiltrate both major political parties and seek influence from within.

"The awakening will come too late for their plan to pay off," Hawke said. "And a few Pioneer Little Europes in the Northwest won't save us. It's up to the radical wing of the movement to take control."

"I thought that was happening," Jude said innocently.

Hawke snorted. "We can't fund a new world order by robbing banks and stealing credit cards from old ladies." He was warming up, his brow aglow with perspiration. "I would not say this outside these four walls, but since Pierce and Butler passed to Valhalla, our movement has lost its way. What are we now but a social club for white trash and prison inmates?" Bitterly he added, "That fiasco in Kalamazoo was a new low. What was the turnout? Ten? Maybe twenty?"

Jude nodded. "What an embarrassment."

"A public face-off between factions! Bill White in his brown shirt and swastika armband behaving like a child because he wasn't invited to speak. Is that what we want the unawakened to see?"

"What are you suggesting?" Jude asked.

"The Christian Patriots Alliance. A new political organization."

"You're dissolving the CRAP?"

"No, we'll have two arms. One political, one security. I intend to implement the Führer principle."

Jude hoped she looked suitably impressed. "I thought the NSM tried that."

Hawke dismissed this idea with a faint sneer. "Those amateurs. No, I'm going to hire experts and pay for an advertising campaign."

"Won't it take a lot of money to get this off the ground?"

Smugly, he replied, "I have that taken care of."

Jude could tell he longed to let slip the name of his benefactor. With a note of disappointment, she said, "It's better that I don't know any details."

Hawke responded to her reticence with a hint. "Let's just say we have the support of a man who understands firsthand what we're dealing with." In case she didn't follow his meaning, he added, "This is a man familiar with blood and honor, the grandson of a Third Reich hero."

Wondering which SS criminal he was referring to, Jude prompted, "And you think the timing is right?"

"I do. I've handpicked my leadership cadre and I'll organize a rally in April. That's when I'll make the unification announcement." He crossed the room to stand before her. "With you at my side, we could set an inspiring example. The Aryan leader and his Valkyrie. The future of a cleansed America."

Wincing inwardly, Jude braced herself for a marriage proposal. She couldn't get a girlfriend, but the crazy men were lining up. It was time to change the conversation. Before Hawke could continue she said, "Oh, Harrison. If only we lived in a different time where none of this was necessary and all the peoples of the world could live in peace."

He patted her shoulder, and struck an avuncular note. "Your compassion is a virtue, *Fräulein*. Even though you know it's impossible, you still yearn for all races to share your noble spirit. That steadfast heart of yours longs for a safe place in which to rear your children." He stared up at the Hitler portrait once again, drawing strength. "Yours is the hope of all Aryan women and the driving inspiration of our struggle. A future for white children."

Jude touched his hand before he could continue with the speech. "I'm worried for your safety, Harrison."

Her soft tone made him flush. "Every true leader must accept the risks that come with his destiny."

"I understand, but there's something I have to tell you."

Hawke sat down next to her and seized both her hands. His palms felt clammy. "Don't be afraid to confide in me. Every word spoken is strictly between us."

As if she could hardly wait to unburden herself, Jude said, "I was at a briefing yesterday about the Telluride Film Festival. You won't believe this, but there's some kind of plot to attack the festival. The ASS is behind it."

At the mention of these CRAP traitors, Hawke released her hands and brought a fist down on his thigh. "What kind of plot?"

"It involves a chemical weapon. That's what they're saying. We're on a Homeland Security alert. I just wanted you to know because you'll be—"

"Under close scrutiny," he completed in disgust. "A suspect."

She nodded sympathetically.

"Those morons," Hawke ranted, leaping to his feet. "They're going to spoil everything. An attack on a few Jews and their commie elite friends. Very smart." He paced back and forth.

"It means I won't be able to come out here during the investigation," Jude said. "I shouldn't be here now, actually."

Hawke stopped pacing and searched her face intently, no doubt seeking signs of betrayal. Jude held his gaze steadily, thinking, *Arbiter, you owe me a pay raise.*

Finally, with a quick flash of relief, Hawke said, "Your loyalty at this critical time means more than I can say."

Jude fidgeted like she was stressed out. "What are you going to do?"

"I'll tell you what I'm not going to do," he said coldly. "I'm not going to allow a few retards to destroy this movement. We are not going to play into ZOG hands this time." He stomped over to the barred window and stared broodingly toward the desert. "Timothy McVeigh set the racialist agenda back by fifty years. It can't happen again."

"Do you think this could be some kind of setup?"

Hawke's gleaming head spun her way. "What are you saying? Do you know something?"

"I used to work for the Bureau, remember? I know how they do business. Maybe they have a mole in the ASS. Someone they've turned. Think about it. How did they get their information?"

Hawke stared into space, his Adam's apple bobbing in his thick neck. Purple blotches appeared on his angry red face. "I see your point. The feds instigate the plot, then look like heroes for stopping it. No one gets hurt, but we're publicly disgraced and half our movement is arrested."

"They'll blame you," Jude said. "You'll be guilty by association." She played the card Arbiter had insisted upon. "This is all about you. Don't you see? The government doesn't want you to lead. They know you're a threat."

Hawke's face went rigid with shock before settling into the fatalistic frown of a man who realized he had a choice to make in his own dramatic destiny. He stalked to Jude's side and bent to kiss her cheek. "Rest easy, *mein Schatz*. I'll take care of this."

Ushering her from her seat, he led her to the sideboard to collect her weapon. As they walked to the Dakota, Jude said, "If I can, I'll update you on the briefing."

"Take no risks on my behalf." He opened the door for her. "One day, God willing, I will be in a position to show you the full extent of my gratitude."

Not a prospect Jude wanted to dwell on. She glanced at the underling standing a few feet away, as if his presence was a factor in her reserve. Hawke clutched her hand to his chest in a rare public display of devotion.

"Be careful," she told him. "Call me if there's anything else I can do."

Hawke returned her hand and stepped back. To the young man in uniform he said, "Take note, *Oberschütze*. This is how a proud Aryan woman conducts herself."

"Yes, *Herr Oberst*."

Jude put on her sunglasses, thankful to screen her gaze. As she waved good-bye, both men saluted. She waited until she was ten miles from the compound before she moved to the shoulder of the road and called Arbiter. "He went for it," she said. "What now?"

"We find out how smart he is."

"Don't hold your breath."

"I think you underestimate him."

Scary thought. "We'll see. Are you going to bring him in?"

"Hell, no. We need him."

"I'm never going to turn him into a cooperating subject," Jude warned. "He's hardcore."

"That's okay, we have other assets. Hawke is going to plug us into a laundering op out of Argentina. Al Qaeda uses the same network."

"I'm not making any headway in that department," Jude said.

Hawke was fond of mouthing off about the future of the white race, but he knew how to shut up when it came to his support network.

"On the contrary," Arbiter said with silky satisfaction. "He now trusts you completely. It's only a matter of time before he starts talking."

"This isn't about Telluride, is it?" Jude supposed she should have guessed her masters had a larger agenda.

"Telluride's a win for us no matter what happens," Arbiter said. "If the place goes up in smoke, we can name our terms for Patriot Three. If it doesn't, we come out smelling of roses for arresting a bunch of terrorists."

"I have a feeling Hawke is going to take the law into his own hands."

"Still a win," Arbiter said. "Because if he does, you'll be the loyal girlfriend who helps him get away with it."

A debt of gratitude Hawke would want to repay *very* personally. Jude cringed. "If that's how it ends up shaking down, I want your orders in writing. On the record."

"We'll cross that bridge when we come to it."

"Just so you know, I won't be hung out to dry. If I go down, it'll be noisy."

Arbiter chuckled softly. "Relax. You're in good shape."

"And I plan to stay that way."

Jude ended the call and deleted the record on her disposable cell phone. She didn't want to be part of a screwup. If this operation went south, she would be given a security transfer to another location, far from the Four Corners. The thought troubled her. She wasn't ready to leave.

"Miss Harwood is having a soirée next Saturday," Tulley said as soon as Jude's shadow fell across his desk. "We're invited."

As he'd expected, his boss received the news with a pained expression. She was unmoved by independent cinema unless Bruce Willis was in it, and she thought Elspeth Harwood was overhyped.

"That thing is about to fly off its bracket," she said like she had more important things to worry about than the social event of the year.

She took off her sunglasses and stared up at the ceiling fan. "I suppose if I don't fix it myself one of us is going to get decapitated. Remind me—why do I have a big, strong twenty-seven-year-old deputy sitting around this office? Other than feeding pig ears to his dog, of course."

Tulley said, "I put in a maintenance call to Montrose. They said it's on the fall schedule."

They also said the Paradox Valley substation was low priority being as it was a fully renovated building, unlike some of theirs that were about to fall down on the heads of female deputies. Was that what Tulley wanted? No sir, he told the supervisor.

The stationhouse used to be a school until the Montezuma and Montrose sheriffs' joint initiative. Now it consisted of an office, an interview room, a couple of holding cells, and a utility room out back. Jude kept her Bowflex in one of the cells since her house was too small for serious gym equipment. Tulley was thankful about this because having the Bowflex in plain sight gave him the motivation to improve himself. He worked out every day and could press two hundred pounds, a weight most MCSO deputies would never lift unless they had to rescue their wives from a burning building.

Tulley smoothed his shirtsleeves over his biceps and wondered if he should buy a bigger size uniform now that his was getting really tight. His best buddy, Bobby Lee Parker, said ladies like to see shirt buttons popping across a man's chest instead of his gut. Tulley could accept that, but he wasn't sure if he looked professional with his shirt all stretched.

"No one ever filled out a T-shirt like Marlon Brando," Miss Benham said from the counter in their tiny kitchen. She must have noticed him feeling his muscles. "Women fainted in *Streetcar Named Desire*, did you know that?"

"Yes, ma'am. But ladies were shy back in the old days. Not any more." To make his point, he said, "They weren't fainting in *300*, they were *panting*."

"*300* indeed," Miss Benham sniped. "They should have gotten their historical facts in order before they made a film about Sparta."

"It ain't supposed to be a documentary." Tulley was surprised that Miss Benham didn't appreciate the film for its artistic visual style even if she thought the men were too naked.

"It's pro-war propaganda," she said with a delicate sniff.

"It's a legend," Tulley argued.

"You've been duped."

"You sound like a schoolteacher." That always got her. Miss Benham had taught right here in this room for about fifty years before she retired.

"I liked that movie," Jude said. "I got it on DVD. Big screen would have been better."

"Oh, man, it was awesome at the Regal," Tulley told her. "Me and Bobby Lee went three times."

"Why doesn't that surprise me?" Jude zapped hairs off her seat with a sticky tape roller. "Has that hound been sitting on my chair again?"

Tulley patted his thigh and Smoke'm got up from his bed and plodded across the office for a smooch. "It's mostly from his ears. He was laying his head there."

"I don't care where it's from. I'd appreciate not having dog hair all over my butt every time I walk out of here."

"Coffee, Detective?" Miss Benham already had the mug in her hand. She placed it in front of Jude along with the invite they'd received that morning.

Miss Benham said she was going to keep the card for a souvenir since Dr. Westmoreland had handed it to *her*. Tulley couldn't see as that was fair. The envelope was addressed to him, too. It was handmade. That was one of Miss Harwood's hobbies. A gifted actress like her, always in the public eye and working on two movies at once, longed for time out. Miss Harwood relaxed by squishing rags and paper into a pulp and making her own cards and envelopes. Only special people received them. Everyone else got whatever the publicist sent out. That's what it said in the latest *Vanity Fair* magazine. Bobby Lee brought in his copies for Tulley when he was done reading them. He subscribed.

Now that Miss Harwood had moved here from England, she was in all the magazines. The fact that she'd just married Dr. Westmoreland from the ME's office in Grand Junction was big news. No one in the Four Corners would have guessed they'd have a famous lesbian couple living here, of all places. Some people around the area had come out of the closet to show their support. Tulley thought they'd probably regret their noble impulses. It was all very well to flaunt your personal preferences when you were rich and famous. Regular people had to think about their paycheck.

Miss Benham said Dr. Westmoreland was a self-defining woman and Miss Harwood was a creative artist from London and therefore had Bohemian sensibilities and fluid taste in partners. She wouldn't expect the Philistines in the Four Corners to understand such things. But she sure had that wrong. No one Tulley knew was offended by idea of Miss Harwood and Dr. Westmoreland together. Most guys at the MCSO said it was hot. Live and let live.

Tulley glanced over at Jude. She had a strange look on her face as she read the invite, and she'd had her hair cut again. Miss Benham thought it made her look too stern, but she about lived at the Le Paradox hair shop. Bobby Lee said with unique looks like hers, fancy hairdos and lipstick were pointless. Miss Benham said Bobby Lee was biased because he was her boyfriend. She thought the people who cared about Jude should encourage her to make more of her attributes. Tulley could see her point. It was one thing for a guy to be tall, dark, and handsome, but people wondered about a woman who looked like that. Things being the way they were, however, Miss Benham was dreaming if she thought Jude would ever wear a dress.

"I guess you two can hardly wait to rub shoulders with the Hollywood crowd." Jude dropped the invite on a stack of files like it smelled bad.

Miss Benham snatched it up. "We're one of the select few to receive this invitation, I'll have you know."

"I wish that did it for me," Jude said.

"Philip Seymour Hoffman will be there," Tulley said. "And they're going to do a computer uplink to Lars von Trier."

Miss Benham sighed. "All those phobias of his. If he could only bring himself to get on an airplane and leave Denmark, he could come out here and find out what this country is really like. Generalizations are the province of the uninformed."

"Von Trier's the director of *Dogville*," Tulley informed Jude. He didn't think much of the USA Trilogy so far, either. He wasn't surprised when he found out von Trier was brought up by nudist, communist parents.

"I don't watch animal movies," Jude said.

Tulley caught Miss Benham's eye and they both kept quiet. He fed Smoke'm some Zuke's PowerBones, a treat Bobby Lee's mom had told him about. She was a pothead, but she sure loved her dogs and she knew plenty about canine health. She was the one who told him that there was way too much stuff from China in dog food. She said they still ate dogs over there so why would they care if our pets got sick? That was before the recalls. Ever since then Tulley had been shipping Smoke'm's food from a natural pet store run by hippies in Boulder.

"I'm going to Montrose to buy a new dress for the soirée," Miss Benham said. "Something bright. Why should women of my age have to settle for mauve?"

"You don't look a day over sixty," Jude said.

Tulley had seen old photos of Miss Benham when she ran the schoolhouse. She looked exactly the same now as she did back then in the dark ages. He wasn't sure how to turn that observation into a compliment, so he kept quiet.

The phone rang and Jude picked up. After a short silence, she asked, "When did she leave?"

Tulley recognized the tone. Normally Jude's voice was low and husky. He and Miss Benham argued over who she sounded like most, Kathleen Turner or Barbara Stanwyck. When something came up, her tone flattened out and she seemed to bite the ends off her words. From the few things she said, he could tell there was a problem, so he got to his feet and combed his hair in the wall mirror just in case they'd been called out. He could do with a haircut, he thought, moving his thick black waves first in one direction, then the other. Sometimes he went to Le Paradox, but only if that weirdo friend of the hairdresser's wasn't around.

He wasn't sure what he'd done wrong, but Sandy Lane had taken a dislike to him. She called him "Pretty Boy," which, despite Floyd Mayweather's accomplishments in the boxing ring, was not a nickname most guys would appreciate. Tulley thought she was deliberately egging him on, but he wasn't about to pick a fight with her. If there was one thing his ma taught him, it was to never lay a hand on a woman.

Jude asked a couple more questions, then said, "Okay, I'll be over in ten minutes."

Miss Benham poured coffee in a paper cup to go. As she squeezed the lid down over the rim, she asked, "Shall I accept Miss Harwood's invitation for all three of us? We're invited to bring a guest each, as well."

"Count me out," Jude said. "Tell her I have a headache."

"It's a week away. You can't predict headaches in advance."

"Trust me, in this case I can guarantee it."

"It's not because of their sexual orientation, is it?" Miss Benham asked. "No one worries about that type of thing anymore. Besides, creative people have always explored boundaries and defied social mores."

Jude rolled her eyes. "Agatha, I don't give a rat's ass about anyone's sexuality. Bobby Lee will drive you. He can go in my place."

Miss Benham stared at Tulley like he knew why their boss got irrational every time Miss Harwood's name was mentioned. He said, "Dr. Westmoreland asked for us to tell you she hopes you'll come."

"Yeah, I'll bet she does." Jude swapped her uniform shirt for plain clothes.

Tulley checked out her muscles. His were bigger these days. In comparison to both of them, Bobby Lee look like a weakling with his Pilates for men.

"Will you be needing me and Smoke'm?" he asked.

"No, that was Debbie at Le Paradox," Jude said. "Some kind of security issue. I'll go take down the details and check the locks. That'll keep her happy."

"Your hair's short enough," Miss Benham said.

Jude smiled. It wasn't much of a smile, but the sun lines crinkled around her eyes. Over time, Tulley had gotten used to her serious look, but when they first started working together he always thought she was mad at him. Jude didn't put on a happy face like most people. Folks that didn't know her wouldn't see the little changes that gave her thoughts away, but Tulley had learned to recognize them. Her mouth was straight and hard-looking, and when she pressed her lips together in anger her chin tightened slightly. When she thought something was funny, the small hollows at each corner of her mouth deepened a fraction.

Tulley had a theory that most people didn't notice Jude's mouth because they were too busy staring at her eyes, which were flat-out beautiful. He wished he could stare right into them for as long as he wanted, but he only got to do that with Smoke'm. All the same, he took advantage when she didn't realize she was being watched. It wasn't just their mossy granite color that was unusual. She had a mess of eyelashes most females would flutter all the time, but that wasn't her style. Instead she watched everything with a sleepy gaze that gave no clue as to her thoughts. Bobby Lee said she had bedroom eyes. Tulley had never understood that expression until he met Jude.

After she left the stationhouse, he said, "What's with her and Miss Harwood?"

"It's that dark side of hers," Agatha said. They often talked about Jude's silences and her tendency to go off into the mountains alone. "I suppose she has things on her mind."

Tulley considered telling Miss Benham about the terrorists, but Jude said there was no reason to worry a woman of seventy-two with frightening information. Miss Benham was looking forward to the Telluride film festival and Jude was damned if a few cretins planning a bio-attack would spoil it for her.

"Deputy, that dog bed is filthy." Miss Benham frowned at him across her glasses. "Take it outside and shake it right now before it gives me hives."

Tulley said, "Yes, ma'am."

He never argued about doing the chores. His ma had taught him better than that. He picked up the denim-covered beanbag and whistled to Smoke'm. Once they got out into the parking lot, he shook the bed into some bushes and gazed up at the huge Marlboro Man sitting on his horse, overlooking the station. That, Tulley thought, was a real man. Tough guys like him were the bedrock the West was built on. While Smoke'm lifted his leg at the base of the billboard, Tulley struck a pose like that of the bronzed cowboy. He couldn't help wondering what the Marlboro Man would say to someone like Crystal Sherman.

Every time he saw that female, Tulley got embarrassed. She always pretended to flirt with him, saying she wanted to watch when they took his picture for the fund-raising calendar and such. Tulley wished she'd quit. Her husband was a buddy of his. Deputy Gavin Sherman had a seven-thousand-dollar Belgian Malinois detection dog from Adlerhorst International. That was one super-smart animal. He'd never track a felon like Smoke'm and he wasn't a cadaver dog, but he could get around an agility ring like he was on banned substances.

Tulley was helping Gavin train him for the canine world games in Scottsdale in a couple of months' time, so he stayed at their house when he was in Cortez. He wasn't sure if that was such a good idea. Crystal had a habit of walking around in little tiny shorts when they were working the dogs. She was always bending down to pick up throwtoys and leaning seductively against the ramps and weave poles. The last time Tulley stayed overnight she walked in on him when he was taking a shower. He didn't think it was an accident.

Taking another look up at the billboard, he tried to guess what the Marlboro Man would say if Crystal Sherman ran her hand over his butt while he was flipping burgers on the grill. The ideal brush-off came to mind and Tulley rehearsed the words in a convincing cowboy drawl.

"Darlin', while I'm flattered, I think it's time you ran along back to your *husband*."

CHAPTER THREE

The midsummer sun burned a hole in the afternoon sky, its molten glare too much even for Pippa Calloway's high-tech sunglasses. Squinting, she rested her head on the steering wheel and contemplated her situation. She was parked at the side of the road in the middle of nowhere, her cell phone was almost out of juice, and she was low on water. This was truly the road trip from hell.

A deep voice over the windshield repeated, "Recalculating."

"Hal," the voice of her Garmin GPS unit, liked to point out the error of her ways. Pippa extracted a fresh bottle of water from her cooler, took a few gulps, and then splashed some on her face. All she could think about was sleep. She'd left Connecticut five days earlier for her two-thousand-mile odyssey to the Southwest. Her Mazda CX7 looked like it belonged to a homeless person, with personal possessions piled to the roof. Pippa had crammed five years of her life into the car, forcing herself to throw away everything she hadn't worn or looked at for a long time.

She pictured Uncle Fabian's smooth, tanned face as she lugged all this crap into his spare room. He always rolled his eyes over her pack-rat habits, but he never made her feel unwelcome. Pippa had an open invitation to come to him anytime, for any reason, and stay as long as she liked. Usually, when family life got unbearable, she fled to Maulle Mansion, his home in the Garden District of New Orleans. This time, however, she wanted to put several thousand miles between herself and her parents.

She'd never been to the log cabin in the San Juan Mountains and had the impression that her uncle preferred to have the place to himself. Still, she had a front door key, one of the four he'd given her to his various homes. Earlier in the month Uncle Fabian had suggested she fly to London to chill out in his pied à terre near St. James Park. But her parents thought nothing of "hopping across the pond," as her mother put it, to shop and go to the theatre. If Pippa wanted to avoid them, she would have to hole up some place her mother wouldn't be caught dead in. Looking around, she knew she'd found that exact place.

As she left Farmington, she turned off the GPS and slid a couple of old Rolling Stones CDs into her player. The route was depressing, lined with a succession of pawn shops, junked cars, decrepit mobile homes, scrawny dogs, and scenery that was nothing like a western movie. She had expected red canyons, tall cactus plants, and cowboys on horseback. Such vistas were the norm somewhere around here, if Uncle Fabian's e-mails and photos were any indication. Meantime she was driving toward an ochre-toned netherworld beneath a vast blue sky, a place where time and human foibles made only a transient impression on nature.

To her left loomed Shiprock, a dark bluish gray monolith that seemed to float above the desert plain. According to a brochure she'd picked up at a trading post en route. The Navajo had named the landmark *Tse'Bit'Ai*, or Rock with Wings. Pippa pulled over and found her camera. As she took photos, she thought she could almost see the wings of a celestial being struggling to break free of the volcanic stone. The illusion sent a small thrill of pleasure through her body and she squeezed her hands closed, imagining the feel of clay between her fingers. It had been months since she modeled or sculpted. She could hardly wait to get started again.

Wiping perspiration from her forehead, she got back in the SUV and set off once more. If she hadn't driven through Kansas before detouring through New Mexico, she might have mistaken the benighted vista around her for the worst hellhole in the galaxy. But having endured hour after hour of highway hypnosis in the flat monotony of the Sunflower State, she had a whole new perspective on the meaning of doom. The distance markers never seemed to change, and she'd even started to suspect Hal of some kind of robotic revenge: force the know-nothing human to drive in a daze, seeing nothing but white lines, until she drifts into the path of an approaching semi.

A shattering horn evicted Pippa from her fugue state and she swung her gaze from a saw-toothed zigzag of sunburned rock to a sign that announced "Entering the Navajo Indian Reservation." A few cars parked along the highway offered kneel-down bread from their open trunks. Pippa wasn't hungry but the poverty around her made her sad, and she wanted to buy something from the people who lived in this miserable place.

She stopped under the shade of a twisted tree and requested some of the delicious-smelling bread. As the Navajo woman wrapped the filled corn husks, Pippa asked, "Do I just stay on this highway to get to Cortez?"

The woman turned her head to the right and seemed to point with puckered lips, her hands still busy.

Not sure if she'd been given directions or the brush-off, Pippa said, "Thank you," and overpaid for the bread.

"Highway 491," the woman said. "*Hágoónee'*."

Pippa repeated the Navajo farewell. Her version sounded weirdly mechanical and unmelodic. She took some lip balm from her top pocket and applied it as she returned to the CX7. The afternoon heat was intense, 104 degrees outside, according to the temperature reading on her radio display. She was ready for her trip to be over, but it would take another two hours to reach her destination.

She drove until a sign directed her to H-491, a lonely two-lane road through a cratered landscape. A procession of power pylons followed the highway, providing an incongruous but welcome reminder that civilization lay somewhere beyond this desolation. Strange square rimrocks rose ahead, and far beyond them a mountain range undulated in the haze like a violet mirage. She passed broken bottles, torn tires, and occasional wreaths at the side of the road until finally she cracked up over a shabby wood sign that proclaimed "Welcome to Colorful Colorado."

She could see why this dismal stretch of road, once Highway 666, was known as the Devil's Highway. A waitress on the New Mexico side of the state line had told her it had been renamed to ward off a satanic curse. When she heard this superstition, Pippa thought the girl was kidding. Now, as an odd waywardness entered her steering, she was not so sure. A few hundred yards past a sign that read "Toad Porter's Haysales," Pippa pulled over onto the gravel shoulder and got out of the SUV. A quick look at her back tires confirmed her worst fear. She was stranded in the desert with a flat tire.

She stared at the hay sales sign in puzzlement. There was no evidence of hay, or fields it could grow in, or a store that might be operated by a man called Toad Porter. The only other vehicle on the road was a truck with tinted windows, slowing down as it approached. Pippa didn't know if that was a good thing or a bad thing. She tried to look like she had everything under control as the vehicle stopped and a tall man with straight silver-white hair to his shoulders got out.

He approached the SUV in a casual gait. At his heel loped a gray dog with a heavy mane and a hind leg missing. The man wore jeans and a dark red shirt with a silver bolo tie engraved with a bird. His broad-brimmed black felt hat had a turquoise-studded leather braid around the crown. A cream and brown striped feather hung from a leather thong at the side of his face.

"Flat tire?" he asked.

"Yes." Pippa waited for an offer of help.

The stranger looked past her into the back of her car, then returned his quiet-eyed stare to her face. His expression was unchanging. "Got a spare?"

Pippa hesitated. How many times had her father told her what to do in the event of a breakdown? She was supposed to call AAA roadside service and wait for them to arrive. Who knew how long that would take? She would probably be a skeleton picked clean by buzzards when they finally showed up.

"Yes, it's in the back."

"My name is Eddie House."

The man seemed to expect her to trust him. Irrationally, she did. She stretched her hand out into the golden glow of the late afternoon sun and shook his briefly. "I'm Phillipa Calloway. I'll get my stuff out so we can reach the spare."

As she opened the rear hatch, a second person emerged from Eddie House's truck, a gangly fair-haired youth in cargo pants and a T-shirt. The three-legged dog nuzzled him.

"My boy, Zach," Eddie said. "This lady is Ms. Calloway. We need to change her tire."

"Want me to fetch the tools, sir?" Zach patted the animal's pale lupine mane and smiled tentatively at Pippa.

Eddie gave the young man a nod and helped unload boxes from the back of the Mazda.

"I can't believe I got a flat." Pippa sighed. "I've been driving for five days and I'm so close now, it's insane."

Eddie lifted the floor panel to extract the spare. He didn't ask where she was headed.

Feeling the need to let this stranger know that she wasn't just a lost tourist no one cared about, she said, "I'm on my way to the mountains. I have family past Dolores." She fished her cell phone from the side pocket of her jeans as Eddie wheeled the spare alongside the SUV. "I should let them know where I am."

She took a few steps away, avoiding broken glass and discarded soda cans. She'd called Uncle Fabian earlier in the day to warn him about her imminent arrival, and he'd told her to drive carefully once she reached the mountain roads. He sounded really happy that she was coming. She waited for him to pick up but the phone cut over to voicemail. He was probably out buying her favorite foods. He always did that just before she arrived. There didn't seem much point leaving a message, but she wanted Eddie to see her talking to someone. Just a simple precaution.

Cheerfully, she said, "I'm just a few miles south of Cortez on the Devil's Highway and a man called Eddie House is helping me with the tire. I guess I'll reach your place in about an hour."

Zach returned with a jack and a steel toolbox and the two men set about swapping the wheels. For family members they bore no resemblance.

Pippa said a few farewell pleasantries to the imaginary person at the other end of the phone. "My uncle offered to drive out here," she informed her rescuers. "But I said everything was fine."

Zach grinned at her. "We'll have you all set in no time."

"What's your dog's name?" Pippa asked, disconcerted by the pet's intense tawny-eyed stare.

"He's a wolf."

Pippa froze the hand she was about to extend. Laughing nervously, she said, "Well, that explains the big teeth."

"He won't harm you." Eddie made a hand signal and mumbled something guttural in another language. The wolf crouched to rest on its belly. "His name is Hinhan Okuwa. I told him you're a friend."

Pippa decided Eddie was a Native American and his son must be some kind of albino. She asked, "Do you folks live on the reservation?"

Eddie didn't answer for so long that she thought she must have offended him. Was it wrong to ask?

Zach said, "Our house is a ways out of Towaoc going toward Cortez."

Not exactly an answer, but Pippa nodded as if everything was now perfectly clear. Feeling the need to explain herself, she said, "It's just that I've been driving through the Navajo Nation. I wasn't sure if I'm still on tribal land."

"This is the Ute Nation," Eddie said.

Zach explained, "The Weeminuche live here, in the Four Corners, and the White Mesa people have their lands in Utah. There's about two thousand Ute left."

Pippa gazed around at the barren plateau extending east to west. What would two thousand people do on land like this? She couldn't see many signs of habitation, only litter and abandoned cars. "Where does everyone live?"

The men got to their feet and Eddie lowered the jack. As they gathered their tools, he said, "There was no water on the reservation for a hundred years, then we made a deal with the government for water, so the people can return."

With a note of pride, Zach said, "Most everyone can get a job. There's the casino, and the ranch project, and the construction company. Dad makes pottery. He's famous."

"You're an artist?" Pippa smiled. Uncle Fabian had a huge collection of Native American pottery. He displayed stunning examples in each of his homes. "I'm familiar with some of the Southwestern styles. Santa Clara. Acoma. San Ildefonso. My uncle is a collector. Perhaps you've met him. Fabian Maulle."

Eddie's gaze was suddenly more personal. "Yes, I know him." He glanced down at her hands. "Are you the sculptor?"

"He told you about me?"

"He showed me one of your heads." Eddie peered deeper into the vehicle, his face concerned.

"Don't worry, I didn't try to move any of my works. If I decide to stay, I'll have them shipped out here."

"You're coming to live in the Four Corners?" Zach sounded astonished.

"Possibly. It depends." Pippa started lifting her stuff back into the SUV.

Eddie helped her, then handed her a card. "Come to the pottery factory. I'll show you my work."

"I'd like that." Pippa smiled. "Thank you for your help. It was very nice of you."

Eddie and Zach farewelled her solemnly.

Zach advised, "It's best you don't drive out here at night in the future, ma'am. We get a lot of accidents on the triple six."

"Drunk drivers." Eddie's voice was very flat. "It's a problem."

"I'll keep that in mind." Pippa got back in the CX7 and lowered her window, allowing a rush of warm air to invade the SUV. She started the motor and turned the a/c up high.

Eddie and Zach waited until she was on the road before getting in their truck. She gave them a wave and turned on the GPS.

With gloomy disapproval, Hal said, "Recalculating."

"Knock yourself out," Pippa told him.

Staring at a bizarre chimney-shaped rock formation ahead of her, she hit the random setting on her CD player and cranked up the volume. As she drove toward the future, she sang along to one of those maddening White Stripes tunes that would lodge in her brain until something genuinely compelling drove it out.

Lonewolf watched a group of black helicopters buzz overhead as she mouthed the lyrics to yet another moonbat anti-war song. As the final off-key notes faded, she offered her "War Profiteers" placard to a protester standing in the shadow of the ten-foot-tall Dick Cheney effigy. He looked about twenty. Sierra Club ballcap on back to front, souvenir T-shirt from a Washington peace march, shoulder bag weighed down with peacenik buttons.

He thanked her for the placard and offered her a bottle of Gatorade in exchange, saying, "If I drink any more I'll have to go pee again."

"Yeah, me, too," she said, declining the drink. They joined the chant of "Down with the dictator."

Around her, so many people were recording the event on cell phone cameras and videocams that it was hard to identify the professionals. But Lone had no doubt that the Secret Service and the FBI had plants standing out in the sun in disguise, pretending to care that their country was becoming a fascist dictatorship right under their noses. She'd been surprised by the turnout for the peace rally. Over two hundred. Quite a showing for Jackson Hole, Wyoming, the summer golf retreat of the man she intended to neutralize.

She'd arrived two days earlier and had spent some time getting the lay of the land and experimenting with different looks. After several dry runs she found she attracted the least attention dressed as a man in baggy khaki shorts and a tee. The red Nike ballcap she'd chosen for the rally was emblazoned with "OU" and "Sooners," identifying her as a misguided Oklahoman to the hirelings who would later analyze event footage.

She'd dyed her short, nondescript mouse hair dark brown and tinted her eyebrows a few shades darker. The color was temporary and she planned to get rid of it before she drove back to the Four Corners. She kept her Oakley photochromic sunglasses on at all times. Anyone in a security detail paid close attention to eyes in a crowd. No one would notice anything special about hers even if the glasses came off. Contact lenses had dulled her distinctive bright blue to a mundane shade of gray.

Lone had distorted her muscular build with fake flab around the middle, but she couldn't do much about her height. She had lifts in her hiking boots and walked tall, trying to give the impression of five ten instead of five eight. She wore an iPod and made a point of tapping her feet and looking lost in her music, so she didn't seem as focused as some of the rally-goers. That was another thing agents watched for—the stillness of the predator, an unconscious byproduct of intense concentration. To blend in, she needed to move, but not with any obvious sense of direction. As she drifted toward the gates of the poncy Teton Pines Resort and Country Club, she kept her head down and her iPod in her hand, as if her playlist was more interesting than the events unfolding around her.

"Hey, is that the Nano?" A guy with designer stubble and artfully tousled brown hair sidled up to her. Beneath the baggy pants and T-shirt, he was built. The backpack slung across his shoulder looked new. So did his sneakers.

"Yeah, it's fucking awesome," Lone replied in the deepest version of her unfeminine voice. "Hey, pal, have you seen a blond chick in a pink top?"

The guy gazed around, bringing his backpack into view. The peace sign in the center was a recent addition and the patches were extremely clean. He pointed to a young female waving a sign. "Over there?"

"No, that's not her. Damn."

"Girlfriend?"

"Fuck, no." When the guy looked confused, she said, "Get with the program, man. Look around. It's Babe Central and we're in the minority. Know what that means?"

Her companion acted cool. "Oh, yeah, you gotta love the peace movement."

Lone angled her head a little. "Check it out. Yellow placard. 'Bring My Brother Home.' Don't let her see you looking."

As her companion took a moment to ogle the braless female, Lone checked out his ankles for a concealed weapon. One hem lifted slightly, telling her all she needed to know. Anyone who had worked in covert ops developed certain instincts. Most often, she had no idea how she made someone. Her mind seemed to process the subtle clues unconsciously, and by the time she carried out a closer inspection she was simply working through a checklist, making sure she wasn't mistaken. For this operation, agents were fair game, innocent civilians were not. She wondered which branch of Big Brother this faux peacenik took his orders from.

"Do you think the Democrats will impeach?" he asked in an unsubtle attempt to place her on the threat assessment spectrum. Liberal tree-hugger, crazy commie, or neurotic screwball with a martyrdom complex.

Lone hoped she would fall into that other category: horny loser. She wondered why she'd been tagged for closer inspection and decided she was just a statistic, one of the twenty percent of this crowd identified as a male between eighteen and forty-five. No one looked Middle Eastern enough to have earned instant arrest.

"Impeach?" She let a disgusted sneer show. "No way. Those pussies aren't gonna strap on balls anytime soon."

"I guess." Her new best friend glanced around. "Do you know which house is the VP's?"

"Nope, but if you find it let me know. That's one doorstep begging for a steaming pile of dog turd." Snorting with laughter, she continued, "Hey, Cheney steps out for another day at the golf course and 'Fuck—what's this on my shoes? Call the feds. Shoot some old guy in the face. It's a fucking terrorist attack!'"

Her comedy skit raised a phony laugh from her companion and he glanced past her, no doubt lining up his next target. Lone could tell she'd been dismissed as a dork who should have auditioned for *American Pie*. All those years in high school drama had paid off.

The protestors wheeled the effigy closer to the stone-pillared gates of the tony country club and tied a rope around its neck. Lone stared up at the papier-mâché face of evil. Here in the midst of a beautiful, natural wilderness lurked the draft dodger who had cynically sent thousands of servicemen and women to their deaths. He knew all along that Iraq would be a quagmire. That's what he told ABC news in 1991, explaining why we didn't occupy Iraq in the first Gulf War. He repeated the same opinion over the years until he became VP of the Bushdom, then suddenly his rhetoric changed.

Lone knew why, and it wasn't because Iraq was any different. The men of the evil alliance knew the American public had a short memory. They figured, after 9/11, they could sell anything with enough patriotic spin—invading counties, sidelining army generals who disagreed with them, torturing prisoners, suspending habeas corpus. Of course the decision to invade Iraq had been made long before the Twin Towers came down. Anyone who bothered to inform themselves could ascertain that fact. Not that the so-called "news" media would ever join the dots and ask tough questions. Those lackeys knew the truth, but they would never print it. They were in the propaganda business.

The simple fact was, war profiteers didn't get to walk away with billions during peacetime. Lone's family was dead because bloated fat cats didn't have enough money. They needed to play golf on immaculate greens beneath majestic mountains while soldiers on extended tours of duty swallowed dust and sand with their jerky. Cheney "had other priorities" when his country was at war with Vietnam and had obtained five deferments. Nothing had changed. He was still out to lunch while heroes were paying for his comfort with their lives. He was eating lamb chops when Private First Class Brandon Ewart was being dragged out of a poorly armored Humvee by insurgents before they cut his throat.

Lone thought about her partner's suicide note. Madeline wrote: *What did my son die for?* The answer she and every mother deserved was that her child had given his life for a noble cause. That he was defending his country, and there was no higher calling for a patriotic American. Brandon had died a Marine, and proud, and no one could take that away from him. But the truth was unspeakably banal. Brandon had died because war was good business and a few corrupt men were drunk on power.

Lone hadn't always known what she knew now. She used to laugh at conspiracy theorists. She thought Iraq naysayers were deluded fools who refused to accept post-9/11 reality, misguided liberals who didn't understand what was in their own best interests. People like her were trained to protect American interests even when they received no thanks for doing so. They were the active patriots, the bulwark between a free society and the external forces of hate that sought its undoing. She was proud to wear the uniform. She could look anyone in the eye and defend her beliefs, knowing she was right.

When Madeline started spouting left-wing rhetoric about blood for oil, Lone had tried to make her see sense. Back then, the commander in chief had her loyalty, and she gave him credit for knowing what he was doing. She couldn't believe that a president would take the country to war without an imminent threat. Even if the bullshit about WMDs was just a smokescreen and the real reason they were there was to secure oil resources, Lone could have accepted that. She just wanted to be told the truth, to know what she was risking her life for.

Soldiers like her obeyed their commanders' orders without question, but mutual trust was fundamental to that equation. The commander had to rely on the loyalty and obedience of his troops, and the troops had to believe their commander would only send them into harm's way if there was no other choice. The idea of an elective war, a war to make money for friends in big business, was such a dire breach of trust that Lone had refused to entertain the possibility. Even after she lost Brandon and then Madeline, she thought if she got to the truth of the matter her beliefs would be vindicated. She simply couldn't accept that she'd been duped and that the weak-kneed liberals she despised had been right all along.

A sob closed her throat as she thought about the facts she'd uncovered. The truth was hard to accept not only because it made a fool of her but because it changed everything. Ego was not an indulgence an honorable soldier could afford when her country was at risk. An evil alliance of men had stolen America out from under the feet of her citizens, using lies and propaganda to hide their real agenda. Now that she understood what was really happening, she saw evidence of their strategies wherever she looked.

There had to be a war so the big donors to the Bush presidential campaign could get their payday. The "plan for a post-Saddam Iraq" memo laid it out right there six months before 9/11—troop requirements, war crimes tribunals, and divvying up the oil assets. According to Paul O'Neill, the memo was all they could talk about at the National Security Council meeting that February. Screw the information about an imminent terrorist attack; they had more important things to think about, like which of their pals would get the Iraqi oilfield contracts.

Besides, back in 2000 Cheney and his neocon friends in the PNAC had lamented that American world dominance would progress slowly unless there was "some catastrophic and catalyzing event—like a new Pearl Harbor." Would they stand in the way of the dream-come-true scenario they hoped for? Lone seriously doubted it.

Every time she thought about the real reasons her country was at war, she was consumed with a wintry rage that made her physically ill. Some days she felt so angry she wanted to harm herself. She couldn't believe she'd stayed in her brainwashed bubble for so long. Like others who'd drunk the Kool-Aid, she reacted like a wind-up doll to the familiar refrain: patriotism, American values, fight them over there so we don't have to fight them here. Her adamant beliefs had blinded her to Madeline's despair. She'd read into her lover's angry words nothing more than the grief of a mother who'd lost her child. She had kidded herself that time would heal and Madeline would come to terms with her loss.

Lone felt sick and her hands began to sweat. In her arrogance and blindness, she had invalidated Madeline's feelings and left her terribly alone in her unbearable knowledge. The day she'd killed herself,

Madeline left her diary open on the nightstand at Lone's side of the bed. A quote was penned in the middle of the page:

> Nothing is so unworthy of a civilized nation as allowing itself to be "governed" without opposition by an irresponsible clique that has yielded to base instinct.
> —White Rose Society. Germany, 1942

Several weeks after she dropped dirt into Madeline's grave, Lone finally Googled the source of the quote, a leaflet written by a handful of Germans who resisted Nazi ideology and dared to say so. They were executed, of course. Beheaded. Kids who dared to question the corrupt beast of National Socialism. Their story made her think about how an entire nation could be coopted and coerced into accepting the unacceptable. Her country could not be compared to Nazi Germany, but the lessons of history were undeniable. People could rationalize almost anything, even act against their own interests, when they buried their common sense under layers of fear, self-deception, obedience, and misguided patriotism.

Lone had done exactly that, and she had failed the woman she loved. She was not going to make the same mistake twice. She had Debbie to think about now, innocent, trusting Debbie Basher, who knew nothing about politics and saw only the good in people. Whatever happened, Lone was going to keep her safe. She would never let Debbie down. When she was done, Debbie would be proud of her. And so would Madeline, if she was looking down from heaven.

A loud cheer rose around her, calling her thoughts to order. Lone added her voice absently to the chants as the Dicktator effigy was pulled, Saddam-style, off its pedestal. She pictured the real VP there, toppled from his lofty perch, facing the fury of the little people whose lives he trampled as he pleased. Would he expect mercy, or would he concede that criminal conduct should have consequences? Even Nixon had finally understood that America was a precious idea and that the office he held should not be defiled by the dirty dealings of corrupt men. He'd had enough shame to resign.

Aware that she was standing too still, Lone followed a young woman dawdling away from the rally. She'd seen enough to know that this was not the right place for the delivery phase of Operation Houseclean. Jackson Hole was deceptively open and tranquil, but now that the millionaires had been driven out by billionaires, the area was knee-deep in private security. Of the three Cheney residences she'd scoped out, this one offered the easiest access but it wouldn't suffice. The chances of getting her target close enough to a van packed with C-4 to be killed by the explosion seemed poor and the opportunities to get a clean head shot were extremely limited.

She considered the option of rigging a golf cart to explode. She could gain access to the eighteenth hole via one of the upscale houses that backed onto the green in that area, but escape would be impossible and she needed to get away so she could move quickly to the next name on her list of first-wave targets.

Talk about shock and awe.

Americans thought Republican sex scandals were shaking things up. They were startled by the departures of Donald Rumsfeld, Karl Rove, and Alberto Gonzales. Well, she had news for them. They hadn't seen anything yet. The evil alliance would thrive with impunity no more. Their days of gluttony at the trough of greed, amorality, and excess were numbered.

The men leading this country toward doom so they could wallow in wealth thought they were entitled. For them, the means always justified the end, when the end was about their wealth, power, and privilege. Screw the other ninety-nine percent of the population, they were just there to be used. The cabal that had stolen the country slept like babies. They threw sticks for their dogs and bounced their grandchildren on their knees. They could look at themselves in the mirror and ignore the blood on their hands.

Well, not for much longer. When she was done, the blood would be their own.

CHAPTER FOUR

D ebbie Basher hung the Closed sign on the door of Le Paradox and gazed up at Jude. Her hazel eyes were bright with tears. "Thanks for coming."

They both heard the tremble in her voice. Looking embarrassed, Debbie tucked her wavy chestnut hair behind her ears and clasped her hands together. She was not one of those women who could hide emotional turmoil behind a placid veneer.

"What's wrong?" Jude asked.

Debbie's mouth trembled. "Where are my manners? Coffee?"

Jude lifted the paper cup Agatha had placed in her hand as she left the stationhouse.

"Oh, silly me." Debbie's eyes darted left and right.

Jude always had the urge to hold her and stroke her hair, as one would a frightened child. "Let's sit down," she said.

Over the past months she'd befriended the sweet-natured hairdresser, hoping to get a fix on her taciturn lover, Sandy Lane aka Lonewolf. Debbie's name had popped up on the FBI radar when someone purchased two hundred pounds of C-4 plastic explosive in her name. It wasn't rocket science to figure out who made the buy. Jude was still amazed that Sandy had implicated her girlfriend. She probably thought anyone following up on the purchase would take one look at Debbie and assume identity theft. This woman wouldn't know plastic explosive from tofu.

Debbie had no idea that she and her beloved were under surveillance, and Jude had no plans to tell her. She wanted to find out what Sandy Lane was up to and talk her down before she did something she would regret. So far, she hadn't come close to gathering any hard intelligence. The woman was a survivalist with a cabin somewhere in the San Juans. Jude had attempted to followed her down there on several occasions, but Sandy wasn't stupid.

It wasn't easy to hide a Dakota with patrol markings in a single, slow-moving lane of traffic on the narrow, winding mountain highway, and Sandy always seemed to know when she was being followed. Last time, she'd stopped at a rest area and waved as Jude approached. Jude had pulled over to greet her as if the encounter was mere coincidence. She said she was on her way to Cortez for a meeting. She could tell Sandy didn't buy it.

The FBI kept files on thousands of antisocial loners. Admittedly most weren't building C-4 stockpiles. But Sandy seemed to be lying low, and since she could not be tied to any watch-list organization, all Jude could do was wait for her to make a move.

"Would you like a donut?" Debbie asked as Jude followed her to the tiny staff area out the back of the shop.

"No, thanks." Jude sat at one end of the scuffed leather love seat that took up most of the room. "You said you haven't heard from Sandy for a couple of days?" she prompted.

Debbie perched on the edge of the cushion next to Jude's like she might have to flee at any moment. Jude wondered what kind of childhood could have left her so painfully vulnerable and lacking in confidence.

"I feel silly calling you." Debbie give a jittery shrug. "I'm sure she's perfectly fine and I'm worrying for no reason."

"You're entitled to be concerned."

"It's just…" Uncertainty pinched Debbie's small face. "This isn't the first time. It's been going on for months."

Jude waited, wanting her to work through all the usual rationalizations until she arrived at the gut fear that made her seek help in the first place.

"She goes away for days at a time and never tells me where, and she doesn't call till she gets back. She keeps changing her cell phone number." Debbie covered her mouth with both hands, smothering a sob. "Do you think she's having an affair?"

An affair was probably the best scenario. "What do you think?" Jude asked.

"I don't think she's seeing anyone. I think she loves me. But everyone says this kind of thing is a sign." Debbie gave a self-deprecating smile. "I'm probably just being paranoid because of what happened with Meg."

Before moving to the Four Corners three years earlier, Debbie had lived with a woman in Denver. She'd walked out when she discovered her partner had been cheating on her for months. Meg had promised to buy her out of their house, but that never happened and Debbie struggled along in rented accommodation, trying to make ends meet by working part-time in another woman's hair shop. In the meantime, her father had died and she wasn't close to her mother. Her only sibling, an older brother, was pastor of an evangelical church in Greenville. He had numerous children, but Debbie, the "homosexual sinner," was not allowed near them for reasons of family values.

Jude wasn't surprised by her dependency on Sandy. Who else made her feel loved? An ugly thought unsettled Jude. What if the relationship was just an expedience for Sandy? Could she be using Debbie, even setting her up?

With deep unease, Jude said, "Let's assume she's not having an affair. What else could she be doing? Does she have a hobby she wants to keep to herself? Is she going away to visit a sick relative?"

"Not that I know of. I was hoping she might have said something to you."

Jude stifled a laugh. The last thing Sandy Lane said to her was, "If anything ever happens, make sure Debbie's okay." Not the words of a woman whose partner was nothing more than a convenience, surely.

That was six weeks ago, at a community cookout Agatha organized for the Fourth of July. Jude had dragged Sandy aside later and asked her point-blank what she thought might "happen." She had fobbed off the question, saying she was just feeling gloomy after she saw a collision on the highway.

"There's something else." Debbie's voice tightened. "This time, before she left she said we're moving to Canada when she gets back."

"Canada?" Jude's pulse jumped. Sandy was planning an exit strategy that involved vanishing across the border. And she was taking Debbie.

"I don't want to live in Canada," Debbie said, wringing her hands. "My boss and her husband have an alpaca farm and they're expanding.

She wants to sell the shop. I'd get it for peanuts. Nobody wants to buy a business out here."

"That sounds like a good opportunity if you think you could make a living."

"I thought I could add some other services. Manicures. Facials. I'm a trained aesthetician as well as a hairdresser."

"You'd probably do okay," Jude said. "Have you talked to Lone about it?"

"No. I was planning to and then she started with this Canada idea. She's acting like it's definite."

"What's in Canada?"

"She has a property there. She bought it after her partner died."

"Where is it?" Jude asked casually.

"I don't exactly know." Debbie met Jude's eyes, as if seeking understanding. "She's such a private person. You know, she really needs her space. I respect that, so I don't ask a lot of questions."

"But this is not just about her." Jude spoke evenly, keeping incredulity out of her tone. "She wants you to go live in another country with her. I think you have every right to ask questions."

"I tried to talk with her. I mean, what am I supposed to do for a job? But she said I don't have to think about any of that. She can take care of both of us."

"How's she going to do that?"

Debbie looked embarrassed. Jude had already concluded that she was afraid of driving her lover away and avoided any kind of confrontation. Sandy didn't seem abusive toward her, quite the opposite. As far as Jude could determine she was very tender and devoted. But she also treated Debbie like a child. A possession.

"Does she ever talk about her time in the military?" Jude asked.

Arbiter had finally tracked down Sandy's service records, only to find most of her file content was unavailable. "Alexandra Lane Cordell" was indeed known as Sandy Lane to her buddies and had served in the 82nd Airborne, as she'd told Jude. But she'd refrained from mentioning her extensive SOF expertise. Many of the 82nd had been deployed to special ops forces in Afghanistan, waging unconventional warfare alongside elite Green Beret units. Sandy was among them and, according to her commanding officer, she was a brilliant tactical operative and explosives expert. He'd noted in a report that if she were a man, he would have put her name forward as a Delta recruit. That could only mean one thing. Sandy Lane was smart, highly skilled, and a competent killer. Jude had guessed all of those things the first time they met.

Arbiter had since raised the idea that she was now selling her services in the private sector. If so, her C-4 purchase could be tied to a domestic plot. The possibilities were endless. A scare tactic. A hit. Blackmail. Organized crime. Perhaps even a terrorist strike, if it could be believed that she would act against her own country. They'd discussed another possibility, too—that Sandy had been recruited by the Company or the NSA and was active in an operation the Bureau knew nothing about. If so their investigation could conceivably compromise her.

"I think it makes her depressed, talking about Iraq and Afghanistan," Debbie said. "So she keeps things to herself."

"Did something happen there, a particular incident that bothers her?"

Debbie hesitated. "Has she told you about Madeline and Brandon?"

"No."

"Well, I didn't want to say anything. It's not my place. But her partner committed suicide after her son was killed in Iraq. Lone still has nightmares about it."

Holy shit. Jude's gut reacted. So far, Arbiter hadn't been able to verify details of Sandy's personal history beyond information about her parents and upbringing. Because she was gay, the dead ends weren't surprising. The Bureau had tried the usual quasi-legal mail and cell phone intercepts, but their subject didn't seem to receive mail and she barely used her disposable cell phones. Every time Jude wheedled a number from Debbie, it went out of use before they could trace it. Arbiter got antsy about that. Civilians, unless they were criminals, tended to leave a big, clumsy footprint. They did nothing to guard their privacy and were easy to monitor. Sandy knew better. She behaved like a spook. Arbiter was reluctant to put her under heightened scrutiny for that reason; the Bureau found it wise to avoid blundering into other intelligence agencies' operations.

He would rethink his assessment now. The new information brought Sandy's profile into focus for the first time. The deaths could be precipitating stressors. Combined with her personality, military background, and social isolation, the personal losses could trigger a volatile response. Sandy, whatever her status, was a walking time bomb.

"I'm sorry I didn't say anything before," Debbie continued. "I thought she might tell you about Madeline once she got to know you better."

"How would you describe her mental state?"

Debbie paled and her mouth shook. "What do you mean?"

"Listen to me." Jude took Debbie's hands. "I care about you and I care about her. I think Sandy could be...unwell. With all she's been through personally, and her experiences in battle, she might have PTSD or at the very least, she needs counseling. Do you know if she's seeing anyone?"

Debbie blinked in alarm. "Do you mean a psychiatrist? I don't think she'd ever go for that."

"She won't accept help?"

"She thinks it's weak." Forlornly, Debbie said, "She gets in these moods. It's hard to explain. I can tell she's angry. Not at me, but there's something deep down inside." A shrill laugh died as quickly as she released it. Tears sprang to her eyes. "I know, it sounds silly. But I know something's wrong. I just *know* it."

"I believe you." Jude sipped her coffee while she contemplated how to handle the situation. If she was going to escalate, she had to know Sandy's whereabouts. "This trip. Was she planning to drive or fly?"

"She was driving."

Naturally. And she would be using cash, not credit cards. Jude hadn't taken the risk of planting a GPS device under Sandy's pickup; her subject was sufficiently paranoid that she would anticipate the obvious. "Did she say where she was going?"

"No, but one evening I saw her on the Internet looking at accommodations. I didn't pay much attention."

"She was on your computer?"

"Yes, she left her laptop power cord at home accidentally and her battery got low. Normally she never uses my computer."

Something in her tone suggested she found this odd. Jude suspected it was one of many little things she would start piecing together, attempting to make sense of behavior that made her uneasy.

"Can I see your computer?" Jude stood.

"Yes, of course." Debbie took her purse from the counter and fished out a set of car keys. "I don't have another appointment until late. Would you like to stay for an early dinner?"

"Sounds like a plan. Thank you." Debbie was a great cook and Jude figured she was going to need some time at the computer. She would have to search everything Sandy stored at her girlfriend's place.

As Debbie locked the shop, she said, "It's not just me, is it?"

Jude could feel the anxiety radiating from her. "No. It's not just you."

A sense of dread washed over her as they walked away from the hair shop. She'd been in a funk ever since the Corban Foley case was wrapped up almost a year ago. It was one thing trying to move beyond the acquittal of the toddler's killer, but dealing with the foibles of her fickle ex had preoccupied her far more than was acceptable. And while she was feeling pissed at the world in general, and Mercy Westmoreland in particular, she had allowed Sandy Lane to slip out of focus.

How had she not known about the trips out of town until now? She should have noticed the absence of Sandy's truck, which was a fixture outside Debbie's home most evenings. She'd been hanging out for an opportunity to search Sandy's mountain hideaway, assuming she could find it. Sandy's trips away offered the ideal opportunity. The thought that she'd already missed several chances aggravated her.

"Debbie, where does Sandy live?"

"I don't know."

"You must have some idea." Jude could hear her own impatience. Softening her tone, she said, "I'm worried about her. I think we should check to see if she's at home."

Debbie hugged herself, plainly mortified. "I thought she was ashamed because she doesn't have a nice place. So I stopped asking if I could visit with her. I know I should have pushed harder."

They stopped at Debbie's car, a beat-up Toyota.

"If she says she's coming over, how long does it normally take for her to arrive?" Jude asked.

"More than an hour."

"Okay." Jude backed off. She didn't want to pressure Debbie too much in case she relayed their conversation to Sandy.

She waited for Debbie to start her car before getting into the Dakota. She wished she'd tried harder to talk to Sandy, but very few women unsettled her as the former paratrooper did and she'd been reluctant to push her luck during their private interactions. They always seemed to be circling each other in an unspoken ritual of dominance, sniffing out weaknesses, testing will.

By stepping back and letting Sandy move out of reach, Jude had blinked first.

❖

"Finally." Pippa honked her horn and almost fell out the driver's door.

The car bays in front of Uncle Fabian's log cabin—more of a log mansion, really—were arranged in a semicircle and were all on an incline. She hoped her SUV wouldn't roll down the hill onto the main road. Her mouth watered at the prospect of a long, cold drink. The kneel-down bread, with its sweetcorn and green chilies, had made her so thirsty she'd even guzzled a can of warm Diet Coke that had been rolling around under her seat since she left Boston.

Pippa bounced up the front steps, marveling over the turquoise-inlaid handrail. She paused on the front verandah and turned around to take in the view. On the other side of the highway, the Dolores River ran through mountain meadows and tall pines. Above her, the San Juan Mountains loomed like silent guardians of a hidden world. She felt incredibly lucky to be here.

There was no doorbell, just a cast-iron knocker. Pippa tapped it out of good manners. She had a set of keys, but it seemed rude to barge in when she'd never visited before. There was no answer to her knock and no barking from her uncle's poodle, Coco. She called out a couple of times, then wandered along the verandah and looked in the windows. Her uncle was probably out shopping. Coco would be with him.

Pippa tried the door and was surprised to find it unlocked. Uncle Fabian tended to be paranoid about security because he had so many valuable art works. Pippa stepped into a slate-tiled entry hall and called, "Uncle Fabian, it's me."

She stared around a great room to her right with a wall of floor-to-ceiling windows. Pippa took the steps down to this huge L-shaped entertainment area. A moss stone fireplace occupied the center of the room, above it a huge portrait of Geronimo her uncle had commissioned when Pippa was just a kid. She could still remember an argument over dinner between Uncle Fabian and her father about Geronimo. Uncle Fabian said Prescott Bush and several other members of Yale's Skull and Bones society desecrated the chief's grave and stole his skull and other relics. Her father, a Yalesman, said the story was just a myth.

Pippa listened for the sound of her uncle's voice from somewhere in the huge home. Logs were stacked on either side of the fireplace, which was shielded on all sides by decorative guards. High above, a second-story mezzanine stretched the length of the great room. A few armchairs stood in one corner, arranged around a low table. Pippa heard a slight thud and recalled her uncle mentioning his office was upstairs. She strolled over to the wide staircase and began climbing, gazing down into the incredible room.

Her mother would have dismissed the décor as "basic." She'd crammed their home in Chestnut Hill with antiques and Persian rugs. But Pippa could see why her uncle had chosen simplicity. With such majestic views, it would be silly to clutter the room with ostentatious furnishings. A few rugs were scattered around the timber floors, various Ute and Navajo artifacts hung from the walls, and the sofas and chairs were upholstered in leather or fabric, in earthy colors. The sensibility was perfect for the location.

For a few seconds, Pippa thought about phoning her parents to let them know she'd arrived safely, but she decided to spare herself. They'd probably forgotten she was even on the road, and she couldn't stand the thought of another conversation with her mother about the mistake she was making. Her parents blamed Fabian for her decision not to accept the job they'd arranged for her even though she hadn't told him until after she'd rejected the offer.

Fabian was the black sheep of the family, and no one would tell her why. Pippa once asked him and he said her mother thought a gay man shouldn't have inherited Maulle Mansion in New Orleans. It had been passed from father to son for over two hundred years and since he wasn't going to have children, she thought the house should be hers. The place was falling apart and Pippa knew her parents planned to sell it if they could overturn the will. Their lawsuit had been thrown out and Fabian spent the next fifteen years restoring the home to its former splendor.

No one knew exactly where he got all his money. Her dad said he'd made a fortune in real estate and venture capital, and even more in hedge funds. He was a philanthropist, which peeved Pippa's parents because it meant, in the end, he'd leave everything to the poodle rescue or some foundation for orphans in Darfur. They thought her brother Ryan should get everything.

As she reached the top of the stairs, Pippa almost tripped over her uncle's antique ebony cane. Ever since a skiing accident, he'd had a knee problem and used the cane. She reached down for it but froze, her fingers hovering inches from the smooth silver ball head. Her heart raced at double time. Even as she registered the wet, red smear over the silver, her mind only foggily interpreted what she saw. Blood.

Pippa clamped her hand over her mouth, stifling her instinctive cry and listening intently. Something crawled from the eerie stillness, stealing the air from the upstairs hallway. She tried to breath but all she could do was gasp. Panic jerked her into motion. She rushed along the hallway. Her foot slid on something. More blood.

A wail rose in her throat. There'd been an accident. "Uncle Fabian, I'm here," she cried, pushing the nearest door wide, expecting to see her uncle wrapping his hand in a bandage.

A voice croaked, "Pippa?" and she stumbled across the room to the man sprawled on the floor.

"Oh, God. What happened? Oh, my God." She didn't know where to look, what to touch. She lifted her uncle into her arms.

A wet groan rose from him. "They killed Coco."

"Who? Who did this?"

He forced out the words, "They don't know anything."

Her mind screamed *Help! Someone, please help!* She had to call 911. What was she doing holding him instead of getting an ambulance? She freed a hand and pulled her cell phone from her jeans. Her mouth shook so much she had trouble speaking.

"Don't try to talk, Uncle Fabian. I'm calling 911. You're going to be fine."

"It's too late." He lifted a hand but it fell back. Blood ran from the corners of his mouth. His shirt was soaked. "I'm dying, sweetheart."

Pippa jabbed the numbers. "No, you're not. Don't say that."

"Ask Oscar," he choked. A violent tremor shook his body.

"Uncle Fabian," Pippa wailed.

She dropped the phone and bent over him, trying to hear his heart. The position was too awkward. He was slipping away. His face was chalk white beneath the blood and bruising. Frantically, she laid him flat on the floor, desperate to revive him. She didn't know where to start. She tore open his soaked shirt. Blood welled slowly from several different places on his torso.

She snatched up her cell phone again. Thank God. Someone was waiting at the other end. "Hello," Pippa gasped.

"Dispatch. Can I help you?"

"Send an ambulance. Oh, God. I can't remember the address. It's on Railroad Avenue, near Stoner. A big log home on the left. Please hurry."

"Calm down," the operator said. "Tell me what's happened."

Fabian shuddered and Pippa juggled the phone so she could hold him again.

"Ma'am?"

"Someone's hurt my uncle," Pippa sobbed. "I think he's been stabbed."

She bent low over the bloody man in her arms and urged, "Just hold on, Uncle Fabian. The ambulance is coming."

Her uncle blinked through the blood that coated his eyes. He spoke in short bursts. "Ask him…where the box is…"

"Don't worry." Pippa glanced up at the birdcage near the windows. Her uncle's beloved African Grey cowered where the cover formed a shadow. "I'll take care of Oscar till you're better."

Fabian's mouth moved in what seemed like a smile. "I love you, Pip."

"I love you, too." Tears poured down her cheeks.

The dispatcher said, "Ma'am. Talk to me. Is the person who attacked your uncle still on the premises?"

Pippa stifled a scream of fright and stared toward the door. "I don't know."

A wet, soft gurgle sounded in her uncle's chest. "Ask Oscar," he said one more time, then his eyes rolled back and he relaxed in her arms.

Pippa sank down over the one person in the world she felt truly close to. Through a web of tears and snot, she cried, "He's dead. Oh, God. He's dead."

CHAPTER FIVE

"That's the niece?" Jude asked, indicating a chalk-faced young woman wrapped in a blanket and sitting on the front step with a female paramedic.

"Yeah, Phillipa Calloway. She's the one called it in." The state patrol trooper handed her ID back.

Jude wasn't first on scene, by far. The driveway leading up the log home was lined with black and white Dodge Durangos, the patrol vehicles used by the MCSO. The house was taped off and the surrounding area crawled with deputies and state troopers. Sheriff Pratt had summoned her, as he did for any homicides out of the ordinary. This one promised to be a high-profile case. The dead man was not just wealthy, he was a respected benefactor of local causes. Fabian Maulle purchased state-of-the-art medical equipment for Southwest Memorial, paid the college fees of several Ute kids nominated by the Tribal Council, and supported police charities. Around the Four Corners, the very private millionaire was seen as a real philanthropist, a man in a different league from the hedge-fund honchos who threw their weight around every ski season.

Sheriff Pratt stepped away from a group of detectives at the command post. Approaching Jude, he said, "Looks like a robbery gone bad. They broke in thinking the place was empty and Maulle interrupted them. Wrong place, wrong time." He pointed to a sheet-covered shape in the parking area. "Poodle took one to the head. Point-blank. Slice of bologna in its throat."

"The burglar fed it a treat, then shot it? Jesus, that's cold." Most times the family pooch was shut in a laundry room or let loose on the property.

"Yeah, tell me about it," Pratt said grimly. "What happened to honor among thieves?"

"Where was the dog shot?" Jude asked.

"Out back." Pratt pointed. "There's just some cats and a parrot in there now. We put a call in to animal control."

Jude glanced at the young woman once more. Phillipa Calloway was just a kid. Eighteen, or maybe a little older, but so slight she could pass for a high school kid. "Was she on the premises at the time?"

"First responders arrive and she exits the house, covered in blood. Says she found Maulle wounded."

"Who conducted the field interview?"

Pratt glanced toward a tall man with a black handlebar mustache. "Sergeant Pavlic took down her details. She's too shaken up to give a full statement. The victim died in her arms."

"Do we have a cause of death?"

"I'm gonna say multiple stab wounds. The coroner isn't here yet." Pratt rolled his eyes expressively.

Until the official pronouncement was made, no one could move the body or start processing the scene in any comprehensive way. Dr. Norwood Carver, the Montezuma County coroner, was usually the last to arrive at a scene. He liked everyone to remember who the real star was. Carver was one of those rare birds, an elected county coroner who was also a forensic pathologist, thus unusually well qualified for his job. If he couldn't attend a scene when it was necessary, he arranged for someone from Durango or Grand Junction to stand in for him. That could take hours.

"Any sign of the murder weapon?" Jude asked.

"Not yet. We put out a BOLO for a male acting suspiciously."

Long shot, but fact was stranger than fiction. Suspects did stupid things, like stopping at a gas station for cigarettes before they remembered to change their bloodstained garments.

Jude glanced toward the other detectives, "Who's the primary?"

"That would be you, Devine."

"Sir, with all due respect. I'm going to be tied up with the Telluride operation once the FBI arrives."

"You're the one with major crime experience," Pratt said. "And we're not talking about your average Joe here."

"I can see that, but—"

"No, what I'm saying is Maulle had juice. He knew the governor. I'm going to have bigwigs on the goddamn phone every day until we get a result."

"So partner me up with the primary. How about Pete Koertig? He's earned it." Jude lowered her voice. "Media-wise, it could be a good move to have a local man lead this one."

Pratt hesitated for a split second before conceding, "Good thinking."

"Have we ruled out Ms. Calloway?"

Pratt regarded her like she was crazy. "There's no way she did it. Look at her. Ninety pounds wet. Hysterical with grief. They had to give her a shot to calm her down."

None of which proved anything. Patiently, Jude said, "We're going to need her clothing. When is she being transported to headquarters?"

"We're not going that route tonight. I want her taken to the hospital. We can get her statement tomorrow.'"

"Sir, she's probably the last person to see the victim alive."

"Which is why we should show some sensitivity." Pratt sounded protective. He was the father of several girls, one of whom looked a little like their witness. "She's not a suspect. But if you want a quick word with her, I'll go give Koertig the good news."

Relieved, Jude took the steps onto the verandah and strode over to Phillipa Calloway. After identifying herself, she said, "I'm very sorry for your loss, Ms. Calloway."

Upon closer inspection, the young woman was probably in her twenties. Corkscrews of auburn hair framed the face of a dreamer. Even puffy from crying, her eyes were a beautiful almond shape, their shade a dark aqua blue that reminded Jude of the Colorado spruce trees around her house. Her coloring was Celtic, the skin a milky tone that would never tan. Red blotches marred its translucent perfection. From the tear-ravaged look of her, she was every bit as innocent as Pratt claimed.

"Who would do this?" She directed her anguished question at Jude.

"We want to find out as much as you do," Jude replied.

The answer was standard, but she always meant what she said. Her sincerity seemed to calm Calloway. The paramedic seized the opportunity, jumping up like she was relieved to escape.

"I need to check on a couple of things," she said, patting their witness's shoulder. "Can I leave you here with the detective, Pippa?"

Calloway nodded vaguely and Jude took the responder's place. "This must have been a terrible shock," she said.

"I had a flat tire. Otherwise I'd have been here. Oh, God. Maybe I could have done something."

Or maybe they would be taking two bodies to the morgue. Jude kept the thought to herself. "Where did the flat tire happen?"

"On the Devil's Highway. There was a sign. Toad Porter's Haysales."

"Not far from Towaoc?" Jude knew the area well. She drove out that way to visit her friend Eddie House.

"Yes. A couple of guys stopped to help me. A father and son. They mentioned they lived somewhere nearby."

Jude was relieved that someone would be able to verify Calloway's story. Piecing together the rest of the alibi, she asked, "Do you remember what time that was?"

"Yes. I saw it on my cell phone while they were working on the tire. 3:26 p.m."

"Ms. Calloway—"

"Please, call me Pippa."

"Thank you, Pippa. Did you get the names of the men who fixed your tire?"

"Yes." She frowned as if she'd been about to speak but the words had slipped from her mind. With a dismayed "Oh" she stared at Jude in confusion.

"Don't worry if you can't remember right now," Jude said gently. "You've had a terrible shock. Do you remember anything about them?" If they lived around Towaoc, it would be pretty easy to track them down.

Pippa frowned. An edge of frustration lifted her dull tone. "Why does it matter? Shouldn't you be thinking about who did this?"

"I am," Jude said. "But one of the first things we have to do is rule out the people closest to your uncle. I know it's upsetting to have to think about all this now, but you were the last person to see Mr. Maulle alive."

Pippa's frown gave way to comprehension. "So I need an alibi for when he was attacked?"

"In a nutshell, yes."

"The father looked Native American, but the son was blond. They had a three-legged wolf."

Jude veiled her astonishment. "Is the name 'Eddie House' familiar?"

Pippa looked startled. "Do you know him?"

Jude kept their personal acquaintanceship to herself. "Mr. House is a famous Ute pottery-maker."

"He knew my uncle," Pippa said. "Uncle Fabian collected pottery. It sounds like he bought some of Mr. House's pieces."

"Did you happen to notice if any items are missing from your uncle's collection?" Jude couldn't imagine a burglar killing a rich collector and walking away empty-handed.

"I didn't look. And this is my first time here. I don't know what he kept in this house."

Her tone was so weary and despondent, Jude said, "We can talk again later, Pippa. I'll need to take a statement from you about finding your uncle. For now, can you confirm what time you arrived here?"

"Around 4:40. I kept phoning once I reached the mountains, but he didn't answer. The last time I called was just a few minutes before I found the house."

"Thank you, that's helpful." Jude stood. "I need to go talk with the other detectives now. Do you have some clean clothes to change into?"

"All my stuff's in there." Pippa pointed toward the Mazda SUV parked below the house. "I didn't even bring my bags up."

"I'll have someone fetch a change of clothing so you can get more comfortable. Is there a family member we can call?"

"My parents are in Boston. Uncle Fabian is all the family I have... had, out here."

"Then we'll help you get situated until you decide what you want to do."

"Thank you. Everyone's been very kind." Pippa stared out at the mountains. Wistfully, she said, "It's so beautiful here, I can't believe this could happen."

"I'm very sorry," Jude said once more. "People thought highly of your uncle."

Before Pippa could give into tears once more, Jude moved away and signaled a female deputy to sit with Pippa. Stepping under the tape, she stepped into the house, acknowledging several members of the Crime Scene Unit. They'd set up a portable workstation near the entrance for their equipment and evidence inspection and were milling around waiting for the coroner to arrive. Jude pulled on latex gloves and a pair of boot protectors, and picked up a bunch of evidence pouches and security strips so she could offer an extra pair of hands. Pratt, already garbed, fell into step with her as she moved farther into the house.

"What's your take on the niece?" he asked.

"Same as yours. Innocent family member. She has an alibi. We'll have to confirm her story, but that shouldn't be difficult. I'll take a full statement once they're done with her at the hospital?"

"Let's give her some time to get over the shock. Maybe she'll remember more."

"I'll be in town for a while." Jude had expected to stay in Cortez for several days after the Telluride briefing. She was thankful she'd packed extra clothing. With the homicide landing in their laps as well, she could be stuck down here for a week.

"Your FBI friends arrive tomorrow, don't forget about that," Pratt said.

Jude wasn't sure if Arbiter intended to inform the left hand what the right hand was doing. He'd been cagey when she asked, saying if too much was divulged they would know he had an asset in the mix. It was better for all parties if her cover remained intact. She wondered how long it would take the task force to discover that she was a "friend" of Harrison Hawke. Once they made the connection, what then?

She took a few cautious steps into the living room and absorbed the million-dollar view. Even in the fading light the panorama held her spellbound. The San Juans rose dark purple against a red-streaked sky, stretching north toward Telluride. She could imagine the owner of this house sitting in the single black leather armchair opposite the windows, soaking up the splendor. She picked up a book from the occasional table next to the armchair and checked the cover. *The Dance of Anger.* Yep, that made sense. Who wouldn't want to dive between the covers of a self-help bestseller when they had this house and this view?

She slowly absorbed the rest of the room. Nothing seemed out of place. Fabian Maulle's log home was photo-perfect and belonged in a ritzy real estate show on TV.

"Nice life," she said.

"I met the guy a couple of times. Not your typical loud mouth fat cat." Pratt picked up the book and thumbed through it, pausing occasionally like the contents spoke to him.

Jude picked a careful path toward a display cabinet in the adjoining dining area. The contents had to be worth a fortune, but there was no sign of a smash and grab or even an attempt to force the door. Either the burglar was in a hurry to leave, or he had no clue what antique Pueblo pottery was worth.

"The attack occurred in Maulle's office upstairs." Pratt placed the self-help book back where he found it. "The place was ransacked. They were probably looking for cash. A safe, maybe."

They climbed the stairs, avoiding photo evidence markers and tape barriers. Deputy Belle Simmons met them at the top where a large area of blood spray and bloody footprints had been marked. Belle was in charge of the MCSO crime scene technicians and was one of the few officers with major crime scene experience. As usual, her makeup bore testimony to hours in front of a mirror. Jude had never seen her without the works. She was still in her summer shades: bronze foundation, frosted copper lipstick, and green eye shadow. In winter, she favored coral lips and more dramatic eyeliner. Her bold red curls were scraped into a bun and adorned with a spangled pink hair net.

"How's it coming?" Pratt asked.

"Well, it's quite a blood scene. Everything's taped off and we've taken the wide-angle views. Just waiting on the coroner now." Belle gave Jude a smile. "Good to see y'all, Detective."

"You, too. How are the kids?"

"I'm about ready to send them back where they came from." To Pratt, Belle said, "Count yourself lucky you just got those gorgeous little girls to worry about, Orwell."

The sheriff looked smug. He and his wife had daughters so sweet and well-behaved that Belle wondered if they were quite right in the head, at least that's what she'd confided to Jude. She and her mild-mannered husband, refugees from Louisiana, had two boys who didn't know the meaning of discipline. One of them, the twelve-year-old, had recently driven the family car onto the street and rear-ended a neighbor's BMW. Luckily, he wasn't injured and they could afford the repairs. Belle's husband had an Internet shoe business and did okay.

Jude was always surprised when good people had monsters for children. There was a time when she blamed parents for every failing of their children, but that didn't explain all the creeps who came from good homes, or the responsible adults who had shitty childhoods. The more homicides she investigated, the more she believed in the idea of evil in its many facets. What else could explain the brutal banality of the Menendez brothers, or the calculated sadism of a child killer?

She hoped Belle's boys were just going through a phase. She was a good woman and a good cop. She deserved kids she didn't have to apologize for.

"Are you hanging around after you finish with the scene?" Belle asked.

"I can if you need an extra pair of hands." If there weren't enough technicians, Jude sometimes helped out, labeling bags and sorting evidence.

"No, we're okay," Belle said. "Three more deputies finished their CSI certificates this year, and one of the guys added a bloodstain analysis course."

"There's plenty for him to do here," Jude remarked.

Pratt excused himself to answer his cell phone, returning a moment later to announce, "If you'll excuse me, ladies, the media's here, and the coroner is on his way up."

Jude's stomach stopped curdling when she heard the word "his." She would have been surprised if Mercy Westmoreland attended a Montezuma County crime scene at this time of day unless no one else could be found. But the Maulle killing would be a high-profile case, and the sheriff liked to involve Mercy in those. Thanks to regular stints on Court TV, her name had courtroom cachet, a state of affairs that bugged other hardworking but unglamorous forensic pathologists in the Four Corners.

She and Belle stepped back as the wiry figure of Norwood Carver came into view downstairs. Jude knew exactly what he was wearing under his bunny suit: high-priced cycling apparel he didn't care to sully on the job. No doubt he'd pedaled up here on his carbon-framed racing bike, complete with support crew bringing up the rear in an SUV with a spare bike strapped to the roof. The sides of Carver's vehicle bore the legend I BRAKE FOR CADAVERS, his idea of sophisticated wit.

Sure enough, a red-faced dweeb Jude recognized as a pathologist's assistant from Carver's office came panting up the stairs after his master, weighed down with body bag and field kit. Carver occasionally glanced back at him with the cheerful disdain of a man accustomed to leading the meek.

"Dr. Carver. Good evening. Thank you for coming so quickly," Belle said deferentially. "This way please."

Carver marched toward the room at the end of the hallway. Jude always had the impression that he was driven by a mental stopwatch that never stopped counting off the seconds until he could return to the real work of fitness training.

He called over his shoulder, "Step on it, Fritz, or that's your brain in the next jar on my desk."

The coroner called all his assistants "Fritz" in honor of the only one he thought was worth a dime, a minion who had laid down his life on the altar of science, stung to death by a wasp colony at a crime scene.

Picking his way across the ransacked office to the man lying in a dark pool of blood on the floor, Carver said, "I understand we have a positive identification."

"Yes, the victim is Fabian Maulle," Jude said. "His niece ID'd him and recorded time of probable death at 4:46 p.m. She was with Mr. Maulle when he stopped breathing but did not attempt resuscitation."

"Has the body been moved?" Carver asked.

"The victim was dying when his niece discovered him," Belle said. "She held him in her arms. This is the position she placed him in after he appeared to be deceased."

Carver took Maulle's pulse, tested for rigor, examined the torso wounds and what appeared to be blunt force trauma to the head, looked down his throat and up his nose, then crisply announced, "It would seem money doesn't buy happiness. Wrongful death."

He rose and moved away from the body, signaling "Fritz" to complete the initial tasks. The ruddy underling took a series of in situ photographs, then rolled Maulle on his side, arranging his clothes to obtain his core temperature.

"He's still warm. Rectal is ninety-six point two degrees and room temperature is sixty-eight."

Jude did the math. In an air-conditioned room like this, the normal body temperature of 98.4F would drop at slightly less than one degree per hour. Maulle's temperature was consistent with the time of death Pippa Calloway claimed. At the postmortem they would get an estimate of how long exsanguination had taken. Depending on which internal organs were affected and which arteries were severed, stabbing deaths often occurred in a minute or less.

While Fritz scraped beneath Maulle's nails, fingerprinted him, and bagged his hands, Carver admired a parrot staring from a birdcage near the desk. "African Grey. Smart bird. Thinks like a four year old, so they say. Which makes him roughly the equivalent of Fritz here."

"Great," Jude muttered. "Our eyewitness has feathers."

"All yours, Detective." Carver waved a hand expansively around the blood splattered scene, indicating they could complete their processing. "I'll notify the sheriff."

As soon as Carver departed, the photographer took over the crime scene and began setting up his tripod and lights. Jude and Belle issued some instructions and left him to it. The fewer people in the scene at any one time, the more likely that evidence would be preserved. Jude glanced toward Fritz, who was roaming the hallway with his body bag. A couple of paramedics trudged up the stairs with a stretcher, ready to cart Maulle off to the morgue as soon as the detectives had seen all they wanted to see.

Pete Koertig followed them, his ruddy face scrunched with the effort of containing his glee. "Meet your primary," he told Jude.

With his scalp aglow beneath the fuzz of short blond hair, and his big white grin, he looked more like a college football player than a detective. His heavyset build made him intimidating, and his general clumsiness gave the impression of a guy who wasn't the sharpest crayon in the box. As a consequence he was often underestimated, a factor in his impressive confession record. When suspects thought they were smarter than the cop doing the interview, they lowered their guard.

Jude had worked several cases with Koertig, and once they got beyond first impressions, they'd settled into a productive camaraderie. She found him methodical and hardworking. He was also self-aware enough to capitalize on his own strengths and weaknesses, something more egotistical males found difficult.

"I thought you'd catch this one for sure," he said. "All the guys did."

Jude shrugged. "I'm not the only show in town. Congratulations, boss."

Chortling, Koertig dragged on a pair of gloves, which promptly split. "Shit." He grimaced. "Excuse my French."

Belle took a spare pair from her pocket and checked the sizing on the bag. "These are extra large."

Koertig peered into the office. "Burglary? I don't think so."

"No, the place was tossed." Jude studied the chaos. Papers spilled from the filing cabinet. Every bookshelf had been emptied onto the floor. Expensive looking paintings were stacked carelessly behind the door. No burglar would have walked out of Fabian Maulle's house empty-handed if he knew enough to target it in the first place.

"No sign of forced entry," Koertig said. "I checked all the outside windows and doors."

This wasn't Washington DC. Violent crime was rare enough that people felt safe in their own homes. Maulle probably didn't lock his front door while he was at home. Jude made a mental note to ask Pippa about her uncle's habits.

"The killing seems personal," she said.

Stabbings usually were. Aside from serial offenders whose crimes were sexually motivated, it was rare for a stranger to invade someone's home and kill him with a knife. Guns or blunt instruments were the norm, and Maulle's killer had coldly shot a dog, execution-style. How did such a calculated act jive with the messy killing of Maulle himself? Had the gun jammed when he tried to shoot Maulle?

She considered the burglary-gone-wrong theory carefully. It was conceivable that a robbery had been interrupted. The intruder could have picked up a knife at the scene. Perhaps he'd been near the kitchen and Maulle confronted him. There was no sign of a struggle downstairs, but she and Koertig would walk the scene over the next hour and come up with an initial theory. The next day, once Belle and her team had collected all the forensic evidence, they would return for a more thorough search of the house, looking for anything that could suggest a motive for the crime.

"We'll need a warrant," Jude said.

While a warrantless search could keep things simple, she always thought ahead to courtroom challenges. The defense invariably raised questions about the competence of investigators, evidence collection, and chain-of-custody issues. The legality of the search could become an issue. Obtaining a warrant with the broadest possible scope was a good way to sidestep at least one hurdle. Prosecutors appreciated when detectives dotted the i's.

Belle gave the photographer a few more instructions, then looked toward Jude and Koertig. "Why don't y'all make your notes before I get started in there."

A couple of flash pops were followed by a raucous squawk, and the African Grey shook the bars of his cage.

"We ought to remove the bird," Jude said. "If he keeps flapping around all kinds of crap is going to fly out of his cage. Let's get animal control up here."

"I can carry him out," Koertig said. "That cage lifts off the stand."

"Put the cover over it," Jude suggested. "I think that's supposed to calm birds down."

"Hang on. Let me dust it first." Belle picked up her glass fiber brush. "If only he could talk. He saw everything."

❖

"Check this out," Koertig said, moving to the far end of the kitchen.

After they'd taken a close look at Maulle and left the body to be removed, they started their assessment downstairs, examining possible points of entry. As they worked, the forensic crew dusted for prints and collected trace.

"These French doors are deadlocked, but there's a pet door in the laundry." Koertig pointed to custom double swing doors. "Someone could crawl right on in."

Jude looked out the laundry window. A fenced dog run occupied most of the backyard, a sensible precaution in the mountains, where pets were often attacked by wild animals. "Maulle's poodle was out back when the killer arrived. And no one carries a pile of bologna in their pocket because they like the smell. He came prepared to deal with the dog."

"He must have cased the place ahead of time," Koertig said.

"Or he knew about the poodle because he and Maulle were already acquainted."

"Do you think Maulle let the guy in?"

"If he did, why shoot the dog? No, I think our perp entered via the pet door and exited out the front."

"So the dog barks, he feeds her bologna and whacks her, then he comes in the pet door on his hands and knees—"

"By which time, Maulle is on his way down with his walking cane," Jude said. "He must have heard the barking and the shot."

"So the killer takes a knife from the block on the kitchen counter," Koertig said.

From the looks of the block, each slot was usually occupied. There were two knives missing. The larger one was in the sink.

"Why take a knife when he already has a gun?" Jude asked.

"He's freaking out because Maulle caught him. Something goes wrong with the gun, maybe."

"That's a possibility. Or he had a change of heart. His plan was to execute Maulle just like he executed the dog, but for some reason he got angry. A shooting would have been too quick."

"He chased Maulle up the stairs," Koertig mused aloud. "They wrestled for control of the knife. Maulle took a stab wound."

"I think he hit the killer with the head of the cane first," Jude said. "Then the killer got mad and stabbed him."

"So, Maulle staggers along the hallway to his office—"

"Accounting for the blood and the sets of bloody footprints." There were three, from what Jude could see. One set was significantly smaller than the others. Pippa's.

"Why did Maulle make a run for the office instead of the bathroom?" Koertig asked. "He could have locked himself in there and called 911."

"Self-defense," Jude said. "He keeps a gun in the top drawer of his desk."

"You looked already?"

"Yes, and there's a bloody handprint on the desk and blood on the drawer handle. Maulle was clutching his abdomen. He put his left hand down to steady himself while he opened the drawer with his right hand."

"But the killer aimed his gun and told him to freeze," Koertig conjectured. Maybe he convinced Maulle that if he cooperated he wouldn't be shot."

"Or it could be the other way around," Jude said. "Maybe Maulle reasoned with the killer. A rich guy like him could offer money."

"Why didn't the perp cut a deal?" Koertig strolled through the kitchen once more. "Either this hump is the dumbest burglar alive, or robbery definitely wasn't the motive."

It was too soon to rule anything out entirely, but Jude thought they were pretty safe excluding the burglary angle. As they analyzed the evidence, their theory of the crime would evolve, but for now, she was pretty sure the killer had some kind of connection with Maulle.

"I don't think this was random," she said. "Maulle had an enemy. So, we're looking for a motive." Murder 101: motive plus opportunity equals suspect.

Koertig stared around. "No one gets this rich without trampling on a few toes."

"How do you want to do this?" Jude asked, reminding herself that she wasn't the primary this time. "We'll need to interview Pippa Calloway and get the search started ASAP."

"You take the girl. She might be more comfortable with a female." Koertig checked his watch. "Belle's going to be on scene all night. I'll pick up the warrant first thing tomorrow after the briefing and meet you here when you're through with the niece."

"Works for me."

They walked through the huge living room once more before heading out the front door. The outdoor lights were on and people were leaving. Animal control had caged Maulle's three cats and were loading them into the back of a van. The K-9 units had found no sign of the assailant in the heavily wooded vicinity. They'd be back in the morning to resume searching for evidence. The few reporters who'd shown up for a statement from Pratt had left with breaking news to report.

A gust of wind stirred the treetops, causing mournful creaks.

Night birds cried. The thin, waxing moon was obscured by a drift of cloud cover. Around the staging area, the temporary lighting seemed garishly overbright. Jude shivered slightly. Fall was in the air, making the temperature drop sharply at night. She was puzzled to see Pippa Calloway sitting on the verandah where she'd left her.

Approaching Sergeant Pavlic, she asked, "Why haven't they taken Ms. Calloway to the hospital yet?"

"She won't leave the bird, and they wouldn't take it in the ambulance with her."

"Well, she can't stay here all night."

"We're waiting on the grief counselor," the sergeant said, plainly thankful that a caring professional would soon show up to deal with the stalemate.

Jude watched Pippa Calloway press her cheek to the cage and stroke the bird's cloud-colored breast feathers. In response, the parrot leaned into her and ran its beak across her lips.

Jude wasn't the only one staring in astonishment when it crooned in a soft masculine voice, "I love you, Pip."

CHAPTER SIX

Jude escorted Pippa Calloway to Southwest Memorial in Cortez and waited while the doctor examined her. She sent a deputy out to Eddie House's place with the parrot. Eddie was an expert in rehabilitating birds. When she called him he seemed excited, or that was Jude's interpretation when he said something long and pensive about the mysterious telepathy of the African Grey and its single-minded devotion to its humans.

Jude planned to escort Pippa to the Holiday Inn once the she was cleared by the doctor. She was staying at the same hotel, her usual accommodation when she had work to do at the MCSO headquarters in Cortez. Pippa would have to remain there until her uncle's house could be occupied or she made other arrangements. Sheriff Pratt had called her mother, Maulle's next-of-kin. Mrs Calloway was planning to fly to Durango with her husband tomorrow. According to Pratt she was "the snooty type."

Jude hoped Pippa would be comforted to hear that her folks would be in town soon. After she'd signed off on the paperwork and picked up a sleep aid prescription, they strolled out to the parking lot and she told Pippa the good news.

"Your parents are flying in tomorrow."

Pippa's reaction was interesting. She said, "Of course they are, the vultures."

"You don't sound pleased."

"I just escaped from them." With the melodrama of youth, Pippa added, "They ruined my brother's life by making him marry my sister-in-law. I'm not letting them ruin mine."

Jude wondered how bad it could be. During the conversation with the grief counselor before they left for the hospital, Pippa had described graduating from Harvard and realizing, after a few trips abroad to various European capitals, that she could never face being a dentist. Her parents had arranged a cushy job for her and were angry that she was throwing her training away. Not that she needed to work, anyway, she'd pointed out. She had a small annual allowance from her grandfather's estate, enough to scrape by on if she lived somewhere inexpensive and grew her own vegetables.

Her plan had been to stay with her uncle for a while and pursue a career as a sculptor. Obviously she wouldn't have to worry about ending up on the street if that didn't pan out.

"Your uncle never married?" Jude asked as they climbed in the Dakota and set off for the hotel.

"He was gay."

"Is there a partner?"

"Years ago he was with someone. That didn't work out and since then I don't think there's been anything serious."

"It sounds like you were close to your uncle."

"Yes." Pippa's voice was husky. "He's the only person who really cared about me. I mean I know Mom and Dad love me, it's just that it feels totally conditional. They want me to be a certain way, to have certain people as my friends. My first serious boyfriend was African American. You wouldn't believe what happened."

"Try me," Jude prompted.

She could sense that Pippa was chattering to distract herself from all she'd been though. In this state, she could reveal quite a lot in an interview. Jude was tempted to drive direct to headquarters and make the most of the opportunity. On the other hand, just talking like this would establish a rapport and build trust.

"Dad got him into Vanderbilt and paid his tuition for a year," Pippa said in disgust. "That was the deal. We break up, he gets ahead."

"Well, if he agreed to that—"

"I made him agree. Things weren't going to work out anyway." Anger sharpened her tone. "Not that my parents could see that. I thought he may as well get a parting gift at Dad's expense."

"Pippa, I'm going to ask you this question again down at the station tomorrow, but do you have any idea who killed your uncle?"

"I wish I did."

"Even a vague suspicion. Just a feeling."

Pippa shook her head. "I really don't know any of Uncle Fabian's friends. He kept family separate. I mean, I met people sometimes if we were out and ran into them. But honestly, I don't know much about his life outside of home."

"You spent time with him regularly?"

"Usually a couple of vacations each year and some long weekends."

"Did you ever notice anything odd? Phone calls late at night. People dropping off parcels to the house, and your uncle acting strangely. Anything like that?"

Pippa was silent for a long while. "I don't know if this counts, but after Katrina, something happened at the house in New Orleans and all of a sudden Uncle Fabian hired a security guard."

"Do you know what occurred?"

"No. It was in November. He said I didn't need to worry about it."

"When Detective Koertig and I were examining your uncle's office, we found his computer was dismantled and the hard drive removed. Do you know when that occurred?"

"No, but Uncle Fabian would never have done that," Pippa said with certainty. "He was the ultimate technophobe. He wouldn't have known what a hard drive looked like."

"Would he have backed up his computer onto a CD or a memory stick?"

"No, I did that for him when I stayed. I showed him how, but he never got organized about that stuff."

"He had computers in both his homes?"

"In all four houses. And he had a laptop. I helped him buy that around Christmas."

Four homes. What was he, head of a drug cartel? Jude decided to leave that intriguing question unanswered for the moment. She turned into the Holiday Inn parking lot and took her bag and Pippa's from the back of the pickup. After the exhausted young woman had settled into her room, Jude handed her one of the sleeping pills with a glass of water.

"I don't do drugs," Pippa said.

"You need to rest so I can pick your brain in the morning. I want to catch the guy who killed your uncle."

Pippa took the pill and flopped dejectedly onto one of the armchairs in front of the TV. "I keep thinking I'll wake up and this will all be a horrible nightmare."

"Take a shower before that pill makes you woozy, then get into bed and close your eyes," Jude instructed, surprised at herself. She sounded like someone's mother.

The young woman nodded absently. "He spoke to me before he died. I asked him who did it but he didn't say. All he talked about was Oscar."

"You were there with him at the end." Jude soothed her as best she could. "The last thing he saw was the face of someone he loved. I know it's not much, but most victims of violent crime are not so fortunate. I'm sure it was a comfort to him."

Tears drenched Pippa's deep-sea eyes. "Yes, I hadn't thought of that. Thanks, Detective Devine. You've been really nice."

Amazing, Jude thought cynically, *some of us are human beings.* "Is there anything else you need before I go?"

"No, thank you. I'll be fine."

Jude wrote her room number on the hotel notepad and said, "Just in case."

As she left, she glanced back before closing the door. Pippa was hugging herself like a hurt child, tears rolling down her face.

❖

"What does it take for you to answer your phone?" Mercy's throaty tease made Jude's skin prickle. "I've been calling all day."

Jude deleted the voicemail message without listening to the rest of it. She wasn't in the mood to deal with her ex. Not today, and probably not tomorrow, either. Mercy had been phoning her and stopping by the stationhouse on flimsy pretexts ever since she returned from her honeymoon in March. Jude wasn't sure why Mercy wanted to pretend they could be friends. She'd never been suckered into that lesbian daydream, herself. When it was over, it was over. Whatever "it" was.

By any definition, she and Mercy didn't have a "relationship."

A relationship implied emotional connection, a togetherness that existed on more than one plane. Jude didn't know how to categorize their liaison. She supposed the term "hookup" could be applied to a series of nonexclusive sexual encounters with the same person. Zero commitment. Fun while it lasted. Anyway, she was a free agent now.

Unenthralled by the thought, Jude tossed her cell phone on the bed and stalked into the tiny bathroom. She turned on the shower, stripped, and stuffed her dirty clothes into the laundry bag she'd brought with her. She always felt disgusting after walking a crime scene, as if death had soaked into her pores. For that reason she kept a scrubbing brush and loofah mittens in her overnight bag.

After she'd gone through the motions of cleaning her body, she toweled off and checked out her physique in the mirror, a habit she ascribed to common sense, not vanity. If she wasn't well toned, she was vulnerable, and Jude didn't like feeling subpar. She turned slowly and saw powerful shoulders and arms, but a belly and hips that needed work. Since her broken ankle she'd slacked off and it showed.

Irritated, she scrubbed her teeth. She needed to get back into her old routine, taking long hikes whenever she had a couple of days off. That was one thing she loved about living in the Southwest. There was always something new and wonderful to explore. She could always find solitude and silence.

Her cell phone rang, and she spat the foamy toothpaste and rinsed hastily. It was probably Koertig or Pratt calling to see how things were going with Pippa Calloway. She rushed to the bed and flipped the phone open before voicemail could pick up.

"Jude?" came a soft query.

Horrified, Jude lowered the phone from her ear and peered at the caller ID. In her haste to take the call, she hadn't checked before answering.

"Is this work related?" she asked, just in case the Fates had decided to torture her and Mercy had been assigned to conduct the autopsy on Fabian Maulle.

"If I say yes will you talk to me?"

Jude hated Mercy's habit of answering a question with a question. "I don't have time for this. What do you want?"

"Why won't you come to the soirée?"

"Oh, for crying out loud." Jude plunked herself down on the bed. "Is that what you're calling about?"

"Jude, we have to move beyond this. It's been months since the wedding. Your behavior only draws attention and makes people wonder."

"Like attention is a problem for you. Was I on drugs or did you and Elspeth go on TV to announce your wedding?"

"I wasn't referring to myself," Mercy said. "You're the one who's paranoid about being outed."

"Funny, that's not how it seemed when we were seeing each other."

Mercy had flatly refused to go on social outings in case they were spotted together. Jude had respected her wishes. After all, they didn't live in San Francisco. This was the Four Corners, right next to Utah, not exactly a bastion of tolerance and diversity. The few gays and lesbians Jude encountered were not out publicly, although friends and family usually knew. Durango had a visible LGBT community and a PFLAG branch, adding fuel to the widely held view that the place was a hotbed of liberals and rich lefties, destined to become just like that hippy-infested Sodom in the east, Boulder.

Jude didn't have a problem with being discreet, and besides, it suited her agenda. Being open about her sexual orientation would compromise her undercover operation. There was no way Harrison Hawke would bare his soul with a lesbian, so Jude had gone to some trouble to establish heterosexual credentials, including a bogus boyfriend. The mutual "beard" arrangement she had struck with Bobby Lee Parker was in part to help her cover, but she had also gone that route to shield Mercy. Not that it made any difference. Mercy still wouldn't share even the kinds of social outings that were normal for women whose paths crossed professionally. Now, all of a sudden, she was out and proud. Married, no less, to the woman she'd been sleeping with throughout her nonmonogamous unrelationship with Jude. Elspeth Harwood, phoniness personified.

"Elspeth and I are willing to let bygones be bygones," Mercy said.

Jude was ready to puke. "I'm going to hang up now."

"No! Please. Wait."

A soft rush of breath poured into Jude's ear, filling her with unbearable longing. She still missed Mercy so badly she could forget to breathe. Hating that sorry fact, she forced her lungs to process air and said, "Could we just let this go? I'm not coming to your party. I'm not into the movies your wife makes. I have nothing in common with her or her friends. Why would I torture myself by spending a whole evening with those people?"

"To see me," Mercy said.

"Are you serious? You think I'm that desperate?"

"Yes."

Infuriated, Jude said, "Fuck you."

"Yes, fuck me."

The husky reply made the blood rush to Jude's head. She sagged back against the pillows, willing herself not to hear Mercy repeating those very words as their bodies danced in carnal rhythm. She wanted to hang up, but the sound of Mercy's breathing stopped her. Thanks to a marvel of technology, their voices could bounce from earth to space and back again. Yet they still weren't communicating.

Jude forced herself to lower the phone before Mercy could speak again. Staring at the display, she placed her finger on the End button and severed the electronic pulse that connected them.

❖

Lone turned in her rental Toyota at Provo, took a cab to one of several Starbucks in the vicinity, and walked for twenty minutes to reach the garage she'd leased for the past year under the name "Houseclean Enterprises." She swapped the plates on the Honda Accord she'd left there on Thursday, then drove to Monticello, not stopping at any time during the four-hour trip. As she approached Madeline's tidy suburban house, she checked her wristwatch. Taking this route, the trip home from Jackson Hole was around seven hundred miles, just over twelve hours on the road, counting the stopover in Provo. It was now 0320 hours. With the final leg to Rico, she would be home before six in the morning, exactly according to plan.

She parked in the garage and closed the door by remote. At this time of night the neighbors were all asleep. Hopefully no one would notice her arrival and even if they did, they wouldn't think twice about it. She made a point of visiting the house at least once a month, like any absentee owner, staying for a couple of days to make sure her property was in order. During that time, she would come and go occasionally, including late at night. Routines were important. People paid no attention when they seemed familiar.

The house was silent and had a musty, unoccupied smell. Lone turned on the kitchen light, took a bottle of juice from the fridge, and sat down at the table. As she drank, she reviewed her decision to execute the first phase of her mission at an event instead of at one of the three Cheney residences.

The drawbacks were obvious. Heightened security. Greater risk of collateral damage. Late notice—most Cheney appearances weren't announced publicly until close to the date, so last-minute logistics hassles were inevitable.

Yet there was an upside. Security would be tight. It always was when the VP left a secure location for one of his carefully orchestrated glimpses of the outside world. Yet the Secret Service's successful record in protecting vice presidents could create a chink. Cheney's detail thought they had the threat assessment formula down. They believed they could single out the kind of individual who could be gunning for their man. Audiences were handpicked and subject to intense screening. Only the party faithful and big donors were allowed up close.

By controlling access, the Secret Service had the battle half won. Their man would never veer off script and break through the perimeter of his protection on some random whim to speak to a veteran in a wheelchair, or kiss a baby. Such impulses were driven by curiosity or an innate empathy for others—human sentiments that would never afflict the Dicktator. This was a man who shot captive quail from the safety of his car: why not stalk hamsters? If there was one thing Lone could count on, it was that Cheney's actions in a crisis would be driven by self-interest, cowardice, and paranoia. He was completely predictable, and that made her planning easier.

To neutralize him, she intended to exploit the one vulnerability all high-profile targets shared. Arrival and departure. The Secret Service could control access in a contained space, but out in the open the environment was unpredictable. Massive advance planning was always undertaken and plans were made for all kinds of contingency. Routes were kept secret and streets and buildings around the venue were cleared. But there was no way to guarantee security. The unexpected could happen and Lone planned to make sure it did.

She knew exactly how to create the opportunity she needed. Chaos would be a factor. Wherever Cheney went, there would always be protestors, and in certain cities the turnout would be optimum. A frightened crowd could be counted upon to create a commotion. A van full of plastic explosive would deliver mayhem, even if no one was hurt. Lone had spent the past year observing the security measures at Cheney appearances and making advance plans of her own for five potential venues. By her calculations, he would appear at one of these in the near future, and she would be ready. She even knew where she would park the van and which building she would hide in ahead of time.

Lone poured the rest of the juice down the drain and walked through the house, making sure all the doors and windows were secure. She paused in the bedroom she'd shared with Madeline and picked up a framed photo from the dresser. Madeline and Brandon, heads tilted close. From each face, the same serious brown eyes regarded her with deep affection. Mother and son smiled with the joyful surprise of people whose lives hadn't been easy and who cherished the good times when they came along. Lone dusted the picture against her T-shirt and replaced it on the wood surface. Despite her lack of faith, she believed they were together now, in heaven. Surely, if there was a higher being, they had been granted peace.

Sitting on her side of the bed, Lone dwelled on her undertaking. She knew it was wrong to take the law into her own hands. But the men of the evil alliance did not respect the law or the constitution. They were bereft of honor or conscience, and entirely corrupted by power. Their stranglehold on the country had to end, and surely it was the duty of any true patriot to see that it did. Lone took that duty seriously. Operation Houseclean was now in transition. Her planning was complete, her rehearsal phase was in its final stages. Within weeks, she would be ready to execute.

There were eight names on her list. Nothing excessive, and all extremely deserving.

❖

"What's the time?" Debbie blinked and rubbed the sleep from her eyes, almost dropped the phone.

"Just after six. Hey, Debbie doll, how are you?"

"I was worried about you."

"Why?"

"Wouldn't any woman be worried if her partner went away for days and never called?"

She felt guilty for talking to Jude about her relationship and for letting her go through files on the computer. If only Lone communicated more, she wouldn't have involved their detective friend.

"I told you I'd be out of range. I can't keep trying my phone just in case there's a signal."

Debbie didn't believe Lone had tried her phone once. "Where were you?"

"In the mountains." Lone's voice softened. "Sweetheart, I told you not to worry. Don't I always comes back?"

"Yes, but what if you didn't? What if you were lost? Imagine how stupid I'd feel trying to report you missing, not knowing a thing about where you were hiking." Feeling like a nag, she said, "It doesn't help that you keep changing your cell phone number. What if I lost the new one? Not that you ever answer my calls anyway."

Lone sighed. "You're angry."

"Yes."

"Then I'd better make it up to you."

Debbie's stomach dropped. Lone knew exactly how to reduce her to putty. It happened every time they had words, and what they usually fought about was Lone's obsession with privacy. Debbie felt incredibly shut out. It occurred to her that she would trust Lone with her life, yet she didn't trust her completely as a partner. What was wrong with her? After all Lone had done to help her and make her feel good about herself, it didn't make sense.

She came right out with her worst fear. "Is there another woman?"

"No." The denial was swift and emphatic. A soft chuckle followed. "Is that why you're upset? You think I'm seeing someone?"

There was a patronizing note in her voice, like she thought Debbie was being ridiculous and had no right to question her. Debbie had heard the same tone before. From Meg. Her ex had always gotten self-righteous when Debbie challenged her. She'd hidden her cheating behind lies and guilt trips, making Debbie feel like a bad person for being untrusting. Lone was completely different from Meg, and Debbie couldn't believe she was fooling around. But when your partner keeps on disappearing and not answering the phone, what other explanation is there?

She knew Lone was waiting for her to crumple like she always did, and she knew how this conversation would end. Lone would be in her house and in her bed, and she would push her concerns to the back of her mind yet again. Well, she was fed up with that game. Lone felt far away, even in their most intimate moments. The distance between them made Debbie question everything. Did Lone even love her?

"I don't know what to think," Debbie said, adding wordlessly, *Because you don't talk to me.*

"Don't you trust me?" Lone sounded hurt and genuinely shocked.

Normally Debbie would be apologizing by now, she was such a sucker. With a flash of anger, she said, "I think I'm the one who should be asking that question. If I went away for days without telling you where I was and never phoned, wouldn't you want an explanation?"

"Debbie doll—"

"Don't," Debbie said sharply. "You always turn things around as if I'm the one who's being unreasonable. You act like I'm silly because I want you to tell me what's going on."

"I don't think you're silly. I love you."

"Then how can you talk about us moving to Canada without even telling me where we're going? What if I have other plans? Are you just going to go without me?"

"I'm coming over," Lone said stiffly.

"Don't bother," Debbie flung back, furious that Lone still hadn't answered a single question. "I won't be home."

"Okay, I'll come to Le Paradox."

"I won't be there, either."

"Calm down, baby. This isn't helping."

Debbie wasn't sure what had possessed her, but suddenly she wanted to make Lone walk a mile in her shoes. Lone thought she could come over and make love just to avoid the issue. Well, not this time. Forcing a flippant note, Debbie repeated the words Lone casually threw at her every time she went away. "I'll call you when I get back."

Lone still wasn't hearing her. "I think we should talk. How about if I bring over a couple of steaks and put them on the grill."

Debbie's hands shook. "Do what you like. You're welcome to use the house while I'm away, if you want."

"Away?"

"That's right." Using the same excuse she'd heard from Lone on several occasions, she said, "Something came up and I have to be out of town."

"It's not Meg, is it?" Irritation drove the tenderness from Lone's voice. "I told that lawyer of hers if she ever hassles you again you'll take her to court."

"This isn't about Meg." Debbie got out of bed and took clean clothes from her drawers.

"Then what's up? Where are you going?"

Debbie laughed. "I can't believe you're asking me to explain myself. Haven't you heard anything I just said?"

A stony silence followed, then Lone bit out, "So, this is some kind of tit for tat?"

Tears blurred Debbie's vision, but she kept control of herself. "Lone, you know everything about my life, and I know nothing about yours. You know where I am every hour of the day, but I never have a clue where you are unless we're together. You sleep in my house, but I don't even know where you live. You tell me we're moving to Canada. You don't even ask if I want to. And you accuse *me* of not being trusting?" She gulped in a breath. "*You're* the one who doesn't trust. *You're* the one keeping secrets, and I've had enough. Do you understand?"

A heavy silence stretched between them. Debbie watched the digital clock count down the seconds. When it became clear that Lone didn't intend to meet her halfway, she said, "Just so you know, the silent treatment is getting old and it's childish. I'm going to take a shower now."

Still no reply.

Debbie gathered her clean clothes despondently. "I love you,

Lone, and you're hurting my feelings. Think about that when you shut me out."

This time she didn't wait for a reply. Dropping the receiver into its cradle with a sharp thud, she stared at the pillow Lone slept on. They'd been sharing a bed for more than a year, but it only dawned on her now that she didn't really know who her lover was. She just hoped she did.

CHAPTER SEVEN

The interview room smelled powerfully of chemicals and lemon deodorizer, the scent having built up overnight after the cleaners shut the door. Pippa sneezed and blew her nose. She looked like she'd cried all night.

Jude took the seat across the table from her and said, "Are you sure you don't want to speak with your lawyer before we begin?"

"I don't have a lawyer. Do I need one?"

"That's entirely up to you. We don't have to do this now. If you'd rather wait for your parents—"

"God, no. Let's get it over with."

Jude went through the formalities, explaining that the interview was being taped and that Pippa could be asked to give evidence in court.

"That's fine," Pippa said. "I don't know anything. But whatever."

"I want you to relax and think back to yesterday afternoon," Jude said. "Just tell me everything you remember. Even the little things that don't seem important. Let's start with driving to the house. In your 911 call, it seemed like you weren't sure of the address."

"I'd never been there. I overshot twice trying to find it," Pippa said. "I turned around at Stoner and came back down the road. But by the time I saw the house I'd already gone past it again, so I pulled into a driveway. I remember the ranch. *A River Runs Through It.* Very original."

Jude smiled. "I know the place. Did you have to wait for any cars to pass before you could make the turn?"

Pippa stared into space for a moment. "Yes, there was a white family car heading north, and two other cars passed on the other side going toward Cortez. One was an old Cadillac with a wobbly back wheel. The other was a Lexus. An LS 460. Dark gray with tinted windows. I thought it was going to smash into the back of the Cadillac."

"It was in a hurry?"

"Yes, it was trying to pass the Cadillac. The driver was pissed and flipped the bird."

"Are you sure it was a Lexus?"

Pippa nodded. "My sister-in-law has the same model. Dad says it's a status car made for dummies. She's a terrible driver."

"Do you remember anything else about either car?"

"The Cadillac had all kinds of bumper stickers. Nascar. Playboy. Immature stuff. The Lexus had a Colorado plate. I looked at it because I thought if there was an accident I might have to come forward."

"Did you get the number?"

"I was going to write it down when I got to Uncle Fabian's but with everything that happened I forgot. There might have been an 'X' in it."

"That's helpful." There couldn't be too many of the luxury sedans registered in Colorado. The color and plate details would narrow down the search. "So, you drove up to your uncle's house, arriving at around four forty p.m. on the afternoon of Saturday, the eighteenth of August. How were you feeling?"

Pippa blinked, as though she'd anticipated a different question. Jude deliberately tapped into different areas of memory during a cognitive interview with a witness. If a person got into a pattern of describing only what she saw, she could forget to mention something she heard or smelled. Asking Pippa to recall her feelings would keep her from settling into a groove. With most witnesses it also helped build rapport.

"I was happy. Incredibly relieved. I'd been driving for days."

"I'm sure you couldn't wait to get inside," Jude affirmed.

"I knocked. I guess I waited a minute, then I looked in the windows and I couldn't see anyone so I went in. Coco wasn't there." Her face contracted. "Why do that? Why kill a sweet old dog like her?"

Jude passed Pippa a tissue, agreeing, "It's unforgivable. I really want to catch the creep who did this."

"I called out and walked around and then I went upstairs. I thought I heard something. A thud. It must have been my uncle. When I got to the top of the stairs I saw his cane and I knew something was wrong. There was blood on it."

"Did you pick it up?"

"No, all I could think about was finding him. There was blood on the floor. I stepped in it." She paused. "I probably ruined evidence. When I saw him I just grabbed on and held him. Was that the wrong thing to do?"

"Not at all. You did what anyone would do."

"I called 911. He was trying to talk to me."

"Please think very carefully, Pippa. You were right there, holding him. What were his exact words?"

"He said they killed Coco."

They.

"I asked him who hurt him and he said something like 'nobody knows.' And then he told me he was dying and he got worried about Oscar. He was talking about his food box, like I'd let him starve. He was…going. I could feel it."

"Did he say anything else?"

"Only that he loved me." Pippa buried her face in her hands. "I should have tried to stop the blood, but I panicked."

"Pippa, you did all you could. Your uncle died because a criminal stabbed him."

"The sheriff said it might have been a robbery and my uncle interrupted the burglars."

"It's too soon to guess at what really happened. But it's certainly important for us to examine every possibility. If fingerprints and DNA are present we might get a match in our databases."

Pippa seemed buoyed by this idea. She took another tissue from the box.

Jude waited for her to blow her nose and calm her breathing, then asked, "Another possibility is that the killer was known to your uncle. Going back to that incident in New Orleans you mentioned last night. What can you tell me about it?"

"Uncle Fabian was worried. And he was angry. I could tell."

"Do you know which security company he hired?"

"Yes, Counter Threat Group. I remember because it was weird. You should have seen those guys. They carried machine guns."

Jude didn't comment. She recognized the name. CTG was one of the more prestigious global private security firms specializing in close protection. Why would Maulle have hired heavy hitters like these guys? And why weren't they still with him? Did he think he'd dealt with the threat, whatever it was?

"Do you have any theories about what happened?"

Pippa looked pained. "I wish I'd paid more attention. There was one night…I heard Uncle Fabian talking on his cell phone. That was just before the CTG guys arrived. All I can remember was something about Anton's people and how Anton could crawl back under his rock."

"Do you know who Anton is?"

"Human slime. That's according to one of the guards. Hugo. I don't know his other name. He was South African."

"Do you remember anything else?" Jude would have to track Hugo down. Hopefully, he hadn't joined the countless mercenaries in Iraq.

"I know Uncle Fabian was upset," Pippa said. "Normally we went out a lot when I stayed, but not that time. I had to drag Hugo if I wanted to go anywhere, and Uncle Fabian wanted me to stay at home, so it was a pretty boring vacation."

"Did he tell you anything else about Anton? Like a last name, for example?"

"No. I was kind of distracted. My final year and so on. I wasn't paying much attention."

"Actually, what you've remembered is very useful." Jude took a sip of water while she gathered her thoughts. "Your uncle was a wealthy man. What line of work was he in?"

"I think some of his money came from investments, although he was always making jokes about hedgies. He said they would still get to keep their fifty-million-dollar houses even if they lost all their clients' money, and that's why he didn't do business with them."

"So he wasn't involved in hedge funds?" If any other form of legalized gambling returned the kind of cash Maulle appeared to have, Jude wasn't aware of it.

"Not anymore. All I know is that he traveled overseas a lot on business, but he never told me what kind of business he was in."

"What were his interests?"

"He collected art, mostly paintings and pottery. He was into opera and ballet. I guess you could say he was an elitist. But he wasn't a snob, not like my mother."

"You mentioned his former partner when we spoke last night. What was his name?"

"I'll write it down. The spelling is weird."

She took the pen and notepad Jude passed her and wrote "Yitzhak Eshkol."

"They were together for ages. At least ten years."

"When did the relationship end?"

"Maybe 2000 or 2001."

"Did your uncle have casual partners?"

"Yes, but I never met any of them."

"Did your uncle live with Mr. Eshkol?"

"Yes, at his London house. I think he did that deliberately so he wouldn't have to put up with shit from my parents. Bad enough gay, but a Jewish boyfriend? Ohmigod."

"Your mom and dad are anti-Semites?"

"They wouldn't see it that way. You know, it's fine to have dinner with one, but we don't marry them." Perhaps reading something into Jude's steady gaze, she said, "It seems so yesterday, doesn't it?"

Jude kept her opinion to herself. She was never surprised by anything people did or thought. "So your parents and your uncle didn't see eye to eye?"

"That's an understatement."

"Any idea who's likely to benefit financially from his death?"

Laughter broke through Pippa's melancholy, brightening her eyes. She was immediately contrite. "God, listen to me. It's not funny, is it? I mean, you have to ask about family. They're the usual suspects."

"It's strictly routine," Jude said. "We start with the people closest to the deceased and work our way out."

"Now that you ask, I guess he might have left Mom some money, and he always said he'd leave me his pottery collection. I don't know what I'm supposed to do with it since I don't have a house."

"Your brother?"

"Mom thinks Ryan will get Maulle Mansion, but I seriously doubt that's going to happen. I think he'll get a car or a painting. Something token. Uncle Fabian was okay with Ryan, but he called my sister-in-law a grasping shrew and she called him a fag, so there was a rift between them."

"Families, huh?" Jude commiserated. "Any idea what your uncle planned to do with most of his estate?"

"If I had to guess, I'd say he left everything to charity." She glanced toward the door as a sharp knock interrupted their conversation.

A metrosexual in a shiny Italian suit and black cowboy boots sauntered past a deputy. "Detective Devine, what a pleasure." Griffin Mahanes removed his dark glasses and offered Jude the tiger-eyed stare that captivated female jurors.

Mahanes was a criminal defense attorney with an upmarket practice in Denver. Occasionally he showed up in the Four Corners if there was a high-profile case he thought he could win. Mahanes proclaimed a passion for the west, and had even packed a Colt six-shooter for his recent appearance on Suzette Kelly's *Colorado Connoisseurs*, a celebrity gossip show on Channel 8. Whenever he honored Cortez with his presence, he made sure to tone down his city accent.

Jude rose, puzzled by his presence when they hadn't made an arrest. "Mr. Mahanes, how can I help you?"

Mahanes sauntered to the table and set his briefcase down on top of Jude's notes. "If I may, I'd appreciate a word with my client."

Pippa stared at him blankly. "Do you mean me?"

"Ms. Calloway is not under arrest," Jude said. "Neither is she a suspect. She's helping us with our inquiries."

Mahanes gave Jude a superior smile, and stuck out a well-groomed hand to Pippa. "Ms. Calloway. My deepest condolences on your loss. I'm Griffin Mahanes. Your parents retained my services."

"What for? I don't need a lawyer. I haven't done anything wrong."

"Of course you haven't, and that's why I'm here. Detectives are always eager to pin a crime on a family member if they can."

Jude shoved his case aside and extracted her notes.

"Have my parents even arrived yet?" Pippa demanded.

"They'll be here in a few hours. Now, we have some important things to discuss, Ms. Calloway, and I know Detective Devine will agree with me that you should be fully briefed on the situation before answering any more questions."

Pippa cast a helpless glance toward Jude. "Do I have to?"

Careful not to sound like she was discouraging a witness from talking to a lawyer, Jude said, "It's your choice, Pippa."

She didn't want to pressure her. They'd verified her alibi that morning and Jude was sure she had nothing to do with her uncle's death.

Pippa's uncertainty showed on her face. "I suppose it's the sensible thing to do."

Touching her shoulder, Jude said, "I'll see you later."

Mahanes walked her to the door. "You know the drill, Detective. Henceforth, you don't talk to my client. You talk to me."

Jude managed to avoid Sheriff Pratt as she left the MCSO headquarters. She drove past the modern gray Cortez PD building and stopped at Centennial Park. Leaving the Dakota unlocked, she strolled across the springy lawn toward the duck pond. The heat was already building and most of the ducks couldn't be bothered leaving the water to see if she had food they could beg for.

She sat on the bench opposite the murky expanse of water and cleared her voicemail.

Tulley: How come he and Smoke'm hadn't been called to the murder scene when Smoke'm was the best tracker dog in the entire state? Also, please reconsider the soirée.

Debbie, in half sentences: Sandy was back and they'd quarreled. She wanted Jude to call her.

The pet-sitter: she couldn't look after Yiska tonight or tomorrow.

Agatha Benham: She'd asked Bobby Lee to come to the soirée. He had other plans. She thought Jude should put her foot down and make him come.

Jude decided to ignore the messages that felt like emotional blackmail, and make other arrangements for her cat. That left just one call she needed to return.

Not surprisingly, Debbie was upset. She wasn't the type who thrived on drama and confrontation. After recounting a garbled version of her conversation with Sandy, she said, "So, now I don't know what's going to happen. She hasn't called back."

"Where are you?" Jude asked, figuring that by now Sandy would be looking for her.

"I'm at the station. Agatha was just telling me about the soirée. It sounds incredible. Elspeth Harwood. She's so stunning. Oh, my God."

Jude resisted the urge to hurl the phone into the duck pond. "You should go," she said. "Agatha would take you. Just ask."

Debbie giggled. "Oh, I couldn't. I'm shy at parties and with all those celebrities, I'd probably get tipsy and make a fool of myself."

Sticking to the subject at hand, Jude said, "Are you really planning a trip somewhere?"

"No, I just said that because I was mad at her. She was acting like I'm the one being unreasonable, so I thought I'd give her a taste of her own medicine."

"Fair enough." Jude could imagine how that went over. "You've been putting up with her bullshit for months. Maybe going away isn't such a bad idea."

"That's what I thought," Debbie said. "The problem is I can't afford it and I wouldn't know where to go anyway. So I feel a bit stupid now."

Jude thought quickly. "I have an idea. My pet-sitter can't take care of Yiska after today and I'm going to be stuck in Cortez until Tuesday at least. Want to stay at my place?"

"Are you sure?"

"You'd be doing me a favor. Tulley will take you over there, and if you give him a key to your place, he'll feed your cats."

"That would be wonderful," Debbie sniffed into a tissue. "I've just rescheduled all my hair appointments. I can pick up some extra clothes and leave right away."

"She'll call you, of course." Jude needed the latest cell phone number so she could throw something to Arbiter. "Let me take down her number."

Debbie hesitated. "She won't like that one bit."

"This is just between you and me," Jude said. "I'm concerned for her well-being, Debbie. It's a precaution, that's all."

"Are you going to call her?"

"No. It's better if she doesn't know I'm involved."

Reluctantly, Debbie supplied the number. "She'll probably change it again soon. You know how that is."

"Have you spoken to her again since the argument?"

"No, I haven't picked up." Anger infused Debbie's voice with strength. "Now it's her turn to wonder where I am."

Jude worked quickly through her options, seeking a way to exploit the situation. If this was Debbie's attempt at leaving a relationship with a controlling partner, Jude would help. But if Debbie wanted to work things out, Jude would also do what she could, including getting Sandy to a shrink before she imploded. Whatever the scenario, she needed information, and the situation was now even more delicate. She wasn't sure how Sandy would react to the quarrel with her girlfriend. Would the extra stress trigger a response? Jude needed to locate her hideaway.

"Here's what we're going to do," she told Debbie, taking a calculated risk. "Don't talk to her today. Not in person and not on the phone. Will you promise me that?"

"I promise." Debbie sounded determined, but she would cave the moment Sandy turned up on her doorstep with flowers. That was their pattern. Jude had heard all about it during haircuts.

"If you want things to change, you need leverage. Right now, you don't have any. She's been pulling this shit for months and you've enabled her."

Not an unfamiliar concept. Jude didn't want to think about Mercy. It still blew her mind that she'd put up with being one of two lovers, pathetically waiting her turn while Mercy saw who she wanted when she wanted. Was she nuts?

"I'm speaking from experience," she said, masking her bitterness with an aura of calm common sense. "If you want a different outcome you can't keep doing the same thing."

"Oh, God. What if she leaves me?"

"Trust me, she's not the type to walk away." Jude framed her next question carefully. "Debbie, are you sure you want to this relationship to continue?"

"I love her. I just want us to be closer."

"That's only going to happen if she starts letting you in more. Give her a chance to realize that she has to make some changes. Then, tomorrow, pick up one of her calls and tell her you'll see her but there are terms."

She could picture the puzzlement on Debbie's face. "Terms?"

"Tell her you're not ready to spend a night with her, but the two of you should talk and it has to be at her place. Period. Not negotiable."

"Why?"

"It's symbolic. She's shut you out of her life and her home. You need to be invited in."

"She won't do it."

"Fine, then tell her there's no meeting. Say it like you mean it."

Debbie uttered a strangled sound.

"You have nothing to lose," Jude said in her most reassuring tone. "If it doesn't work, you can go back to how things were. But if it does, you'll have broken down a big wall."

After a long pause, Debbie said, "I'll try. I really will."

"Good. As soon as you've arranged the meeting, let me know."

Jude wished her luck and ended the call. She watched a couple of ducks circle, then went back to the Dakota and located her latest Bureau cell phone. For a few seconds she deliberated, then she called Arbiter and requested the trace.

"What's cooking?" he asked.

"It's hard to say, but I don't think she's a Company asset. That's just my gut talking."

She knew Arbiter was equally concerned about other members of the alphabet soup, the NSA, NIC, DIA, and DEA, not to mention the offshoots that didn't exist officially. Even if Sandy was exactly what Jude thought she was—a dangerous loose cannon susceptible to external stressors—she could still be working for a government agency at the more clandestine end of the spectrum. Those folks weren't picky about the mental stability of their operatives if they were getting results.

"NORTHCOM has to be a candidate given her background," Arbiter said. "They just asked the Pentagon to formalize CPOC as a separate subcommand and they've been recruiting special ops commandos."

Jude frowned. U.S. Northern Command was the Pentagon's Homeland Security arm. They were supposed to respond to threats, not carry out independent black ops on American soil. As far as she knew, their Compartmented Planning & Operations Cell was a top-secret planning committee inside NORTHCOM.

"What are they up to?"

"Good question," Arbiter said. "They've been running sensitive operations here and in Canada and Mexico for the past few years. We liaise with them, but it sounds like they want more independence."

"So it's some kind of turf war?"

"Our friends at the Pentagon don't like the current accountabilities," Arbiter said. "They've been trying to dump their dependency on the CIA ever since 9/11, and they're not thrilled with the Bureau either."

"Because we're the lead agency? Just a wild guess."

Jude had trouble getting her head around the web of government agencies involved in homeland security, but no one except the FBI was authorized to direct military antiterror operations on U.S. soil. The Domestic Emergency Support Team was a combined Bureau and military special ops strike force formed for that purpose.

"There's buzz that Joint Special Operations Command has something major on the horizon," Arbiter said.

"An exercise?"

Arbiter didn't respond immediately. "So rumor would have us believe. It's hard to confirm since we've been left out in the cold so far." His voice held an edge of irony.

The skin around Jude's hair line prickled. If she was reading her handler correctly, he was telling her that the Pentagon was up to something terror-related and the Bureau knew nothing about it.

"Remember Don's folly?" Arbiter said in a conversational tone.

The euphemism made Jude aware that they were normally less explicit in their cell phone communications. "Don's folly" was Arbiter's code for a new espionage organization proposed by Donald Rumsfeld five years earlier. Among its various functions, the P2OG was supposed to provoke terrorist attacks, or fake them, in order to justify US "responses." The plans were leaked and no one had said much about the P2OG since then, but organization was up and running, having morphed into the Strategic Support Branch. As far as Jude knew, they ran their black ops offshore.

She picked up Arbiter's cue with a phony laugh. "Who could forget Don?"

"I was talking with my farmboy friend last week." For the first time since she'd known him, Arbiter sounded anxious. "He's off-loading some real estate. One of his Mayflower holdings."

Jude felt chills. "I see."

"Farmboy" was a euphemism for graduates of Camp Perry, where the CIA trained its assassins and saboteurs. Reading between the lines, Jude surmised Arbiter's contact had warned him about the Plymouth Rock area. She couldn't come right out and ask why. Their call was probably being surveilled by a rival agency. Joining the dots, she concluded Arbiter was dropping a big hint. He suspected there was a Pentagon plan to instigate a domestic terror incident.

"Do you think our subject could be interested in that real estate?" she asked, thinking about Sandy's mysterious trips away.

"Do us both a favor and find out."

❖

Lone tried to catch a short nap after her phone call with Debbie, but her mind refused to slow down. Her first thought was to drive out to Paradox Valley and make Debbie see sense. She hated hurting the woman she loved, but she had no choice until her primary objective was achieved. There had to be some way to make Debbie happy and to show herself worthy of trust. The answer came to her in a flash. Canada. Debbie resented being kept in the dark about the details, and thinking about it, Lone could see she'd taken too much for granted.

She had tried to introduce the subject over time, talking about moving there and reassuring Debbie that she wouldn't have to earn a living. But she'd missed the perfect opportunity to make Debbie feel included without having to tell her what was really going on. She would be blown away once she saw the property. A hundred acres on a lake, a tricked-out double-wide trailer, and a beautiful log cabin, now half built. Lone was going to sell the Monticello house to pay for the rest of the building as soon as things quieted down after the assassination.

But why wait? She could take Debbie up there soon and convince her to make the move. She would hire a truck and empty Debbie's house, pack up the cats, and it would be a done deal. Debbie would have plenty to do working on plans for the new kitchen of her dreams and shopping online for furnishings. She loved that shit.

Eventually, when the time was right, Lone would tell her about Operation Houseclean. It was tempting to disclose a few general details now, just to test the waters, but she couldn't afford to jeopardize her mission at this critical point. Civilians couldn't be expected to appreciate the necessity of a plan like hers. Debbie had no understanding of politics and Lone was reluctant to destroy her naïveté by explaining how the world really worked. Gentle souls like Debbie made life worth living for warriors like Lone. She refused to imagine a future without that sweet companionship.

Debbie just needed some time to cool off. Her threat to go away was as hollow as it was unlikely. Where would she go? She didn't have close friends, and she had no money for a hotel, or airfare, or the cost of gas for a long trip. She had her cats to consider, and she couldn't just take time off work. No, she would be holed up in her house with the curtains closed, watching that damn *Sleepless in Seattle* DVD.

By this evening she'd be desperate to hear from Lone and regretting every word of that pointless conversation. Lone would head over there with a pizza and Debbie's favorite ice cream, and a bunch of flowers. She would grovel and take full responsibility for being thoughtless and inconsiderate. She'd learned long ago that butches had no other choice after a quarrel. They were always wrong and the girlfriend was always right. The details were irrelevant.

Feeling in control once more, Lone deactivated her close perimeter alarms and traversed the buffer zone to her workshop. She dropped down through the concealed trapdoor into her secure bunker and added her notes and sketches from Jackson Hole to the file on the VP's residences. She then consulted her shortlist of likely event venues for the rest of 2007. The men of the evil alliance were writhing under the bright lights of scrutiny. They had to maintain a stranglehold on power in case the unthinkable happened and they lost the presidential election as well as the house and senate.

Lone felt certain Cheney would soon start raising campaign dollars as he had in 2006, holding thousand-dollar-a-plate chicken dinners to boost the war chests of the most vulnerable GOP candidates. Helpfully, before Karl Rove's departure, his office had released a "priority defense" list. Most candidates were trying to distance themselves from Bushdom and would avoid making a big deal out of a visit by either Bush or Cheney. But they wouldn't say no to money, so there would be discreet events at private homes and hotels.

Lone had compiled a list of the most likely beneficiaries and the locations where Cheney events were normally held in their respective cities. In addition, she'd donated to the campaigns of the top five prospects so she would receive advance notice of fund-raisers. As she did every day, she logged on to the Internet and checked to see if any of her targets was about to benefit from the Dicktator's legendary fund-raising mojo. She wasn't expecting a hit until September, but she was ready to roll anytime.

Smiling, she glanced at the MK-153 SMAW rocket launcher on the bottom shelf of her dedicated Operation Houseclean wall unit. Lined up alongside it was a collection of HEDP and CS rockets, ideal for taking out an armored town car. On the shelves above, Lone stored her sniper rifles and .300 Win Mag rounds, stun devices, assorted tactical weapons, and disguises.

Ideally, she hoped to carry out her mission from an indoor space. She'd purchased several confined-space rockets to eliminate backblast from the equation. But most of the venues she'd scouted would involve an outdoor strike and, regrettably, the killing of the Secret Service sniper whose position she would take over. Lone hated that idea. She didn't want to clip some working stiff who was just doing what he had to do. But as the Dicktator himself said, "There comes a time when deceit and defiance must be seen for what they are. At that point, a gathering danger must be confronted directly."

She agreed.

CHAPTER EIGHT

Griffin Mahanes is here? On a Sunday?" Koertig's pie-dough face was mashed in disbelief.

"Tell me about it." Jude stepped into Maulle's office. The confined space smelled metallic.

"Rich people always go for the cover-up, even when they're innocent," Koertig said. "That's their instinct."

"Her parents retained him." Jude supposed the Calloways were only trying to make sure their daughter didn't implicate herself. In their position she might do the same if a family member stepped from the scene of a murder, covered in blood.

"You get any sense of a motive from the niece?" Koertig asked.

She handed him a copy of the report she'd typed up after the interview. "The family sounds pretty typical. Dysfunctional. Alienated from each other. Just a whole more money than the rest of us."

"Any idea who's likely to benefit from the death?"

"We won't know until we see the will, but Pippa thought her uncle would leave his money to charity." Jude emptied the contents of Fabian Maulle's trash basket onto the floor in an area free of blood. "He only had the one sister. Pippa's mom."

Scanning her report, Koertig remarked, "The vic was gay, huh? That's what I thought." He ran through his reasons. "Closet bigger than my family room. Everything color coded. Kitchen right out of a magazine. And the dog. Your regular single male doesn't have a poodle."

"Which reminds me." Jude deferred the discussion on stereotyping. "Do we have the necropsy report yet?"

They'd sent Coco's body to a veterinary pathologist in Durango. Time of death was always difficult to estimate precisely, but it would help to know roughly when the killer entered the property and shot the dog. They could then calculate the window between that event and Pippa's arrival at 4:40 p.m. There was also the possibility that ballistic evidence could play a role. They'd recovered a 9mm shell casing from the scene, and if the bullet taken from Coco could be matched to a weapon they would have something to take to trial when that day came. Jude was surprised that it wasn't a through and through, but placement was everything. even at point-blank range.

"The vet tech says we can expect it Tuesday." Koertig peered into the gutted computer. "Why take the hard drive? Passwords for bank accounts?"

"Maybe. Or incriminating correspondence. E-mails. Et cetera."

"I guess blackmail's a possibility with him being a homosexual," Koertig said.

"I don't think so," Jude responded. "It's not like he's a pastor or a family-values politician blowing smoke. According to Pippa, he didn't care who knew. He had a couple of long-term relationships, but nothing recently. We need to track down any casual partners."

"Personal motive?" Koertig posited. "Disgruntled ex knows Maulle is loaded and thinks he should have a piece. He shows up and makes threats. Maybe he just meant to scare Maulle, not kill him."

"Four stab wounds doesn't seem like an accident." Jude stared at the desk. "Was his laptop taken into evidence?"

"No."

"He owned one. Pippa said she advised him on the purchase last Christmas."

"That tallies with a warranty in the files. An Apple about eight months old."

"So, the killer took it or it's in another house."

Koertig shook his head. "He'd have it with him. Why bother owning one, otherwise?"

"Apparently he wasn't technically inclined," Jude said. "Pippa did backups for him."

"There's no sign of a zip drive, memory key, or CDs," Koertig said.

Jude found it odd that Maulle was sloppy in that department. He kept his house in perfect order. She inspected the smoothed-out papers he'd discarded. Most were "to do" lists and phone messages.

"Got anything good there?" Koertig asked.

"Plumber, eight thirty a.m. Gym. Pick up cleaning." Jude switched to reading from the grocery list. Maulle had the basic food groups covered. "Asparagus, button mushrooms, basil, cantaloupe, oysters, prosciutto."

"I had that once. Proscuitto. Give me Canadian bacon any day." Koertig set about opening and shaking every book he picked up from the floor. "The guy's fridge is a work of art. Fully loaded, stainless steel. Computer that tells you when the caviar's running low."

Jude conceded this attempt at humor with a brief smile. She'd inspected the glamorous appliance when she arrived, unwise on an empty stomach. Maulle had obviously stocked up for his niece's arrival. Along with the sophisticated delicacies that fit with his discarded shopping lists were various items from the fast food spectrum. Jude had been tempted to sample the shrimp salad. It seemed like a shame to let it go bad.

Koertig was similarly concerned about perfectly good food going to waste. "Did you see the cheese drawer? You wouldn't get an aged Gouda like that in a five-star restaurant."

Jude got a flash of Griffin Mahanes in court describing detectives washing down Brie and caviar with fancy wine purloined from the victim's cellar, said shameless contamination of the scene taking place after they finished disrespecting the man's personal possessions. Could such people be trusted to give evidence?

She said, "I'm sure the family will appreciate the supplies once the house is released."

"You think they'll stay out here awhile?"

"Not if Mahanes has anything to do with it. He'll want them far away and out of reach once we've taken their statements."

Koertig handed Jude an inventory of the desk drawer contents. "So far no date book and no list of telephone contacts."

"He probably used his computer as an organizer."

"Big help."

"Is someone handling the phone dump?" Jude asked.

"Yeah, and we're tracing the Caddy and the Lexus."

"Anything off IAFIS?"

"Not so far."

"Sorry I didn't make it to the briefing."

"You didn't miss much. Belle did the reconstruction. It went down like we thought. Maulle tried to fight off the assailant at the top of the stairs. Hit him with the cane."

"So there's a different blood group on the cane head?"

"Yeah. We won't have DNA results for a few days, but the blood on the floor looks to be Maulle's and the head spray on the banisters belongs to an unidentified male."

"So the assailant is hit on the head, then comes at Maulle with the knife," Jude said. "Why not shoot him?"

"That's the question, isn't it?"

Almost any bullet was far more likely to be lethal than a stab wound. The killer must have made a conscious choice not to kill Maulle immediately.

"She said the perp walked Maulle backward to the office. The rest of the stab wounds occurred there. Plus the blunt force trauma."

"What size feet?" Jude asked. "Eight for the assailant and nine for Maulle?"

"You're good." Koertig grinned. "Maulle's shoes are custom, one foot slightly bigger than the other. Made in London. Same as his suits."

"This is interesting." Jude handed a slip of paper to Koertig. It was dated early in August and was addressed to Pippa.

He read aloud, "'Dear Pip, for unforeseen reasons I need to be in London for the next few weeks. I've reserved a flight for you with British Airways. Put your stuff in storage and come spend a few weeks in Europe before you travel to the Four Corners. We'll discuss future plans once you're in town. You have my support, no matter what.'"

Jude bagged the note. It was the only item from the trash worth following up on.

They spent the next hour searching every crevice of Maulle's office. His paper records were limited to receipts, which he filed methodically according to their type, tax deductible or not. Donations. Tradesmen's quotes. Insurance. Medical. There were newspaper clippings relating to events he attended, a few photographs of himself with politicians and celebrities. Souvenir menus and place cards from meals at embassies and even the White House. His correspondence included letters from charities thanking him for his support, matters relating to his four homes, and a collection of birthday and Christmas cards from Pippa dating back twenty years. These were housed in a file marked "Pip," which was crammed with photos, letters, printed e-mails, cards, poems, school reports, and keepsakes she must have given him. Jude opened a small box.

"It's a tooth and a lock of Pippa's hair." She turned the box over. The inscription read "Pippa 7 yrs."

"No file for her brother," Koertig noted.

"I guess he's chopped liver."

"Sounds like my family. My sister was always the favorite."

"Mine, too," Jude said. She wondered how Pippa's brother felt about being excluded. "That portrait in the formal dining room. It's Pippa, isn't it?"

"Yeah, I just realized."

They exchanged an uneasy look.

"Do you think it's…normal?" Koertig asked.

"I think we need to ask Pippa."

"She's really cut up about the death."

"That could mean anything." Jude leafed through the photos more intently.

Most featured the studied poses of childhood. First day of school. Santa's knee at a department store. Patting a dog. Halloween costumes. Summer camp. Prom. Graduation. The candid shots were equally innocent: Pippa wearing Mickey Mouse ears at Disneyland or running into the surf with a board under her arm. Jude was familiar with the photo collections of abusers from her time in the Crimes Against Children Unit. They were quite different from this assortment of milestone moments.

"I'll speak with Pippa some more," she said. "Just to be sure. But I doubt Maulle was abusing her."

If he was, that would change everything. For a start, Pippa would have a motive and they would have to rethink their theory of the crime. Male blood and footprints were found at the scene. Pippa could have brought an accomplice. Anything was possible.

Koertig returned the last book to its pile and said, "Nada." He ran a finger over the spines. "Normally, your highbrow-type books are just for show, but I think our vic actually read these. Some of them are dog-eared."

"Which ones?"

Koertig handed her a volume, noting, "There's plenty more where that came from."

Jude read the title and glanced at the back cover. *Merchant of Death: Money, Guns, Planes, and the Man Who Makes War Possible.* A book about a notorious arms dealer called Viktor Bout. She glanced at the other titles. Stuff about smugglers and global economics. Apparently Maulle had a lively interest in the politics of globalization. Her mind leapt to Hugo, the South African from the private security firm.

"You'd think a smart guy like him would have had some kind of contingency plan for a home invasion," she mused aloud. "When a guy contracts CTG to get his back, he's not kidding around."

"Yeah, I saw that in your report." Koertig scratched behind his neck. He was always sunburnt there from standing on the sidelines supporting his wife when she ran marathons. "Why let go of the hired muscle when he came out here?"

"False sense of security," Jude replied. "Or he did something to make the problem go away and thought the threat was over."

"This Anton individual Maulle seemed to have a beef with, the human slime. Any thoughts?"

"We'll need to track down that CTG guy, Hugo. I have a few people I can call." Jude reflected that Arbiter had his uses. "So far it's the only wrinkle we have."

"There's always something." Koertig picked a parrot feather off his shirt. His expression was pensive. "Looking around, you'd say Maulle had the perfect life. But someone decided to take everything away from him. This wasn't random."

"No, it wasn't," Jude agreed. "So there has to be a clue in this house. We're just not seeing it yet."

"The boss is never gonna let us travel."

"I know." Searches of Maulle's other homes would have to be conducted by detectives in the respective jurisdictions.

"Pity the niece was never here before," Koertig said. "It would be a help if she knew what was missing."

"I don't buy that Maulle did his own housework," Jude said. "Let's check out the maid services. Someone knows this place pretty well."

"I'm on it," Koertig said. He slid a photo of Pippa back in the file. "You have to feel sorry for the kid. She'll be scarred for life."

"After we've interviewed the parents, I'll talk to them about getting some help for her." Jude finished bagging items she wanted from the filing cabinet and crossed to the door. "You didn't find anything in the bedroom?"

"He was a *very* tidy guy."

"There has to be a safe somewhere. I didn't see any receipt from a home security system company, so it must have been installed when the house was built. Let's get the plans."

Koertig followed her to the master bedroom, another sprawling interior with stunning views. Jude lifted every picture and tapped her knuckles along the wood panels and drywall. The room had a wood floor, like most of the house. The closet was carpeted. It looked like Koertig had already lifted the edges to check beneath.

"Let's move the bed," Jude said.

They squeezed every pillow for foreign objects, then hoisted the mattress followed by the base and lugged them to the nearest wall. The bed was a solid hardwood design like the rest of the hefty bedroom furniture. It had been stripped by Belle's team and the bedding removed for the usual tests. They wrestled the frame onto its side and Jude searched for anything taped underneath while Koertig balanced the weight. She then crouched and tested the floorboards for one that could be lifted. The thought of going through the entire house doing the same thing was daunting. That was a job for junior staff.

"There's nothing in here," she said with frustration.

They lowered the bed and replaced the base and mattress. Puffing, they sat down on opposite sides. Their efforts had dislodged a parrot feather, which fluttered across the satiny floorboards.

"Brains of a four-year-old," Jude said.

Koertig gave her a sympathetic look. "Don't be so hard on yourself. If there was anything to find, we'd have found it."

"I was referring to the parrot."

Koertig regarded her blankly.

"Our eyewitness," she said with grim humor.

"Plus the three cats," he reminded her.

"Yes, and we know how felines love to cooperate with figures of authority."

"Did you hear that bird talking to Pippa?" Koertig asked. "I know they just copy what they hear, but it's still incredible."

"Even supposing that's all they do. What if we could get it to repeat what it heard in the office?"

Koertig didn't respond immediately. "You ever interviewed a bird?"

Jude met his quizzical gaze. "You're right. My neurons aren't connecting. I need to eat something."

"There's this new burger at Sonic. Hot chili with bacon and guacamole."

The merits of that combination spoke for themselves. Jude worked through the rationalizations. They'd searched the most important rooms. Why go quietly insane working through the remaining five thousand square feet of luxury real estate when there were rookie detectives twiddling their thumbs back at headquarters? The outdoor team was still at the scene, gradually fanning out, searching for the murder weapon and any other evidence. The primaries didn't need to hang around.

She peeled off her gloves and got to her feet. "I'd hate for us to fade away while we're snipe hunting."

Koertig sprang up like a man half his size. "I'm supposed to be on a diet," he belatedly recalled.

"Guacamole is health food," Jude said.

They went through all the bagged evidence from the upstairs area, checking that the labels were complete and initialed. In any investigation the paperwork was second nature, but Jude always double-checked her work because autopilot was no guarantee of accuracy. They carried their haul out to Koertig's Durango and unloaded it into a secure storage box ready to be handed over to the evidence clerk back at headquarters.

"Got that knife yet?" Koertig hassled the officers moving slowly up the ridge behind the house.

Jude grinned. She knew he'd enjoy being in charge.

❖

Jude knocked on the door of Pippa Calloway's room at the Holiday Inn. "Do you have a few minutes?" she asked when Pippa's wan little face appeared in the crack.

"Of course." She swung the door wide and invited Jude to sit down.

"I haven't called your lawyer."

Pippa snorted. "He's hideous. Totally reptilian. I don't know where my parents find these people. They're bringing another one with them, did you know that?"

"No." Jude was curious that the Calloways thought they needed an entire legal team.

"The family estate attorney. Because that's what you do at a time like this, you think about money."

Jude wasn't sure how to respond. She'd had family ask if an autopsy was really necessary because they'd heard it could slow down probate. Sticking to her game plan, she said, "I was thinking maybe you'd like to visit with your uncle's parrot."

An elfin smile transformed Pippa's face, carving ten more years off her age. Just looking at her, Jude felt like a decrepit has-been. It crossed her mind that plenty of cops thought about prepaid funeral arrangements. Maybe it was time she looked into the options. She'd contemplated the idea in the past but always felt weird about choosing a casket. If she was iced on the job, wouldn't the people she left behind know better than to bury her in something called the Pink Lady Magnolia?

"I'd love to see Oscar," Pippa said. "Do I have to ask Mr. Mahanes?"

"No, but I'd appreciate if you keep him informed. Call it ego management."

Pulling a face, Pippa located a business card and entered the number into her cell phone. "Mr. Mahanes? I just wanted to let you know I have Detective Devine with me. She's kindly arranged for me to see my uncle's pets." After a few beats, she put her hand over the phone and told Jude, "I'm supposed to say 'no comment' if you ask me any questions, and have a conference call if you want to talk."

"Tell him I'm in awe of his lawyerly prowess and will play by his rules because I can't remember my own."

Giggling, Pippa repeated the words verbatim. As she listened to

Mahanes's closing arguments, she gathered up her wallet and room keys and whispered, "Lead the way."

Jude took the phone from her when they reached the Dakota. "Mr. Mahanes? If you want to come visit with the bird, you're welcome."

"That won't be necessary." He signed off with a slick warning about fruit of the poisonous tree.

Jude handed the phone back and opened the passenger door. "I have a question to ask you. Off the record."

"Okay." Pippa climbed up into the seat.

Jude got in the driver's side, leaving her door open to release the heat from inside the vehicle. She turned on the engine and got the a/c running. As they drove out of the parking lot, she said, "The portrait of you in your uncle's dining room is really wonderful."

"Oh, the Susan Ryder?" Pippa sounded surprised. "I didn't know he'd brought it over from London."

"Did you know your uncle kept all the cards and letters you sent him over the years?"

Pippa was obviously touched. "Oh, that's so sweet of him."

"Sometimes when we find a large collection of photographs of a child in a relative's home, we're suspicious." Jude let the comment hover between them.

"You want to know if Uncle Fabian ever touched me inappropriately?" Pippa's tone was lifeless.

"I'm sorry. I have to rule that out."

"He would not have dreamed of it. Uncle Fabian was disgusted by attacks on children. Anything like that on TV, he was always upset."

"He sounds like a good person," Jude said.

"I suppose in your job you only see the worst," Pippa remarked.

"Unfortunately, that's often true." Jude felt a twinge of sorrow. She wasn't sure if she could remember innocence, it left her so long ago.

"Well, my uncle was a gentleman in every sense of the word," Pippa said with dignity. "I'm not suffering from the Stockholm Syndrome or anything like that. If he was an asshole I wouldn't have been planning to live here for the next year." She stared out the window. "Jesus, what am I supposed to do now?"

"What were you planning to do out here?"

"I'm a sculptor. Not professionally. I haven't sold anything yet.

But Uncle Fabian believed in me. He thought I should explore my talent away from negative outside influences." She gave a bitter little laugh. "By that I mean my parents. They hate that I'm artistic. That's how come I just graduated in dentistry. As if I would ever do that for a living."

Jude thought it must be nice to be a Harvard dental school graduate who could afford to despise the high-paid profession she'd trained for. "I noticed a letter to you among your uncle's possessions, suggesting a delay to your trip to the Four Corners. He said he'd booked a flight to London for you. What can you tell me about that?"

"We spoke on the phone. He said there was a problem he had to handle and he didn't want me to be stuck in the mountains by myself."

"What happened?"

"He called me back a few days later and said everything was fine, so I packed my stuff and got in my car."

"I see." Jude changed course. If she was going to dig any deeper, she wanted Pippa's answers on the record, and that meant scheduling another interview with Mahanes present. "Tell me about your uncle's parrot. Oscar, isn't it?"

"Oh, he's a doll." Pippa livened up instantly. "Incredibly sensitive and loving. I can tell he's devastated."

"This might sound like a stupid question. But do you think he remembers things?"

"Are you kidding?" Pippa laughed. "I'll never have another fight with a boyfriend on the phone in front of him."

Encouraged, Jude said, "There's something I'd like us to focus on during the visit."

Pippa stared expectantly at her.

"Oscar is our only eyewitness."

The sound of a softly expelled sigh reached Jude's ears. "He was hiding in the bottom of his cage, picking out his feathers, when I got there," Pippa said. "And you want to make him remember?"

Jude felt like one of those animal exploiters who sent not-so-funny videos of pet pranks in to Animal Planet. She said "Imagine how proud your uncle would be if Oscar provided important evidence."

Pippa considered this sleazy sales pitch. "Here's the deal. I'll see what I can do to help him connect, but he's not testifying in court. I won't put him through that."

Jude didn't get into discussion about the unlikelihood of a parrot taking the stand. She turned off before Towaoc and bumped along the driveway that led to Eddie House's place. "I can promise you Oscar won't go before a judge. I would never do that to an animal."

"Okay, then." Pippa offered her hand once Jude had parked. "Deal?"

Meeting her determined eyes, Jude agreed solemnly, "Deal."

CHAPTER NINE

While Oscar the parrot repeatedly professed his love for Maulle, Pippa, and nuts, Jude took a call from the sheriff. The feds were in town and she'd drawn the short straw. It was her job to take Special Agent in Charge Aidan Hill to dinner. Pratt thought this would cement mutual respect. Failing that, Jude might be able to get the agent drunk and influence the way chain of command would function. Pratt was gnashing his teeth over the turf issues already.

"You're our interface," he reminded her. "You know how they think."

Jude didn't bother to object. As far as her boss was concerned, she was in the loop. She stared out the window, across the prairie toward the Mesa Verde. The ancient Puebloans had once wandered the lowlands stretched before her. Wild horses had found grazing. Buffalo roamed. This year the fire-scorched mesas bloomed with yellow rabbitbrush and purple tansy after unusual rains. Montezuma County saw more lightning than almost any other place in the nation, but the storms often passed without leaving a drop of water.

Jude glanced up at the bruised clouds rolling in from the east. Today would be no exception.

"Don't ask me to believe this terror plot was all new information to you," Pratt said, letting her know he wasn't stupid. "Ricin. My God."

"You're right, sir. I've been monitoring the ASS for some time now. I guarantee you, these individuals will be in custody before they even make it to Telluride."

"Tom Cruise is building a bunker under his place, you hear about that? Ten million bucks. Some shelter, huh?"

"A lot of wealthy people build secure rooms."

"It's for protection against an alien invasion. That's what they think, the Scientologists." Pratt let go of a barren snort. "The evil Lord Xenu is supposed to attack any day. Instead it's going to be a bunch of Jew-hating dipshits."

"Which is exactly my point," Jude said. "We're talking about a few losers driven by an agenda of hatred."

"Containment," Pratt said. "That's all I'm asking for. How far does it travel by air?"

"Sir, it's not going to come to that. Like I said, airborne contamination is well beyond a bunch of amateurs."

"What if they found someone with brains?"

"Let's wait and see what the FBI can tell us."

"Here's the thing. If it comes down to a choice, that town gets cut off."

"What are you saying?"

"Lock it down," Pratt manfully insisted. "In dire situations, we're mandated to make the tough choices. The loss of a few hundred lives, while terrible, could be a necessary sacrifice to protect the rest of the population. Do you understand me?"

Jude decided Pratt had been overdoing the antihistamines again. They made him fixate on negative outcomes. She said calmly, "I get the picture."

"I was thinking it through last night. You know those movies when the doctor asks the husband to choose if he wants to save the mother or the baby?" Pratt didn't wait for her thoughts on that regrettable patriarchal quandary. "You save the mother, of course."

"I'm not sure how that relates to the Telluride scenario."

"She can always have more babies," Pratt explained. "*And* there will always be more actors. But if no one's left to pay for movie tickets because they all died from ricin poisoning, what then?"

Jude watched the African Grey rest his head beneath Pippa's chin. "Fortunately, we're not facing such a dilemma."

Pratt huffed. "I made certain promises when I was reelected."

Jude remembered them well. A crackdown on public shirtlessness. The upgrading of the posse's saddles and tack. Extra deputies for the greased-pig event at the county fair. "I can see this is weighing heavily on you," she said.

"Our community counts on its leaders to lead when the need arises."

"If my colleagues had any doubts about a positive outcome, the bad guys would be under arrest now. I'm sure they're just building a strong case before conducting a raid."

It entered Jude's mind that her boss could go off half-cocked. If he ignored FBI instructions and rushed in to make arrests and look like a hero, he could blow the lid off a lengthy operation. In the scheme of things the ASS counted for little. They were simply an untidy loose end. Arbiter thought they'd probably poison themselves trying to figure out how to disperse their stock of ricin.

"Sir," Jude said in a soothing tone. "I promise you, I'll personally tear the VIP parking passes from the cold dead hands of every man, woman, and child in Telluride before I allow a whiff of that chemical to choke a gnat in Montezuma County." She met Pippa's startled gaze and placed her hand over the phone, whispering, "Cop joke."

Pratt said, "This is no time for jackass comments, Devine."

"I hear you," Jude said.

Eddie and Zach came back into the room, trailed by Hinhan Okuwa. The gray wolf came over to her, wagging his tail, ears slightly flattened. Jude lowered her head so he could lick her mouth. In the two years she'd known Eddie, she'd reached an understanding with most of his animal companions. Hinhan Okuwa was not an alpha by nature or experience. His demeanor was serious and watchful, but he loved to play. He deferred to Eddie and Jude, and seemed to see Zach and other friendly adults as pack equals. He lifted his tawny gaze to Oscar and the two creatures inspected each other.

"Don't get too close," the parrot warned in an astonishing imitation of Eddie's voice.

Zach grinned. "That's what Dad says when Hinhan Okuwa tries to sniff Oscar."

Jude was impressed. Any parrot that could repeat verbatim what it heard would make a more reliable witness than half the public. It was time to choke Pratt off. "Sir, I have a witness to interview," she said diplomatically.

"Just remember what I said," her boss insisted.

"Got it." Jude closed her cell phone and set it on the table.

Oscar crowed, "What's happening, baby?"

"Human stuff," she replied dismally. "You wouldn't believe it if I told you."

Eddie asked, "Beer?"

"I wish." It had been a long day and the end wasn't in sight. "But make it a ginger ale for me, thanks."

Zach took several sodas from the fridge and handed them out. He and Eddie sat a few feet away in the adjoining room. Jude had asked Eddie to be present. He took in injured wildlife and restored them to health in a small-scale sanctuary on his property. His success with birds had made him famous among protection agencies. Rangers were always showing up with orphaned baby raptors and adults with broken wings.

Jude had told him what she was hoping for from Oscar. Eddie, highly sensitive to the moods of birds, said the parrot was traumatized and had hardly spoken since the deputy dropped him off. They needed to relax him and reassure him that he was not going to be left alone. Bringing Pippa out had been a good move. Oscar was excited to see her and had started talking immediately. Jude wondered if the parrot understood that Fabian Maulle was dead. Or was the concept of death only comprehensible to human beings?

She set up her tape recorder and flicked it on. Nothing would ever be admissible or even accepted as evidence, but if the parrot said anything useful she would be able to listen again. "Pippa, you've known Oscar since he was a baby, haven't you?"

"Yes, Uncle Fabian bought him and his mother from a breeder. Unfortunately she died when Oscar was five." She addressed the bird. "Sad about Loulou."

The parrot made a low sound in his throat. "Loulou can't come back."

"Where's Fabian?" Jude asked.

Oscar bobbed his head and made sounds like he was about to spit up. After a few seconds he stared straight at her and said, "Sad about Fabian."

Jude gazed into the flat, pale yellow eyes. "Fabian can't come back."

"He knows," Pippa murmured. "I can feel how upset he is."

"I wish there was some way to access his memories." Even if he started talking about a person or repeating words from a conversation, they couldn't be sure he was recalling the day of the killing and the people involved.

"He remembers his toys," Pippa said. "And he always remembered where Uncle Fabian put his keys and pens. Things like that. Even a week later, he would remember."

"That's great." Jude got up slowly so she didn't startle him, and went into the kitchen. She found a knife that fitted Carver's description of the murder weapon and returned, holding it behind her back. "I don't want to scare him, but I can't think of any other way to tie his recollections to the scene. I have a knife."

"Keep your distance," Eddie said. "Otherwise he'll see you as a predator."

Jude halted a few feet away and displayed the knife, lying flat on her open palms. Oscar screeched and flapped his wings, then huddled into Pippa.

"Maybe we should forget this," Jude said. "It seems cruel."

Pippa shook her head. "No, let's try for a few more minutes. If he's still distressed we'll stop." She took a bag of nuts from her pocket and Oscar brightened up immediately.

Eddie wheeled Oscar's cage over from the corner of the living room, positioning it a few feet away and leaving the door wide open.

"Good idea," Pippa said. "If he wants, he can go in there. Want cage?" she asked Oscar.

He nestled against her and crooned, "Want purée."

"Dad made some sweet potato for him," Zach said. "He went crazy for it."

Eddie took a Tupperware container from the fridge and set it on the table with a spoon. Oscar hopped down onto the table and wobbled from one foot to the other.

"A hungry parrot is a dead parrot," Pippa said. "That's how they think in the wild. It can make them greedy."

When Oscar had sucked down some sweet potato, he stared intently at the knife, then at Jude's face before announcing, "Wrong one."

"Where's the right one?" Jude pictured herself explaining how she located the murder weapon: *There's this parrot, see…*

But Oscar had no answer. He was suddenly engrossed with Jude's cell phone and burst into speech she couldn't decipher.

Pippa stifled a gasp. "Oh, my God. He's speaking Russian. Something like 'Shall I finish him off?' I could be wrong. It's not my best language, but I recognize *grokhnut*. That's Russian for *kill* or *shoot*."

"Did your uncle speak Russian?"

"Not really. Just a few words. He traveled there sometimes."

Jude had always been amazed by people who could pick up foreign languages. The only one that stuck in her mind was Latin, not the most useful for twenty-first-century law enforcement. She'd spent ten years trying to become fluent in Spanish, but Latinos at a crime scene still looked like they wanted to crack up when she said, "Policía. Había algunos testigos?" Jude had no idea why a request for witnesses would engender instant hysteria. Her attempt to vault the language barrier no doubt led to mispronunciations. She hated to think what she was really saying in her attempts at conversation with the local Hispanic population.

"I speak a few different languages," Pippa said. "We always had household staff from other countries and I just started picking up words. Once they knew I was interested, they taught me. I knew Spanish and Italian before I started elementary school."

"That's amazing," Zach said. If his red face and darting glances were any indication, he was smitten.

Jude figured Pippa had to look pretty good to a nineteen-year-old who'd grown up in a nutty polygamist sect where normal dating was unheard of. Zach had been run out of town, like many FLDS boys. The sixty-year-olds who wanted new brides didn't welcome competition from young males who didn't need Viagra. Zach was a starving, abused misfit when Jude had first asked Eddie House to take him in. Two years later, he called Eddie "Dad" and no one would recognize him. A local teacher had been tutoring him after school and he was ready to take the SAT this year.

Oscar let out a raucous scream and repeated over and over in heavily accented English, "Where is it?" He followed this with, "Talk. Want to live? Talk." He then made a strange sound like chimes.

"I'm sorry, baby boy," Pippa burst into tears. "He's not coming back."

She sagged over the table, her head resting on her arms. Oscar stroked her hair with his beak.

"Okay, we're done with this," Jude said.

Pippa sat up and wiped her face. "I'm sorry. It's just, that was his call for Uncle Fabian. He learned it when he was a baby. It's the sound the old microwave used to make. Whenever the bell went off, Uncle Fabian would go over there."

"So he thinks your uncle will come to him if he makes the same sound?" Jude was astonished.

Tulley would lose his mind if he could see this. She decided to arrange for her animal-crazy deputy to visit with Oscar next time he was in Cortez. He drove down once a week to work with one of the other deputies. They'd entered their K-9s in a dog competition with a $10,000 prize. Tulley had visions of making a stud dog out of Smoke'm. People would pay a lot of money for bloodhound puppies from a champion.

Pippa blew her nose in a tissue. She looked exhausted, her face taut with grief. "Wait," she said as Jude reached out to turn off the tape recorder. "There's something Uncle Fabian said to me before he died. I thought he was talking about Oscar's food. This is probably stupid. I mean—"

"I'm interviewing a parrot in a homicide case," Jude said. "Do you think 'stupid' is a problem for me?"

Pippa gave a teary giggle and carried Oscar to his cage. He sidled across his perch to stare at her with something close to tenderness. "I love you, Pip."

"I love you, too." She blew him a kiss and said, "Question for the parrot."

"How many?" he responded promptly.

Pippa took a couple of nuts from her bag and showed them to him, "Two nuts." Having secured his rapt attention, she asked, "Where's the box?"

Oscar mulled this over, bobbing his head and mumbling to himself in parrot-speak.

Pippa repeated, "Where's the box? Please."

With a satisfied puff of the chest, Oscar replied, "God's in his heaven. All's right with the world."

"Browning." Pippa looked disconcerted. She fed Oscar the nuts.

"Does it mean something to you?" Jude asked.

"Kind of." With a puzzled frown, Pippa said, "Uncle Fabian used to recite that verse to me when I was little. I don't get it. Why would Oscar say that now?"

Pippa was obviously tired and emotional. If there was some meaning in the quotation, it would probably elude her until she'd had some rest.

"Sleep on it," Jude said gently. "Something will come to you."

She slid the cassette recorder into her pocket and picked up her keys and cell phone. Leaving Pippa to say good-bye to Oscar, she walked out to the front of the house with Eddie. They ambled along the pathway between the aviaries and stopped in front of a large enclosure that housed a peregrine falcon with a permanently damaged wing. A gust of wind caught at Eddie's hair, twirling a few straight silver strands around the banded feather he always wore. He adjusted the leather thong that secured it, freeing the beaded ties. Turquoise. Coral. Silver. Jude noticed something new, a pair of silver-capped elk teeth swinging from a braid.

Catching her curious gaze, Eddie said, "Zach went on a hunt. My friends in Craig took him."

Detecting the pride in his voice, Jude said, "His first big game?"

"Yes. Last time he went for five days. Only hit trees. This time a bull elk. Eight hundred pounds. Single shot."

"Sounds like you're out of a job, pal." Jude smiled.

Eddie took his hunting seriously, going out several times a year to bring home the meat that would feed his family and the animals and birds that depended on him. He didn't like buying beef and chicken from the supermarket. The idea of slaughterhouses offended him.

"You want some elk steak?" he said. "I cut a few pounds of strip loin for you."

"Sure beats rabbit." He usually sent her home with something for the pot whenever he successfully hunted smaller game. Jude had gotten past her initial dismay pretty quickly. Anyone who ate commercially farmed meat was on thin ice getting holier-than-thou about others who hunted for the table.

Eddie took a few slivers of meat from the pouch at his waist and fed the falcon. He'd taught it to fly again but it could only manage short distances. The beautiful raptor would never survive in the wild.

As it sucked down the treats, he said, "You've been inside too much."

"That obvious, huh?" Jude sighed. She had full strength in her ankle again, but summer was almost over and she had two major cases to work. At this rate she would be stuck inside 24/7 for the next two weeks and have cabin fever before winter even began.

"Want to come on a cattle drive?" Eddie asked.

"Are you kidding?" Jude had intended to volunteer for a drive ever since she'd been in the Four Corners. "Did you get that gig with that dude ranch?"

City slickers paid handsomely for a few days' relentless toil on a working cattle ranch, and twice a year the local dude ranches moved their cattle to or from their summer grazing pastures. It wasn't unusual to see hundreds of animals marching through the center of town in October. Eddie worked for one of the rangers occasionally.

"Sales are slow at the gallery," he explained, which was his way of saying he needed the money.

"You can sign me up," Jude said.

"It's time for you to get your own horse."

"I know."

Jude hired from the same outfit whenever she went riding. She could stable a horse of her own there if she wanted, but something stopped her from making the commitment. In the back of her mind lurked the knowledge that she could be ordered to leave the Southwest anytime and who knew where the Bureau would send her? She didn't want to gain the trust of a horse and then have to abandon it.

That was the trouble with her life. She couldn't put down roots knowing she'd only have to tear them up again. Yet without roots she was adrift, marking time in a bleak limbo between past and future. The Four Corners was a place of exile, a self-imposed retreat from all that had held her hostage. She had wondered who she could be if she cut herself loose. The last thing she expected was to become little more than a fugitive from the ghosts she'd left behind.

She had failed to reach an accommodation with the past. Its tendrils refused to surrender their hold on her dreams and her conscience. Ben was unfinished business. Walking away was not an option. She had tried, and failed. Yet there was no real alternative. She could sift through the evidence around her brother's disappearance a thousand times over—and she had—but there were no new leads. The case was more than cold, it was mummified. There was no direction to take because each led to the same dead end. No matter how many times she explored the familiar paths, her conclusions were always the same. Ben had been abducted at age twelve by an unknown subject, no body had ever been found, and chances were, after twenty-five years, it never would be. The man who had taken Ben would never be brought to justice. Jude's entire life had been little more than a hopeless quest for the impossible.

A dark inertia gripped her every time she tried to accept that fact, a bleak mood that probably explained the desolate state of her love life. Since her breakup with Mercy and her failure to make something happen with Chastity Young last year, she hadn't dated anyone. And while hookup opportunities weren't boundless in the Four Corners, a determined woman could get laid. Jude hadn't even tried. It wasn't like her libido had gone on holiday, either. She was in a state of pent-up frustration most of the time.

The situation could easily be remedied. She went to conventions, those sex-fests for cheats and desperates. Someone always hit on her. If she wasn't picky she could have an orgy at the next advanced law enforcement seminar series if she wanted.

Jude sighed, and the sound of her own expelled breath called her back to the present. Zach and Pippa stood next to Eddie, chatting about Oscar. Zach placed a package of meat in Jude's hands. She thanked him and praised him for making a clean kill. Eddie said he'd let her know about the cattle drive.

As Pippa got in the passenger door and fastened her belt, she said, "Thank you for bringing me out here."

"You're welcome."

That was something, Jude thought, as she started the engine a few seconds later. For all her failings, she was a good sheriff's detective.

CHAPTER TEN

The woman on the doorstep had probably never spent a moment of her life wondering if she was pretty. Debbie knew the type from high school. They were the ones who dated the boys with late-model cars, married a doctor right after college, and had an affair with the pool guy when they got bored taking their kids to soccer.

Eyes the color of forget-me-nots focused on Debbie. "Who are you?" the visitor asked.

She was beautiful, Debbie decided, not pretty. She wasn't sure what made the difference. The cheekbones, maybe. After years as a hairdresser, Debbie was used to hiding "flaws," but this woman's face was so perfectly structured and her features so lovely, she could shave her head and still stop traffic. When makeup artists raved about porcelain skin, hers was the kind they were talking about. In beauty magazines, her looks were classified as "Nordic." Clients wanted hair like hers, pale honey shot through with platinum and gold, but it would take hundreds of foils to come close to the natural color. She wore it drawn back tightly into a chignon. Very elegant. She couldn't possibly be from around here.

Debbie remembered to answer her blunt question. "I'm a friend of Jude's. Debbie Basher."

The woman didn't offer her name. "Is Jude home?"

"No, she's in Cortez."

"But you're staying in her house?"

Debbie decided she'd had enough of the twenty questions. "I'm sorry, who did you say you are?"

A wintry blue gaze settled on Debbie's face. "Dr. Mercy Westmoreland. I'm with the ME's office in Grand Junction."

Debbie felt instantly foolish. This woman hadn't *married* a doctor, she *was* a doctor. Brainy as well as beautiful. It didn't seem fair. And she was a professional colleague of Jude's, helping solve crimes. Her job was the gruesome one, cutting up bodies to explain how people died. In that moment, Debbie knew where she'd seen Dr. Westmoreland before.

"Oh, my God. Are you Mercy Westmoreland from Court TV?" Flustered, she backed up a few steps. "I'm sorry. I didn't recognize you. On the program you look more…made up. Please, come in."

The lovely doctor didn't move. Debbie's head spun. Not only was Dr. Westmoreland on TV, she was half of the Four Corners' most famous lesbian couple. She'd married a British actress. They were the ones whose soirée Agatha and Tulley were losing their minds over. How could Debbie have been so dumb she didn't know all this immediately?

Dr. Westmoreland seemed to be weighing something in her mind, then she stepped past Debbie and marched into the house like she owned it. Glancing around the living room, she asked, "When are you expecting Jude?"

"Not tonight. She's tied up with a big murder investigation. The one on the news."

Debbie took in the doctor's appearance. Some women were born to wear narrow-fit cream pants with a white shirt tucked in. Mercy Westmoreland had completed her casual chic with a light sweater slung loosely around her shoulders. Debbie had the strange impression that under the sensible outer layer, she wore sexy French lingerie.

"How long have you known her?" Dr. Westmoreland asked bluntly.

Debbie supposed it was only reasonable that a professional colleague of Jude's would want to make sure the person answering the door had a right to be in the house. "For a year. I'm her hairdresser."

"Really?"

Debbie wasn't sure how to read her guest's expression, or lack thereof. Feeling uncomfortable, she offered, "Would you like something to drink, Dr. Westmoreland?"

"It's Mercy, and no thank you." With a long, hard look that

felt like an inspection for flaws, she asked, "Are you involved with Jude?"

Debbie wasn't sure how to answer that. Did Mercy know Jude was a lesbian? Very few people did, and Jude obviously had her reasons for keeping it that way. As for herself, Debbie couldn't afford gossip. If her born-again boss discovered her sexual orientation, she would be out of a job.

Sidestepping a direct answer, she said, "Jude's letting me stay here while the exterminators are in my house. I love Yiska."

To illustrate her point, she stroked the adorable black cat curled on the burgundy leather recliner near the window. Mercy strolled over and they stood in silence for a few minutes, taking in the crimson-rimmed Uncompahgre Plateau. The view was wonderful, but Debbie wouldn't swap it for hers. She loved being nestled in the red sandstone cliffs that rose up around Paradox Valley. That was another reason she didn't like the thought of moving to Canada—all those trees and lakes, far from the desert and the big blue Colorado sky.

She didn't want to be hidden away in a forest somewhere in the cold north. She was used to stepping out each morning into the still of the canyons. She was used to the faded silver cottonwoods and the roll of pebbles beneath her feet. The whisper of the dry wind. The cries of coyotes on moonlit nights. On her days off she wandered familiar paths along the canyon walls, leaving her fingerprints where others had left theirs, tracing the faint stick figures carved into the sandstone. The archaeologists called them petroglyphs, the graffiti of the people whose land she now called home.

"I'm surprised Jude's still living out here," Mercy remarked. "I told her she should move to Grand Junction. There are so few places in this region that are remotely civilized. Santa Fe is a long drive. So is Denver."

"I guess you travel a lot," Debbie said. "With your TV career and everything. Do you go to the movie sets when your...when—"

"Elspeth prefers not to have me around. It cramps her style." Mercy ran her hand over a multicolored glass vase on the window ledge. "And I must admit, I find the filmmaking process excruciating. So much wasted time."

"Well, it must be nice when you can just be at home together like normal people."

"We manage domestic bliss for a few weeks. After that, I want my house back and she wants a director telling her how to breathe."

Debbie didn't know whether to laugh or not. She tried for an intelligent comment. "I suppose she's going to be busy with the Telluride Festival coming up."

With a slight edge, Mercy said, "She's counting the days. And she'll be leaving for another shoot as soon as the festival's over."

What a life that must be, Debbie marveled, jetting around the world to exotic locations to act in movies. Being recognized by waiters in restaurants and having people want your autograph. It would also be pretty bizarre to watch a movie with your partner in it.

"What's it like?" she asked impulsively. "I mean seeing her on the big screen being someone else."

Mercy moved her attention from the evening sky. Regarding Debbie with a mix of amusement and patience, she said, "Actors aren't the gods and heroes they play. The words they speak are not their own. Their gift is in illusion, in making us believe they're not just faking it."

"I haven't seen any of Elspeth's movies, but I've heard she's a wonderful actress."

"Oh, she is," Mercy said mildly. "She's so good, I can't tell when she's for real or just acting."

"That must be really weird." Fearing she'd put her foot in her mouth, Debbie fell silent.

"Yes." Mercy moved away from the window. She glanced along the hallway to Jude's bedroom before returning her gaze to Debbie. "I should get going."

"Is there a message I can pass on?"

"Yes, tell Jude I'm sorry I missed her."

There was an undercurrent in her tone. Anger? Bitterness? Debbie should have shut up while she was ahead. They walked to the door. It was dark outside and the trees around Jude's small house rustled. The air felt heavy, like it might rain overnight. But that probably meant they'd get one of those desert storms, all thunder and lightning but not a single drop of water. Debbie picked Yiska up and the little cat clung to one shoulder as if she was afraid of the open doorway and all that lay beyond.

"I didn't know Jude had a pet," Mercy said.

"She saved Yiska's life." Debbie loved the story of Yiska's brush with death. She and Jude often talked about their cats. "I don't know if you remember the search for that little boy last year, Corban Foley."

"Yes, I performed the autopsy."

Debbie winced at the thought. She and Lone had volunteered for the search-and-rescue operation. Everyone in the Four Corners seemed to be involved, hoping for a miracle. Debbie would never forget the day they pulled that poor little baby from the reservoir.

Avoiding the digression into a subject that still upset her terribly, she continued the happier story of Yiska's rescue. "Jude found her one night during the blizzards back then. She was almost dead and Jude had to drive to Grand Junction in a snowstorm because the Montrose vet clinic wasn't open. They said Yiska wouldn't have made it if she didn't. The weather was so bad she couldn't drive back home so she spent the night on a couch in the vet's office."

"In Grand Junction?" Mercy echoed.

"That's how Yiska got her name," Debbie concluded with the detail she found most fascinating. "It's Navajo for 'the night has passed.' Jude says it was apt because for a while, she didn't think either of them would make it back alive."

"Remarkable." Mercy seemed restless. She stepped onto the porch. The bright lamp overhead bled the color from her face.

Despite a sense that Mercy didn't approve of her, Debbie had enjoyed the unexpected visit and the interesting conversation, and wanted to show her appreciation without sounding gushy. "Thank you for spending a few minutes talking to me. It's lonely out here."

"Have you been staying long?"

"No, just today."

Mercy brushed a speck from her crisp white shirt. "Elspeth and I are having a soirée next Saturday. You're welcome to come if you're free."

Debbie couldn't remember the last time she'd gone to a social event on a Saturday night. She never got invited to anything except potlucks and barbecues. Agatha and Tulley had said she could go with them to the soirée, but it was a different matter to be invited by the hostess herself.

Suppressing giggles of pleasure and nerves, she said, "I'd love to come. Thank you."

"See if you can talk Jude into it." Mercy gave her a smile that belonged in *Vogue* magazine. "Heroes who save small animals deserve time out occasionally."

"I'll try." It crossed Debbie's mind to ask if she could bring her partner, but Lone would never go to a soirée. Getting her to Agatha's Fourth of July barbecue took a solid week of tears and pleading.

Mercy said good night and Debbie waited on the front porch until she got in her big SUV and backed around. The whole time they were talking, she'd felt nervous. Her imagination often ran away with her when she was with sophisticated people. She always had the feeling they looked down on her. For a few minutes she'd even had the impression Mercy might slap her. It was hard to tell what she was really thinking. She seemed arrogant, but Debbie decided that was just her manner. Doctors could be like that, and Mercy had warmed up in the end. Anyway, she'd invited Debbie to her home. She wouldn't do that with someone she took a dislike to.

As she locked the front door, Debbie wondered what she could say to make Jude change her mind about the party so she didn't have to go alone. She wondered what Lone would think if she went with Jude. Probably not much.

Her partner must have picked up her thoughts by telepathy, because the cell phone rang and Debbie knew it was her. For a few seconds, she stared at the phone on the coffee table like it was a grenade, then she rushed over and grabbed it. The caller ID showed no name and a number she didn't recognize, which always meant it was Lone. This was the call she wasn't supposed to answer. Her heart jammed her throat.

"Hello." Her voice came out in a squeak. She took a deep breath and sagged down on the sofa.

"I was expecting a machine."

"No, it's me. How are you?"

"I'm standing on your doorstep feeling kind of stupid," Lone said.

"Why?"

"Because it looks like I'll be eating this pizza and ice cream by myself." There was no anger in her tone, just disappointment.

Debbie felt terrible. Maybe she'd been unfair. Jude was probably right. Lone was suffering from some kind of trauma and that's what made her so detached and secretive. She was probably afraid to open up. "I said I wouldn't be there."

"I was hoping you'd changed your mind. I don't want to fight with you, Debbie doll."

"I don't want to fight, either."

In fact, all she wanted was to be in Lone's arms again and for everything to be the way it was in their first few months together. Nowadays, she only experienced that magical bliss when they were making love. The rest of the time, no matter how hard she tried, she didn't feel close to Lone. Tears started to form as she realized Jude was right. Unless she made changes, her relationship was doomed.

"I'll come get you," Lone said. "I see you left your car behind."

Disconcerted to think of Lone walking around behind the house to peer in the shed where the car was locked out of sight, Debbie wondered how to answer. She couldn't possibly admit she was at Jude's house. Awkwardly, she said, "That's not necessary."

"We need to talk."

"Yes, but I'm tired tonight. Let's see each other tomorrow."

"If that's what you want." Lone sounded completely calm.

Normally, when things didn't go her way, she got tense and her voice altered just enough to warn Debbie that she was crossing a line. At those times she always backed down. Relieved that this conversation was going better than she'd expected, she said in a rush, "Lone, I'd really like if we could meet at your place."

In the long silence that followed, Debbie's mouth went dry and she broke into a cold sweat. Needing to do something other than clutch the phone, she got up to find a drink. As she opened the fridge, Yiska slithered around her legs in a happy feline dance. Debbie poured some special cat milk from the box on the pet food shelf and set the bowl on the floor.

She had cracked up when Tulley first showed her the contents of Jude's fridge. All kinds of fancy food for Yiska. Organic beef. Sliced chicken breast in gravy. Whole sardines. And for Jude: milk, spring water, ginger ale, and a series of plastic containers with heating instructions taped to them. Agatha made home-cooked dinners for her. Twice a week she showed up at the station with a box full of Jude's favorites. The plan was a win/win. Jude didn't have to live on take-out and Agatha earned extra cash, which was a big help.

Debbie took a bottle of spring water from the door and went back into the living room. Balancing the phone, she removed the bottle cap. Lone still wasn't talking. Debbie knew what was going on. Lone would simply wait for her to change the subject, then they would both pretend she'd never suggested meeting at Lone's house in the first place.

Angry with her for refusing to make this one small compromise to improve their relationship, Debbie said, "Well, I guess you're not willing to meet me halfway. Enjoy your pizza."

Before Lone could answer, if she was even going to, Debbie hit End and placed the cell phone back on the coffee table. Lone wouldn't be expecting that. She was used to Debbie apologizing, crying, and blaming herself. Well, new rule: If Lone didn't want to talk, fine—she could have all the peace and quiet in the world.

Debbie turned on the TV and rubbed her tears away so she could focus on the screen. She was hurt. She thought their relationship mattered as much to Lone as it did to her. Apparently not. She turned up the volume and tried to figure out what was going on. The movie was an older one, the colors kind of hazy. Debbie wanted to switch the channel but the TV wouldn't let her. Tulley had warned her about that. Jude had TiVo. When the little red light came on that meant she was taping a program.

Debbie resigned herself to watching and was pleasantly surprised that she started to get involved in the story once she came to grips with the plot. An assassin was hired to kill the president of France for reasons to do with the Algerians. The film wasn't exciting, but it was nerve-racking and Debbie wasn't sure how it would end. She didn't know if it was based on fact and whether Charles De Gaulle was a real man who actually did get assassinated. The security around him was tight, but the Europeans allowed De Gaulle to do risky things so they could avoid arguing with him. Debbie thought an American president would know better.

Sill, the detective trying to track down the assassin was very clever and the cat-and-mouse contest between the two men had her hooked. In the end, she was shocked to find herself half hoping the Jackal would succeed, he'd gone to such elaborate lengths to plan the killing. Of course she was relieved when the plot failed, but she found herself wondering what happened later, who the Jackal really was, and how he ever became such a cold-blooded killer. That was the mystery, she supposed: why people do terrible things.

❖

"Sheriff Pratt says you were with the Bureau before you moved out here."

Special Agent in Charge Aidan Hill moved forward a couple of steps. They were waiting in line for a table at one of the better Mexican restaurants in town.

"Yes, the CACU," Jude said.

"Quite a change of pace."

Jude shrugged. "I was ready to get out."

Hill stared like Jude had just thrown up a hairball on a valuable rug.

A waitress summoned them. "You want a table by the mariachi band or a window booth?"

"The window." Jude glanced sideways at Aidan Hill. They'd given the same reply in unison.

As the SAC strode after the waitress, Jude took full advantage of the view. The agent's butt was firm and toned, even if Hill moved like she had something prickly up there. The walk was familiar. Female agents made an effort to lose their natural hip sway, along with other signs of their gender, in the drive to avoid the "nutty or slutty" label applied routinely to Bureau women. And fraternization was tantamount to career suicide, so no one wanted to be seen as a flirt.

Jude decided no agent who wanted to keep his manhood intact would attempt to grope Hill in an elevator. Her vibe was all work and no play, and she backed up that first impression with a communication style that could only be described as libido-numbing. Pity. Jude could have been tempted regardless of butt tautness. Lately she'd been looking twice at any female under ninety who smiled at her. Not that she would act on her primal urges. For all she cared, Hill could be a half-dressed hottie who only packed a 9mm for the kink factor, and Jude still wouldn't go there. The part of her that wanted to get laid was diametrically at odds with another part that felt physically sick at the thought of any woman getting under her skin again.

Besides, the zone under her skin already had a tenant. Mercy Westmoreland lived there, causing an itchy awareness that Jude could not escape. What would it take to end her fixation? She imagined driving past Mercy and Elspeth's house and seeing Mercy in the yard screaming at a bunch of kids, a cigarette hanging off her lip, saggy breasts, lank hair, and jeans that didn't fit anymore.

Dream on.

Jude ran her eyes over Hill as she slid into the opposite side of the booth. If the brunette was sending any covert sexual cues, she would spot them, and just in case she'd misread her as a sexless drone, Jude sent a subtle signal herself, letting her gaze linger on Hill's shirtfront. She waited for the nipples to react. Nada. Perhaps Hill was wearing those silicone gel nipple covers some of Jude's colleagues in the CACU used. Breast petals. The name made her smile.

Hill gave her a quizzical look. Like everything else about her, the coffee brown eyes transmitted a "hands off" signal. And there was something else, too. Jude's downhill career path didn't sit well with this over-achiever. That she could have traded the Bureau for a two-bit gig in a sheriff's office in Bumfuck, Colorado, was incomprehensible to a straight arrow like this woman. Jude resisted an immediate urge to invite Hill to the shooting range so she could show her how a loser handles a 1,000 yard benchrest in shifting winds. A five-shot group in less than three inches—would that earn a little respect? Or maybe, to even up the odds, they could face off at 600 yards. See who came closest to a sub-inch. Or there was always hand-to-hand combat. Hill had a nice body, very fuckable. But she looked soft. Jude could take her. Ten seconds, maybe twenty if Hill managed a couple of moves.

"Devine?" The tone was sharp. Hill closed her plastic-covered menu with a thwack.

"Something to drink?" the waitress inquired, tapping her pen and sighing like she needed to be somewhere else.

"Go ahead," Jude politely invited her dinner guest.

"She ordered already," the waitress said.

"Okay, I'll have what she's having."

The waitress got perky. "Two frozen strawberry-fuzz-coladas coming right up."

Jude squirmed. She wasn't sure what shocked her more, that SAC Hill had just signed up for a girl drink that would arrive in a huge glass with a slab of pineapple dangling from cherry-studded toothpicks, or that *she* had not been paying enough attention to dodge that unseemly bullet herself.

"Both virgins, right?" the waitress asked.

A nonalcoholic drink, that's what she was talking about. Insult after injury.

"Want to change your mind, Detective?" Hill asked blandly. Something in her tone suggested she thought this was funny.

"No, I can handle a virgin," Jude said. *Take that.*

The unsubtle innuendo was lost on both women. The waitress announced that tortilla chips would arrive momentarily, and Hill asked for an order of guacamole without garlic. Maybe she was planning to kiss someone. Jude almost laughed out loud at that idea. She watched a prom-queen type suck on a straw at a nearby table. In front of her a bowl-sized glass brimmed with icy pink gloop.

"Wait," Jude called the waitress back. There was a fine line between stubbornness and outright stupidity. "Make that a beer after all. Fat Tire, thanks."

"Do you want ice with that?" came the helpful suggestion. "Our beer fridge isn't working that great in the heat."

No, I'll just have Agent Hill blow on it. Jude kept that sentiment to herself. "Sure," she said. "What could be more alluring than warm beer on the rocks?"

As the waitress left them to talk among themselves, Hill said the magic words, "Doing anything later, Devine?"

"What?"

She must have looked dazed because Hill slowed her speaking voice to a village-idiot pace. "I thought we could grab some take-out coffee after dinner and go over the briefing for tomorrow afternoon in my room. Just a preliminary pass. See if I have all the bases covered."

You're shitting me. Jude gave a feeble nod. "Sounds awesome."

And the night was just beginning.

CHAPTER ELEVEN

My deputy has an angle." Jude thought she may as well throw it out there.

She and Hill had spent the past mind-numbing hour discussing the facts that had emerged from the FBI probe into the ASS. Everyone seemed to agree that the men involved were the dregs of the white power movement, none with an IQ over 90. Someone smarter had to be running the operation. The question was who, and what was the agenda?

"He thinks the attack could target a film called *My Enemy's Enemy*. It deals with Klaus Barbie."

"Ah, a Holocaust movie," Hill latched on immediately. "The ASS are Holocaust deniers. They'll assume a Jewish audience. Not a bad theory." With a humorless laugh, she added, "Wait till I tell the team we've been outbrained by a hicktown cop."

"Well, it wouldn't be the first time," Jude said mildly. "I'm curious, are you planning to wait for a body count before you show us some respect and listen to our views, or are we only on board so we can take the heat for screwups?"

Hill didn't bat an eyelash.

Jude thought, *Arrogant bitch*. As usual, that made her look twice at the woman concerned. Hill had gotten comfortable after they adjourned to her room, dumping her shoulder holster and exchanging her crisp shirt and tailored slacks for a faded college sweater and sloppy tracksuit pants. The look had a certain youthful, tousled sexiness that made Jude think fondly back to the FBI Academy.

She'd had crushes on a couple of New Agent Trainees who were probably a lot like Hill. They were deadly serious about their careers even then, putting in extra physical training for the PT tests and practicing defensive tactics with other NATs outside of classes. The only reason Jude got her hands on various lust objects was because she was the NAT to beat in hand-to-hand, so they all wanted to spar with her after hours. Jude had the sense that Hill would like to take her on now just to see how long it would take to disarm her.

She let her gaze drift from Hill's determined face to her sensibly manicured hands. She was the pride of her family, Jude speculated. Her dad was on the job, and one of her brothers was probably a firefighter.

Looking to confirm her guesswork, she said, "My dad was a cop."

Hill drew the wrong conclusion from the remark. "Mine, too, so I have no prejudices in that department, I can assure you."

"Are you an only child?" Jude asked casually.

"No, I have two brothers."

"Cops?"

"Neither of them. One owns a restaurant and the other is a firefighter." Hill tucked a stray lock of hair behind her ears impatiently. "You know, I don't care if we don't become friends for life, so we can bypass the getting to know each other bullshit."

Jude shrugged. "Works for me." She decided Hill was sex starved. She emitted the same tightly coiled frustration Jude detected in herself.

"I'll check in with the festival liaison about that film," Hill said. "It's a definite contender."

"For the record, I don't think Holocaust denial is the issue," Jude said. "If we're looking at an outside party working with the ASS, the film could give us an angle but it's not the usual."

"What do you have in mind?"

"If it's about Barbie and the CIA, you know it has to be about the Cocaine Coup."

Hill gave her such a blank stare Jude had to assume she was new to the counterterrorism division. Apparently it hadn't crossed her mind to explore the intelligence tradition she was now a part of. Maybe that was the norm now that the "war on terror" was sucking up so many agents with limited experience. Jude thought about the chats she and Arbiter sometimes had, just shooting the breeze. The guy was an encyclopedia of counterintelligence history and rumor. She'd learned a lot from him that she never knew when she was working in the CACU.

"Operation Condor?" Jude prompted. Even the general public had heard of that.

Finally, a hit. "Way before my time," Hill noted. "Anyway, that's CIA."

"Yes, but it could clue us into who wants that film shut down, if that turns out to be the agenda." Jude served up a few salient facts. "Barbie's militia brought down the Torres government in Bolivia. They were called the Fiancés of Death, about six hundred Nazis and neo-Nazis."

Disbelief clouded Hill's face. "You're telling me we sponsored an army of Nazis to bring down a government?"

Jude wanted to ask, *Are you that naïve?* Unable to mask her incredulity fully, she said, "Sure we did. It was a big CIA success story. Torres was a problem. He was nationalizing the holdings of big U.S. companies like Gulf Oil."

"Well, we know *that's* an outrage," Hill said dryly.

"Oh, there's more. He thought he could stop the Argentinean cartels that ran the cocaine trade, and cocaine is how we funded Condor. So the guy had to go."

"Okay, now you're going to tell me he was a democratically elected saint trying to do something about poverty in his country."

Jude grinned. "Did I forget to mention that? I guess it just seemed so goddamn obvious."

"This all went down while George H.W. Bush was head of the CIA?" Hill actually sounded disillusioned.

Jude could have rubbed it in with other horror stories from the black ops playbook, but that seemed harsh, so she settled for a simple "Yes" and continued with the coup story. "Barbie's goon squad slaughtered every dissenter they could find. Journalists, intellectuals, nuns, priests, aid workers, children, housewives. It was a bloodbath. Afterward, they marched through the capital wearing swastika armbands and shouting *Heil Hitler*."

"That's what my grandfather died for in the war," Hill said without expression. "Lovely."

"No one ever said counterintelligence was a bakeshop."

Hill's sharp brown eyes bored into Jude's. "You know a lot about all of this."

Jude responded flippantly, "I'm a big reader."

Hill and her team knew only the thinnest details about the Bureau's long-term intelligence gathering operation in the Four Corners. They'd simply received the word from above to deal with the threat. Jude wanted to tread carefully so she didn't blow her own cover with another agent, but she couldn't resist needling Hill a little. A dose of reality never hurt anyone.

"Well, it's nasty stuff, but I don't see how the ricin plot is connected," Hill said.

"Motive," Jude reminded her. "If we want to find the brain quotient, we need to know why he got onboard. I don't know if the film names names, but I can think of one person who doesn't like explaining why he was in La Paz back then. David Dewhurst."

"The lieutenant governor of Texas?" Hill shook her head. "He'd never link himself to morons like the ASS. Are you saying he had something to do with Barbie?"

"The coup was a hands-on CIA op and it happened four months after Dewhurst arrived in town. Do the math."

"No way," Hill said, clearly thrown. "It would be crazy for him to do something like this."

"That's probably true, but we can't rule him out," Jude said, teasing Hill with the unhappy prospect of a sensitive circumstances probe.

Hill wasn't going there. "Who else can we look at?"

"The cocaine trade angle could give us something," Jude said. She'd been thinking about money-laundering operations ever since her uneasy discussion with Arbiter. "Before you fall off your chair, let me just say this. I'm not really a conspiracy theorist."

Laughing, Hill invited, "Come on. Thrill me with your insights."

"The Moon organization was laundering money for the drug cartels back then. Moon was an investor in the Cocaine Coup and he's bought off a lot of people over the years."

"It's past history," Hill said. "Who cares anymore?"

"Do you think it's a coincidence that Carlton Sherwood made the swift-boat video about John Kerry?"

"Oh, God."

"Hear me out. Years ago the very same Carlton Sherwood wrote a book called *Inquisition* about how Moon was being victimized by federal investigators because of his race and religion. The book was part of a strategy to halt inquiries into Moon's operation."

"Moon's evil," Hill said. "We all know that."

"Strange how nothing ever sticks to him, don't you think?"

It was common knowledge that Moon was untouchable. He had served a year behind bars for tax fraud in 1982. Since then he'd continued his illegal activities with impunity.

"He has friends in high places," Hill said.

"John Kerry investigated the contra-cocaine cover up back then and came up with a heap of incriminating facts," Jude said. "The report went nowhere, of course."

"And we ended up with that joke, the 'war on drugs.'" Hill's expression was reflective. "A smokescreen, of course?"

"Is that a rhetorical question?"

"No, I'm just talking to myself. That's how I deal with panic. I'm following your reasoning and it makes sense. I wish it didn't."

"Moon and his pet politicians couldn't let John Kerry get elected and gain control of the Justice Department," Jude said.

"So he was swift-boated by the same stooge who defended Moon," Hill completed.

"Makes you wonder what he would have unearthed, doesn't it?"

"I'm not sure if I really want to think about that. It's so goddamn depressing."

Jude felt the same way. But now that Afghanistan was fast becoming the next narco-state, al-Qaeda was moving a lot of cash and opium. They had to be using experienced money-laundering networks. There were already ties between Muslim extremists and neo-Nazis. Maybe Arbiter was right and Hawke could lead them right to the door of a major network. Jude understood suddenly why he wanted to keep a tight lid on the investigation and behave as though it was completely domestic. If the CIA took over, they would shut it down. The folk who invented contra-entities weren't about to imperil a promising new source of dirty, invisible money.

As far as the Company was concerned, the citizens they protected failed to understand that freedom did not come free. Counterintelligence agencies had to weigh moral dilemmas on a daily basis. The American public could only see things in black and white. Mention tortured nuns thrown from high windows and they lost their minds.

"You think Moon is behind the Telluride plot?"

"His organization could be lending a hand indirectly."

"Interesting," Hill said. "You know we're investigating that NSM crazy, Bill White, at the moment. He has ties to Moon via the *Washington Times*. He used to write for them."

"Out racism seems to be a *Times* hiring parameter." Jude remarked. "The place could be mistaken for a white supremacists' social club."

Hill subjected her to a long, hard look. "You're full of surprises, Detective. I thought we'd spend the whole evening talking about perimeter security and on-the-spot hamburger testing."

"You seemed to have the logistics covered."

"What kind of reading do you do that makes you think like an intelligence operative?"

Jude smiled with breezy innocence. "I get everything off the Internet."

"Bullshit."

"Didn't you know? That's what us hicktown nobodies do in our spare time. We live vicariously through the triumphs of people like yourself."

Hill stood up, stretched, then settled on the one small sofa in the room. Jude remained at the table. She could feel Hill's eyes.

"What the hell are you doing wasting yourself out here?" Hill asked. "What happened? Divorce?"

"Burnout," Jude said. "Just another CACU casualty. There are plenty of us."

Hill was silent for a few seconds. "Want to talk about it?"

"Not really."

"I read your file."

"You what?"

"Your name came up when we started the investigation. The supervisor said we'd be liaising with a former agent. I wanted to find out if that was a good thing."

Jude would probably have done the same thing, but still. She waited for what was coming.

Undoing the single braid that held back her hair, Hill said, "A suspension and FFD examination is no joke. What happened?"

"It's all in there," Jude said coldly.

"Yes, but I'm asking you."

"What do you want to hear—that I shot dead a suspect and regret it on a daily basis?"

"Do you?"

"Yeah, it's almost as bad as missing out on genital warts."

"You have quite a temper, don't you, Detective?"

"Does it say that in my psych evaluation?"

"I'm sensing a certain hostility in you."

Jude stood and gathered up her notes. "If you're done testing me, I need to get some sleep. I have an autopsy first thing tomorrow."

"Was it about your brother?" Hill probed. "The child you found in that apartment bore some resemblance. Twelve years old. Blond."

"What do you want from me, Hill?"

Hill abandoned the sofa and approached her in stocking feet. She was shorter than Jude by several inches. Standing just out of reach, she said, "I'm sorry if I touched a sore spot."

"No, you're not."

Jude had almost forgotten what it was like having to respond to inquisitions from briefcase-holders. She made brief eye contact with Hill and felt almost sorry for her. Hill's mission was as much about making the Bureau look good as protecting the public. If she put a foot wrong she could forget advancement. She would spend the rest of her career in a dead-end job like media spokesperson. In the priesthood of the Bureau, a female agent couldn't afford to make mistakes. Something in Hill's eyes told Jude she thought she was looking at one.

"Listen," Jude said without rancor. "If you want me off the team, just say the word. Plenty of cops round here would love to take my place."

"How many of them are FBI trained snipers?" Hill replied.

"You really did your homework." Jude tried to show unconcern. Arbiter said anyone checking up on her would find nothing in her personnel file. Officially, she was just another former agent.

"Why didn't you simply take a leave of absence?" Hill pressed. "You had cause. If you wanted out of Crimes Against Children, you could have transferred."

"If you must know, Bureau politics make me sick," Jude said. In a way, it was true. If she hadn't found a home in counterterrorism, she would have quit. "Stand-up agents die the death of a thousand paper cuts if they rock the boat, while C-graders ass-lick their way into senior management. Big bonuses, no accountability."

"You're a maverick." Hill bit off the remark as if she'd given accidental voice to a thought.

"And you're to the Bureau born," Jude replied. The phrase was often used by agents, sometimes ironically.

Hill took it for a compliment, which it was in a way. "I like to think so."

In the poor lighting of the room, her features seemed softer than they were at the restaurant. Or perhaps it was late and she wasn't guarding herself so rigidly. Her eyelids drooped, the lashes slowly fanning down as she blinked. When she forgot to compress her mouth, her lips were full and tempting. Jude watched a slight change-up in her breathing and knew Hill was aware of her, too.

Oddly, she couldn't tell if the awareness was sexual or if she just made Hill nervous. She wondered if the SAC saw her as a threat, perhaps even unconsciously. There weren't a lot of female agents, less than twenty percent last time she checked, and instead of being natural allies, they were often competitive, struggling for approval in an organization that still couldn't shake off Hoover's legacy.

Jude suspected that, in her, Hill saw a woman who had let down the side. She'd left the Bureau, proving the conventional wisdom that women couldn't take the heat. Agents like her had questionable loyalties. They were not worthy. True believers like Hill made all kinds of sacrifices to prove themselves capable of the positions they held. To become an SAC, Hill had no life, that went without saying.

Jude toyed with the idea of coming clean with her, just to make her feel better. If Hill knew she was an undercover agent and not a slacker who'd jumped ship, maybe she would chill. Or maybe she would get even more competitive. Jude got a headache thinking about it. Besides, there was nothing to think about. Her cover was intact and had to stay that way. Already, Hill was suspicious of her. She needed to convince the agent that she had nothing to hide.

"I'll tell you something that isn't in the file," Jude said.

Hill was instantly alert, no doubt congratulating herself that she'd broken through and they were now talking honestly. "Yes?"

"After I shot that predator, I knew I'd do it again. I started stalking a subject we were investigating, planning on how I was going to take him out." She paused. "I'm not a vigilante, but if I'd stayed in DC that's how it would have played out. And I'd probably be serving time now."

Hill nodded. She seemed genuinely sorrowful. "Are you seeing anyone?"

Jude knew she wasn't talking about a lover. "For a while I did."

It was the truth. She had discreetly seen shrinks about her nightmares, not that therapy made any difference.

Hill stepped in a little closer, until her physical heat warmed the air around Jude's body. She touched Jude's arm. "I appreciate your honesty, and you did the right thing. It looks pretty bad when an agent goes postal."

Yep, that's what it was all about—protecting the Bureau's reputation. Jude nodded with appropriate shame. She could the relief flooding Hill's body. The agent was happy now that she knew they were on the same page where it really counted. FBI interests came first.

Jude met Hill's eyes and told her what she wanted to hear. "The job I have now is a cakewalk. I catch some decent homicides, but the beat is strictly small town. It's not the Bureau."

"I'm sure it must have its compensations." Hill sought a silver lining. "I got the impression that you're looked up to."

A feeling the SAC would not be familiar with. Females in her position at the FBI were tolerated, not respected.

Jude smiled. "Actually, you're right about that." Disingenuously, she rubbed it in. "Most of my colleagues assume I'll make the calls. They appreciate good leadership. It doesn't seem to matter who provides it, a man or a woman."

"That's good to hear." Hill had probably tried for a patronizing note, but her voice was wistful.

Jude wasn't quite done. "If you get any shit from the locals, come and talk to me. I'll sort it."

Just for the hell of it, she looked Hill up and down appreciatively, before focusing on her mouth. Hill's lips parted. Okay, so fifty percent of the awareness between them was sexual. She still couldn't tell which team Hill batted for, but it didn't really matter. Jude had always been able to make straight women blush, too.

"I'm sure that won't be necessary," Hill said. "I can handle myself."

"Yeah, I guess you're used to that," Jude replied with soft irony.

She watched Hill's eyes flicker as she registered the innuendo, then discounted it as a figment of her imagination. "Thank you for your time, Detective."

"It was a pleasure."

They walked to the door. Hill fumbled with the handle. Jude thought, *I could have you right now*. She took over from her, briefly tempted. The brush of their fingers made her catch her breath and she knew Hill had done the same.

"See you tomorrow," Hill said. Her voice was thin.

Jude said a nonchalant good night. She was a long way down the hotel corridor before she heard the door close behind her.

CHAPTER TWELVE

H ow long would it normally take for someone with these wounds to bleed out?" Jude asked. Her guess was no more than five minutes. In fatal stabbings, hypovolemic shock could kill within sixty seconds.

Norwood Carver's gimlet eyes lifted momentarily from the pale inertia of Fabian Maulle's body. He'd been inspecting the mottled skin surface for several minutes. "Exsanguination was not as rapid as these injuries might suggest at first blush. Of course, two of the wounds are perpendicular to Langer's lines so there's more gaping, and this one is diagonal." He directed their attention to a wound near the center of Maulle's torso. "Note the semilunar curve."

Jude imagined a knife entering across the lines of cleavage. Maulle could have been bending to one side when that one was inflicted. "Single-edged blade?" she asked.

"Yes, very good, Detective. The blunted margin and opposing V-margin are most apparent on the central wound because it's parallel."

"Could it be a kitchen knife?"

"Highly likely. Note the bruising on either side of each incision." Carver gestured with the skull chisel he liked to tap against his thigh during the external examination. "They're not guard imprints. These were inflicted pre-mortem and the configuration is identical for each."

Both Jude and Koertig bent low to squint at the linear discoloration. Each mark was slightly more than an inch in length. Jude had never seen anything like them.

"Possibly an attempt to clamp off the wounds," Carver said. "My guess is bulldog clips. Exsanguination would continue, of course, but death may have been delayed."

"So there was no fatal wound as such?"

"Well, the fellow is dead, so the wounds were fatal. However, I suspect his life could have been saved if he'd received immediate treatment."

Jude would avoid telling Pippa that. "What about hesitation marks or defensive wounds?"

"We took some skin from beneath the nails, or should I say foreign epithelials." He snickered. "Better sound like I know what I'm talking about." Carver routinely mocked the jargon embraced by TV CSIs. "And by the way, Mr. Maulle received regular manicures. He was particular. Take a look."

Jude and Koertig inspected the hands.

"Clear nail varnish," Jude noted. "Trimmed cuticles. Yes, very particular."

"Gay," Koertig said.

"Wealthy," Carver added dispassionately. "Men of a certain status are more likely to be manicured. That's a statistic. Add the homosexual component and we have a formula. Cash plus queer equals kempt."

Koertig haw-hawed. Jude didn't waste her breath pointing out that stereotyping had never solved a crime yet. She noticed something else as she lowered Maulle's hand back onto the stainless steel table.

"Is that a ligature mark on the wrist?" The faint pink discoloration formed a distinctive band.

Carver said, "Fritz, you photographed the wrists, didn't you?"

"Yes, sir."

"It would appear the victim was bound before death, but not with excessive pressure. I'll confirm that in the autopsy report." Carver measured the width and depth of each knife wound and said, "The murder weapon is probably five inches in length. Only one of the wounds indicates any use of force and it's an upward thrust."

"He took that one standing."

"Classic face-to-face. There was some momentum, so the assailant was probably coming toward the victim." Carver probed a wound in the ribs area. "Left side of the body, so your killer is right-handed. The other three wounds are relatively shallow downward thrusts."

"Maulle was sitting or lying down," Jude concluded.

"Sitting for two and probably lying down for the incision parallel with Langer's lines."

"Looks like someone kicked his face in while he was down there?" Koertig said gingerly.

"Multiple blunt force injuries consistent with blows from a fist." Carver took a moment out of the layman's discussion to dictate into his voice recorder. "Abrasion on left lower forehead above eyebrow. Nose fracture. Multiple contusions on left cheek, left upper forehead, back of head." He peered inside the victim's mouth. "Multiple contusions, lacerations, and hemorrhage on mucosal surfaces."

"The killer has to have cuts and abrasions on his hands," Jude murmured to Koertig.

"Any strangulation?" Koertig asked.

"No petechial or posterior neck hemorrhaging," Carver said. "I can't confirm fractures to hyoid bone and thyroid cartilages until dissection. But it would appear your killer had plenty to keep him busy without throttling the victim as well."

He signaled Fritz, who scuttled up and placed a rubber body block under Maulle's back in preparation for the Y incision. Overqualified for the role of *diener*, Fritz was apparently indispensable to his master and pathetically grateful for his own exploitation.

"Sir?" he asked with the breathless reverence of a dullard in the presence of genius.

"Unzip him," Carver said.

Jude took a few steps back while Fritz wielded a large scalpel. Maulle had been dead for thirty-six hours, so the decomposition process had begun, but refrigeration had slowed it. As his flesh was drawn back it gave off the scent of raw lamb. Jude glanced at Koertig, who was pale but stoic. He had only attended a handful of postmortems and had already taken a whiff of the smelling salts Jude carried.

"Do you think he was stabbed by someone familiar with anatomy?" she asked, steering Koertig's concentration away from the more gruesome stage of the procedure.

"Was this the work of a know-nothing amateur or a student of human anatomy?" Some forensic pathologists kept their opinions to themselves, but Carver enjoyed bathing in his own glory. He pitied mortals not blessed with his dizzying intellect, and was always willing to share his godlike wisdom. "One could form that impression, bringing simplistic reason to bear. However, the depth of penetration, the careful placement…suggest control, not stupidity. He didn't slash, or hack."

"Are you saying there was no anger?"

"A flawed deduction." He extended his hand toward Fritz to receive the pruning shears that doubled as rib cutters. "The wounds were ultimately fatal, but the process of death was slow and painful. Whoever killed Maulle wanted him to feel his life ebbing away. That suggests a good deal of anger, wouldn't you say?"

"Very nasty," Jude agreed.

A possibility took shape in her mind, but she kept it to herself since Carver didn't welcome competition. The bulldog clips intrigued her. Would Maulle have had the presence of mind to pinch each wound closed? Nothing in his background suggested he would behave any differently from most victims. Wounded people panicked. They staggered around, clutching themselves. Their first instinct was to grab a towel or garment and hold it to the wound while they called 911. No emergency call had been made until Pippa arrived. Why?

Assuming the killer had already departed by that time, why didn't Maulle save his own life? He had a cell phone in his pocket. Even lying on the floor dying, he could have made the call. He had fought to stay alive with bulldog clips keeping each wound closed, but then gave up while he was still breathing. It made no sense.

She felt Koertig sway at the sound of the ribs being separated from the sternum. Leaning toward him, she whispered, "Did anyone bag bulldog clips?"

As he turned his pallid face toward her, she waved the salts under his nose. "I don't think so," he said.

Fritz took a phone call and interrupted the proceedings. "Sir, the combine harvester casualty arrived. Shall I tell Freddie to weigh the pieces and check if he's all there?"

Carver glanced at the second autopsy table in the room. "No, stick him in the cadaver keep. We'll do him this afternoon. Speaking of harvest." He finished cutting cartilage and lifted the heart-lung tree aloft for inspection. "Premium quality if he was a donor and if this wasn't a homicide. Damn waste."

"The knife didn't penetrate that deep?" Jude asked.

"Remarkably, it did not." He set the organs down and carefully examined the heart. "Very clean. Your man was not an endurance athlete like myself, but he worked out and he ate lean."

"He appreciated living," Jude noted.

"Who wouldn't with his advantages?"

"And yet he didn't call 911," she said softly. Blood loss clouded the mind pretty quickly. Perhaps shock could account for Maulle's behavior after his killer left the house. "After he was stabbed, for how long would he have been lucid?"

"Mr. Maulle was in peak fitness for a man of his age. He could have moved, spoken, and thought clearly enough to act until very close to the end."

Jude walked Koertig to the wall farthest from the autopsy table. As Carver continued his dissection, she said, "Something was going on at the scene that we don't know about. The killer kept him alive for a reason."

"Sadism?" Koertig suggested.

Jude shook her head. "We know the guy was looking for something. Maybe he thought Maulle would tell him where it was. Maybe he was playing chicken. 'If you tell me, I'll call 911, otherwise you'll just die slowly while I sit here.'"

"I checked the plans," Koertig said. "No safe."

"We need to take the place apart. There has to be somewhere a man like Maulle would have kept his most important items."

"His sister's got to know something about him."

"They weren't exactly close. Not according to Pippa, anyway." Jude watched Carver pick up the Stryker saw and go to work on Maulle's skull. When he lifted the top section away, the sucking sound made her wince.

Koertig dry retched and stuck his hand out for the salts.

"I'm ravenous," Carver announced as he cut the spinal cord and removed the brain. Suspending it tenderly in a jar of formalin, he asked, "Anyone want to join me for a steak after this?"

❖

"You did great." Jude gulped some lukewarm coffee. She was due at the MCSO for show and tell in a half hour, then Pratt wanted her to take Aidan Hill to dinner again afterward, since it went so well last time. "So, are you meeting her?"

"Yes." Debbie sounded pleased with herself. "At her place. I didn't think she was going to phone after last night, but she must have realized I meant what I said."

Sandy had caved. Elated and relieved that her gamble had paid off, Jude set her coffee aside. "How far away is she?"

"In Rico."

"That's quite a drive from Paradox Valley." Almost two hours, in fact. No wonder Sandy stayed overnight whenever she visited.

"I didn't realize she was coming so far to see me." Debbie sounded contrite.

"It's beautiful there," Jude said. "You'll love it."

"That's if I can find it. She gave me instructions but it sounds pretty convoluted."

"I know the area," Jude said. "What's the address?"

"There isn't one exactly. You know that old mining road north of the town? The one that's closed?"

"Daisy Creek?" Jude had never hiked in the dense forest up that way. She'd heard there was nothing to see, just a few abandoned miners' shacks. What was left of the steep, treacherous dirt road had washed out a few years ago.

"She says you go as far as the Beware sign, then there's an arrow to Pariah. That was a ghost town. It doesn't even exist anymore. She says I can leave my car in a turnoff and walk on up. She'll meet me on the trail at four this afternoon."

Pariah? Jude had never heard of it. She wondered where Sandy got her mail sent. Did she have a false identity and a mailbox somewhere? These days it wasn't easy to live completely under the radar. She was working pretty hard not to be found.

Jude checked her wristwatch. 12:15 p.m. "I'll send Tulley to pick you up."

"Don't worry," Debbie said. "I've got it all under control. Bobby Lee's bringing my car over, and Tulley's following. He has to go down to Cortez for dog training."

"Okay, so you'll all drive to Rico from my place, then they'll continue on to Cortez?"

"That's the plan."

"How do you feel about seeing her?"

"A bit nervous. I hope she won't be angry at me."

"Well, this is a pretty big step for her," Jude said.

"For both of us."

"Just on that." Jude kept her tone even. "It's probably better if Sandy doesn't know I've played a role in this. She's reaching out to you now, so she'll need to feel she can trust you completely."

"I see what you mean."

"I want things to work out for the two of you, Debbie. She'll need to feel safe about opening up to you."

"I'll be careful," Debbie said. "And maybe you shouldn't say anything about knowing where she lives."

"That's probably wise."

"Thanks for the advice. Oh, I nearly forgot. Mercy Westmoreland stopped by your place last night. She said to tell you she's sorry she missed you."

"Yeah, me, too. Debbie, will you hold a second?"

Jude couldn't think about Mercy now. She rapidly worked up a course of action. Her first priority was a black bag job, searching and bugging Sandy's home. Under the Patriot Act, the FBI could search a residence without the owner's knowledge. They also had the right to obtain personal and financial records without appearing before a judge. All it took was a national security letter, and they had already issued a few NSLs on Sandy Lane. She was up for grabs.

Jude could take her into custody now if she wanted, just on suspicion of being involved in terrorist activity. Sandy could then be held indefinitely while the Bureau figured out if there were any charges to bring. They didn't even have to disclose her name. Basically, she would disappear. No one who knew her needed to be informed that she was under arrest, and she would have no right to legal counsel.

If Jude didn't act soon, someone else would. She couldn't delay telling Arbiter much longer. She'd rolled the dice, hoping to hell that Sandy's love for Debbie would outweigh her paranoia, even briefly, and not inflame it. She had to get into her hideout as soon as possible. Given her workload, she would be stuck in Cortez all of tomorrow.

"I have an idea. Let's all have a potluck at your place on Wednesday night. Watch a silly movie or something. I'll get Tulley to pick up some burgers for the grill."

"That sounds great."

"I was thinking about what you told me. After everything she's gone through, Lone needs support. She has you, but other people care about her, too. Maybe she needs to see that right now."

Sandy wasn't going to drive back to Rico in the dead of night after a few beers and a barbecue. And she and Debbie would be making up. She would probably spend all of Wednesday in Paradox Valley. Jude could nap at the stationhouse for a few hours, then drive down to Sandy's place. By early morning, she could start her search.

"She has such a hard time relating to people." Debbie sighed. "I hope she wants to come."

"We'll keep it casual. I'll try to find out what she's been up to on her trips away. It's probably something she's embarrassed to tell you about and that's why she's keeping it to herself. There's usually a silly explanation for things like that between partners."

"You think maybe she'd be more comfortable talking with a friend about it?"

"That's possible. So far she hasn't been willing to tell you, has she? Maybe that'll change after you visit. We'll see."

"I'd really like if you'd talk to her," Debbie said. "Jude, I appreciate everything you're doing for us. It feels really good to know I can count on you."

Feeling like a jerk, Jude said, "People can make it through rough patches. Good luck this afternoon. Let me know how it goes."

❖

"She wants you." Bobby Lee tousled his bangs in the passenger mirror.

Tulley slowed down with the traffic flow as they reached a line of cars stuck behind a semi. The drive down to Cortez was always like this on the mountain route, which was why he normally went the boring way through La Sal Junction. He didn't know how Jude put up with it on the days she had to drive to the MCSO instead of across to Paradox. She lived in the wrong location, too far from everywhere. She said she was trying to be an equal distance away from both the substation and headquarters, and she couldn't stand to live in Dove Creek, so Montrose seemed liked a reasonable compromise. Lately she'd been looking at places in Norwood. Tulley wished he could afford to rent there.

He slowed down to a 27 mph crawl and thought about hitting his overheads and siren, but people noticed cops rushing to an emergency situation and expected to see all the details in the *Cortez Journal* or the *Durango Herald* the next day. Some troublemaker would remember the K-9 unit and call in and report his misuse of authority.

"She's a married woman," Tulley repeated.

"A hot MILF," Bobby Lee corrected. "I'll take a piece of that action anytime."

"No wonder Jude won't get engaged. She's waiting for you to change your horndog ways."

Bobby Lee looked at him sideways. "She knows who I am."

No clarification was needed. Tulley had heard Bobby Lee's theories about the natural order of things and how as mankind was not genetically designed to be faithful to one woman. How hormones drove the male to fulfill the destiny of the species by spreading his seed, and Bobby Lee was fighting the power of Mother Nature herself if he denied his urges. It was testosterone that prevented inbreeding and made the human race gods of the universe.

Tulley said, "If she walks in on me one more time, I swear I'm gonna tell Gavin what's going on."

"I wouldn't do that."

"Why the heck not?"

"Because he'll fucking kill you."

"Me?"

Tulley put his hand on the horn. The guy in the pickup in front of him kept braking and slowing down, half crossing the yellow lines, positioning to overtake the car in front of him. Like that would gain something. Tulley knew if he was driving an unmarked vehicle, the guy would have flipped him the bird.

"The husband is going to blame the OM first," Bobby Lee said with the certainty of firsthand experience. "In his eyes *you're* the problem."

Tulley concentrated on the road as yet another retard with a death wish tried to pass the semi. "What's the OM?"

"The other man. That's you, buddy."

"Shit! I never even *look* at her."

Bobby Lee cradled his head in his hand. "You worry me."

"He thinks she's so perfect. And behind his back she's flirting and all. It ain't right. I can't respect a woman like that."

"She ain't asking you to *respect* her." Bobby Lee angled his head around. "And take it from me, you're not the first. Chicks who come on like that make a habit of it. This Crystal, she's a bona fide S.L.U.T. The old man's out busting his nuts so she has the nice house and the nice car. She's got him right where she wants him, pussy-whipped and too goddamn busy to notice her extracurricular pursuits."

"I'm sleeping over tonight." Tulley was filled with anxiety. "What if she comes in the guest room? She did that one other time and sat on the bed."

"Man, that's so uncool. You do not want to go there with the hubby in the next room."

"You got that right."

"Pay attention, my friend. This is an opportunity."

"No, it's a goddamn nightmare." Tulley stared straight ahead. He should have known Bobby Lee wouldn't understand. "I'll tell her to quit."

"Good luck with that."

"Thanks, you're a big help."

"Dude, the problem here is you're not handling the situation like you should." Bobby Lee got back to fixing his hair. "Be cool. Get a piece of that ass. Give her what she wants till she loses interest, then she'll dump you and there's no hard feelings."

Tulley shook his head. "I'm not getting shot by a pissed-off husband."

"I can respect that," Bobby Lee said. "Hey, did you ever nail that deputy? What's her name? Serenity or something?"

"She's too aggressive. I want to go back to Denver again."

Recently Bobby Lee had decided to display his tricked-out Chevy Silverado at a custom car show, and they'd spent a few days in Denver. During the vacation, Bobby Lee introduced Tulley to several ladies who made their living in the professional escort business. He spent the night with the one he liked best. It was a positive experience and Tulley was ready to practice his bedroom skills some more now. But not with Crystal Sherman.

"Here's the thing," Bobby Lee said. "You're a good-looking dude.

You don't have to pay for it." He stabbed his thumb toward the caged area behind their seats where Smoke'm was drooling. "And that animal is a major chick magnet."

"I've saved up enough for two more nights with Stormy," Tulley said.

"Oh, man." Bobby Lee put his comb away and got to work with the lip balm. He said soft lips were mandatory if you wanted to make out with chicks.

Tulley accelerated. The truckie had finally found a place to pull over. No one else tried to pass. They had to make way for Tulley. He was the law.

"Like I've been telling you," Bobby Lee said. "I know all the cute chicks in Durango. I can get you hooked up."

Tulley cringed at the thought of sleeping with girls from his best friend's reject pile. He wished he could find someone as pretty and kindhearted as Stormy. After they were finished having sex that night, they cuddled together and got talking about their dogs. She was a big-time animal lover just like him. They agreed that Michael Vick should get death by lethal injection, even though a swift end was more mercy than he deserved.

"Here's what I'll do for you," Bobby Lee said. "I'll take Crystal off your hands."

"Yeah? How do you plan on doing that?"

"Take me over there and tell your friend Gavin some BS about how I'm real eager to see those dogs of yours going though their paces. I'll handle it from there."

"Oh, that's just swell." Tulley decided Bobby Lee was messing with him. He was a mite too casual about going behind Jude's back. If it was him planning to cheat on the detective, Tulley would be terrified.

"Considering I only have your word that this chick's a hottie, that's a generous offer," Bobby Lee said.

"You are actually for real," Tulley marveled.

"I never kid about getting laid." Bobby Lee picked fluff off the black Stetson on his lap. "And don't get yourself worked up on Jude's behalf. I promise you, I could bang every horny housewife in the Four Corners and she wouldn't care."

Tulley kept his opinion to himself. Their relationship was in worse shape than he thought.

CHAPTER THIRTEEN

W
e found the Lexus in Durango," Koertig said.

"That was quick." Jude poured herself a cup of coffee and they took over an interview room for a quick catch-up before they briefed the team.

"It was reported stolen in Animas Valley on Saturday morning. The owner left it idling on the street while she dropped off her kid for a birthday party."

"Where was it located?"

"It's been sitting at an expired parking meter downtown since Saturday evening. We towed it to the garage. Belle's processing it now."

"Anyone see the driver?"

"Eight witnesses so far. They all report seeing two Caucasian males." Koertig consulted his notepad. "Driver is over six feet, 170 pounds, shaved head, goatee beard, pale suit, plain silk shirt open at the neck, cross on a thick gold chain. Passenger shorter, thinner, blond, leather jacket and casual shirt. Neck chains and cross. Rings. Diamond ear stud." He handed Jude a statement. "Waitress at Ariano's. She's our best witness."

Jude scanned the details. The two men ordered veal, paid cash, big tip. Departed around ten. Both spoke with an accent. The waitress thought it was Serbian, Russian, Czech. Something like that. They told her they were from Miami. She described one of the men as having a lot of gold in his teeth and saw tattoos on the fingers and chests of both. The man in the leather jacket had cuts on his knuckles.

"The rose on the shorter guy's chest is Russian mafia," Jude remarked. "The symbols the witness saw on the fingers are probably Cyrillic."

She'd seen a few examples of Russian prison tattoos when she worked in the CACU. Jude didn't know much about them except that they were highly symbolic, a coded language that revealed the wearer's criminal history and gang status.

"Russian mafia in the Four Corners?" Koertig marveled.

Equally amazed, Jude said, "Not exactly their kind of holiday destination. How are the composites coming along?"

"One of the guys is working on FACES now with the waitress."

The men she described would have stood out among the casual Saturday night crowds. Shorts and T-shirts were the norm on warm Southwestern evenings. "Did anyone see them after they left the restaurant?" Jude asked.

"We got a couple of homeless juveniles," Koertig said. "They claim they saw the men getting into a silver Mercedes SUV in the parking lot on Camino del Rio."

"Security cameras? License plate?" A faint hope.

"No, but Durango PD had two patrol cars parked near the lot. They were responding to another son of God incident."

"I thought they sent that guy to the state mental hospital months ago," Jude said.

The offender was a fixture on the streets of Durango. Most of the time he harmlessly panhandled outside restaurants, proclaiming his messianic status to passersby. When he struck a bad patch he got aggressive about wanting to perform miracles and tried to pull people out of wheelchairs.

"They let him out last week," Koertig said. "He stole a mule from the petting zoo. He was riding it through town Saturday night, yelling 'Hosanna.' The homeless kids tagged along for a laugh."

"Where was he arrested?" Jude asked.

"Corner of the 800 block. The boys took off through the parking lot to avoid police. That's when they saw the suspects getting into the Merc. One of the officers also saw the vehicle leave."

"Any idea which highway they took?"

"He thinks they were headed for 160."

"Which would eventually get them onto I-25 and south to I-40," Jude concluded. "So Miami sounds like the truth."

"Do you want to talk to the waitress before I round up the team?"

"No, you did great with her. We better get rolling. The Calloways will be here soon."

"Oh, yeah, and then the joint terrorism task force." Koertig looked her in the eye. "Is it for real or just a practice exercise?"

Jude sipped her tasteless coffee and reminded herself to bring another mug down here next time she made the trip. Her last one got broken and she hated Styrofoam. "I can't say for sure, but it sounds like the real thing."

"What the hell are they thinking?"

"They've brainwashed themselves," Jude said absently. "They lost their way. The blue-collar world is disintegrating around them and they need to blame someone. It's really not surprising that they've latched onto an ideology that makes them feel important and gives them a role to play in something bigger."

Koertig treated this analysis with the solemnity it deserved, concluding, "Numbnuts looking for their fifteen minutes."

"In a word, yes." Jude returned to the topic at hand. "Those two kids. Where are they?"

"Durango PD located them this morning after the Lexus was called in. I sent one of the rookies to take their statements. They're with Child Protective Services now."

Jude sighed. Durango hosted a permanent population of homeless kids drawn by the town's laid-back atmosphere and prosperity. Most had already been through foster homes and skipped town as soon as they were placed in another one. Koertig handed the witness statements to her. They tallied, and the descriptions of the men were reasonable for the time of night and weird lighting. One of the boys had also noticed the tattoos.

"Nice work," Jude said.

Koertig shook his head, still confounded by the idea of Russian hoodlums in their sleepy corner of the universe. "So this was a hit?"

"It's looking that way. If we want to make a lot of assumptions."

"The parrot was talking Russian." Koertig located Jude's notes from the interview with witness "Oscar Maulle."

"Yes, and he used the word *grokhnut*. It means *shoot* or *kill*."

"Maulle had friends in low places. The bulldog clips on the wounds. Is that a Russian thing? I heard they're sadistic."

"I think if they wanted to torture Maulle, they could come up with something more gruesome than that," Jude said.

"Anton...the human slime," Koertig mused. "Is that a Russian name?"

It wasn't Petya, Kostya, or Sasha, but the playwright Chekhov was Anton. Jude remembered that much from high school. "Could be," she said.

"Any progress on the South African security guard?"

Jude had called in a favor with Arbiter. Hugo wouldn't be hard to find. "Not yet, but I should have his details tomorrow."

"I almost forgot, we found the Cadillac, too," Koertig said. "The driver's a moron. They arrested him in Mancos last night. He set himself up under a parachute at the camping ground, smoking weed. It caught fire."

"Jesus."

"Could have been a conflagration, but that old guy who runs the taxidermist shop emptied his waste bucket on the flames."

Jude grimaced. "Striking presence of mind."

"They're enemies," Koertig said. "The moron plays loud music all night so the taxidermist calls the marshall. Last week the moron calls in a complaint about the old guy peeping in the ladies' bathroom block."

Jude drained her coffee and got to her feet. "He's a stellar witness, in other words?"

"Oh, yeah. The kind that makes your Russian mafia psychos look credible."

As they tromped out of the room, Jude said, "You know we're going to have to search that goddamn house again tomorrow."

Koertig slapped the file against his leg. "I had a bad feeling about that."

❖

The Calloways coped better with the death of their relative than the shortcomings of their accommodations. Jude had suggested they interview the family as a whole since they weren't making the cut as suspects.

"I hope we can expedite this," Jim Calloway said. "I have a summit in Dallas starting Thursday, and the bed in our hotel is giving me a neck problem."

"He's talking about a golf summit," Pippa said. "Important stuff."

"You know how long your father's had his name down for this," Delia Calloway chided her. To Jude and Koertig, she explained, "It's a Chuck Cook intensive."

"Three Hall of Famers are doing demos," her husband added.

"You people make me sick," Pippa said.

Jim Calloway continued undeterred. "Inspiration, that's what it's all about."

"Tiger Woods is a guest," Delia Calloway added, tweaking the modest string of pearls at her throat.

"Have you ever met him?" Koertig asked them.

"I've been at the same table." Calloway spoke with the awe of a man who'd broken bread with the Almighty Himself. "Talk about charisma. Talk about class. And his wife. Gorgeous."

"She's European," Delia said as if this explained something.

"He's going to play nine holes with the top five amateurs at the clinic." Calloway practiced his swing sitting down. He was dressed for the part in a mint green and white striped polo shirt and green Bermuda shorts. These showed off a deep tan and a paunch Jude guessed he kept in check with a daily half hour on the treadmill.

Koertig continued with his serious-faced rapport building. "Think you've got the right stuff?"

This foolhardy question was greeted with a detailed account of Calloway's swing evolution and the angst that afflicted him over his shoulder turn. Griffin Mahanes was smugly silent throughout. Jude thought he was probably fondling the calculator in his pocket.

"Are you aware of anyone who had a quarrel with your brother, Mrs. Calloway?" she asked.

"He was disgusted with the company that did the marble for the guest bath at Maulle Mansion," Delia replied dutifully. "He had words with the manager."

"When was that?"

"Three years ago."

"Does the name Anton mean anything to you?"

Delia glanced toward Mahanes, who benevolently invited, "Go ahead."

"Fabian once told me that if anything ever happened to him, the party responsible would be Anton," she said with the same mild distaste that underpinned the bathroom décor revelation. Evidently this disclosure was no more significant in her mind.

"Did he tell you Anton's full name?" Jude asked.

"Yes, but I'm simply dreadful with names. I didn't think anything of it at the time."

"You didn't find it unusual for your brother to speculate on harm being done to him?"

"Fabian was prone to melodrama."

"He was gay," Jim Calloway translated. "Good looking, women all over him, and what do you know? There's your proof."

"Proof of what?" Koertig asked.

"They're born that way. You can't tell me a grown man has beautiful women throwing themselves at him and he chooses a scrawny Jewish geek who plays the goddamn oboe. That's a lifestyle choice? I don't think so, my friend. I call that crossed wires. Genetic malfunction."

"My brother was always artistic," Delia said. "And obsessed with personal grooming. Even as a child he could not abide a crushed shirt."

Jude thought, *Are these people for real?* "He certainly maintained a beautiful home here. Did you ever visit?"

Delia Calloway shook her head, sending a few carefully coiffed strands of ash blond into disarray. She smoothed them immediately. "I didn't even know he owned a log cabin until last Thanksgiving. He said he couldn't join us because he was having some work done and wanted to supervise personally."

"What kind of work?"

"A new concrete floor in his garage."

He poured concrete in late fall, in the mountains? The winter of 2006 was a tough one in Colorado, with the first huge blizzards dumping snow in the mountains in October. Jude glanced at Koertig and knew he'd picked up on this curious fact also. Perhaps Maulle was just trying to concoct an excuse for skipping a Thanksgiving occasion, but as far as bullshit went, the story was an odd choice. He could simply have said he was snowed in. Her first instinct was to dig up the concrete but they would need good reason before they vandalized someone's property. Maulle was a victim, not a perpetrator.

"I understand Mr. Maulle had a relationship with an Israeli, Yitzhak Eshkol."

"That's the oboe player I was talking about," said Jim Calloway. "Do you have an address for him?"

"He lives in Tel Aviv these days," Delia said.

Her husband looked surprised. "You keep in touch?"

Delia gave him a bad-dog look, like he'd just defecated in the corner. "He knows Ingeborg Rennert."

"In case you're wondering who that is," Pippa said, "she's a lady with a hairdo straight out of *Dangerous Liaisons* and a truckload of diamonds. Her husband buys companies that raise untold money from investors and bank loans, he helps himself to as much as he wants, then the companies file chapter eleven because they can't repay what they borrowed. The investors lose everything but Mr. Rennert lives in the world's biggest mansion. He's also the worst toxic polluter in the country, according to the EPA."

"My daughter is a snob," Delia informed Jude. "She suspects all *arrivistes* of criminal conduct."

"No," Pippa said sweetly. "Just the ones that belong in prison."

"If you paid this much attention to your future, perhaps we wouldn't be sitting here right now," Delia retorted. "You'd be home where you belong, enjoying a rewarding career."

Ignoring the family squabbles, Jude set out several photographs they'd found among Maulle's papers. "Do you recognize any of these men?"

"That's Yitzhak." Delia selected one of a very young man. He looked about eighteen. "He's put on some weight since then."

"You've seen him?" Jim Calloway seemed stunned that his wife led a life he knew little about.

"Yes, in Paris last year. He plays for the Israel Philharmonic." Delia glanced at Jude. "I'm sure you can find him through the orchestra, although I can't imagine what you could possibly want to ask him. He hasn't seen Fabian in years."

"We have some routine questions," Jude said. "When was that photograph of Yitzhak taken?"

"Ten or twelve years ago."

"And he was in a relationship with Fabian at that time?"

Delia sighed. "I told Fabian the age difference was absurd. Yitzhak was eighteen and my brother was forty."

"How did they meet?"

"I have no idea. Fabian put him through school and introduced him to the right people. Once Yitzhak had struck out on his own, they parted." Delia paused, and for the first time in the interview Jude glimpsed a flash of genuine emotion. "I didn't agree with my brother's lifestyle, Detective, but one thing I can tell you is he loved Yitzhak very deeply. I think that counts for something, don't you?"

"Yes, I do," Jude said.

Pippa stared suspiciously at her mother. "Why did they break up?"

"There was someone else. That's all I know. Fabian even said he thought it was for the best."

With an uneasy frown, Pippa picked up one of the other photographs. "I've seen him. He was a business associate of Uncle Fabian's."

"Recently?" Jude asked. The dark-haired man in question was weasel-faced and freakishly long-legged. He wore an unflattering burgundy velour jogging suit with cream trim.

"Last year." Pippa twirled a ballpoint pensively between her fingers. "I'd completely forgotten. He came up to us in a restaurant. Uncle Fabian excused himself and they went outside."

"Do you know what they talked about?" Jude asked.

"Zimbabwe. Uncle Fabian was angry when he came back to the table. He said the Russians could have it."

Jim Calloway snorted. "Five thousand percent inflation. Trust me, the Russians wouldn't want it." Plainly bored with the interview, he asked Koertig, "Do you play golf, Detective?"

"I go out with the old man sometimes. He's pretty keen."

"Well, then, you'll appreciate my dilemma being stuck here dealing with this when I should be preparing for the clinic."

Delia patted him. "You'll be fine."

"You think personal situations like this can't affect your game, think again," Calloway said for the benefit of anyone who cared. "First up, you have to keep that tension out of your shoulders or your backswing is screwed. Soon as I get to the resort, I'm signing up for the hot stone massage."

Koertig asked, "Do you own a gun, sir?"

"My client owns a collection of antique pistols," Griffin Mahanes replied.

"And a .45 ACP," Calloway quickly added. "Springfield Armory. Same as the SWAT teams."

"When was the last time you fired that weapon?" Koertig asked.

Calloway sustained the tough-guy act with a halfhearted swagger. "It's not like we have varmints roaming the yard."

"Varmints…" Delia mouthed the word as if sampling a peculiar food.

"Dad doesn't know how to shoot," Pippa said, earning a crestfallen glare from her father.

"You can verify my client's alibi," Mahanes intervened slickly. "Mr. Calloway was on the twelfth hole at Brae Burn Country Club when his brother-in-law was slain."

"Returning to Anton," Jude said. "What exactly did Mr. Maulle say about this individual?"

"They did business. My brother trusted this man and was let down by him. He made some discoveries that poisoned their relationship and I had the impression Anton was making a nuisance of himself."

"So there was no personal relationship?'

"Not that I know of. I can't imagine my brother forming a…liaison with a man from a background like that."

"Please go on." From the corner of her eye, Jude saw Pippa staring in astonishment at her mother. It must have come as a shock that Delia knew so much about her brother.

"He was from one of those Eastern bloc countries." Delia consulted her elegant fingertips. "Russia. Serbia. Liberia."

"Liberia's an African nation," Pippa said.

"They're all communists, aren't they?"

"You're incredible." Pippa stood abruptly. "I need some air."

"Do you know what kind of business your brother was involved in?" Jude asked.

"Oh, yes," Delia said with blithe unconcern. "Military hardware."

Her husband stopped dead in the middle of a lustrous commentary on his best ever personal performance at Pinehurst no. 2. "What did you say?"

"Uncle Fabian was an arms dealer?" Pippa gasped from the doorway.

"Hardware," Delia corrected impatiently. "I assume all those soldiers need a great many tents and toilet seats."

"Excuse me a moment." Griffin Mahanes whipped a buzzing cell phone from the inside pocket of his costly suit and stepped toward the door. He walked Pippa out.

Jude felt light-headed. "Military hardware?"

"That's what he said." Delia sighed. "Of course, he had other business interests in real estate and so forth. But the problem with Anton had something to do with one of the military shipments."

"Did you ever see a photograph of Anton or meet him personally?" Jude asked. She could see Koertig's eyes glazing over as Calloway maintained a steady drone of golf-speak between his occasional contributions to the interview.

"No, he wasn't a friend of the family."

"Can you tell us anything about him?"

"He was too cheap to get his teeth fixed. Fabian mentioned that." Delia stroked her hair back. Her look was deceptively casual, the expensive common-sense attire of the genteel matron. "I formed the impression that he wasn't a people person."

"What gave you that idea?"

"Fabian said he was a liability dealing with the French."

"The French are jerks," Calloway said.

"What was Anton's role?" Jude checked her wristwatch. It would be four soon. Debbie would be meeting Sandy.

"He was some kind of middle man. He flew planes, too. That's all I know."

"Did you ever encounter a security guard of your brother's called Hugo?"

"No, although I recall the name."

"Your brother employed him after an incident at his home in New Orleans. Do you know anything about that?"

Again, Delia surprised her husband. "Someone broke in and defaced several of his favorite paintings. Appalling."

"Looters?" Koertig asked.

"They didn't steal anything," Delia replied as Pippa slipped back into the room. "But Fabian was very shaken."

"Did he say anything else about the break-in?" Jude asked.

"You know about that?" Pippa asked her mother.

"Naturally. Fabian called me in case I thought you should come home. He was worried." Delia adjusted her pearls again. "I don't know if this is relevant now, but the intruders made a threat against you."

"Against me?" Pippa sagged down in a chair.

"What type of threat?' Jude asked.

"I don't know, but Fabian assured me he would take care of it."

"He knew the people who made the threat?"

"It had something to do with Anton." Abashed, Delia said, "I didn't take it seriously until...now."

Jude met Koertig's eyes and signaled that she wanted to end the interview. There was only so much they could cover in one session. When they knew more, they would talk to the Calloways again, Delia especially.

Working her way toward a conclusion, she said, "I just have one other question. The individual who murdered Mr. Maulle seemed to be looking for something. He stole a computer hard drive and a laptop and we think he may have used violence to try to obtain answers from Mr. Maulle."

"Are you saying my brother was tortured?" Delia lifted a shaking hand to her mouth.

Pippa burst into tears.

Wishing she'd been more tactful, Jude said, "I'm sorry. Please understand this is all just guesswork for us right now. Can you think of anything your brother might have had in his possession...even information?"

Belatedly, Jim Calloway demanded, "Do we have reason to fear for our safety, Detective?"

"Can you think of a reason?" she asked mildly.

"I have no idea." Delia placed a hand firmly on Pippa's arm. "And until we know what this is all about, you're coming home with us."

Pippa had the wisdom not to argue. Wiping her eyes, she asked, "Is this something to do with me?"

"Not directly, as far as I can tell." It was too soon to give firm assurances, but the New Orleans incident had occurred two years ago. If there was a threat to Pippa, surely something would have happened in the meantime.

"Should we consider hiring private security ourselves?" Delia asked.

"Hell, no," Jim Calloway declared, sparing Jude an answer. "There's a problem when a man can't take care of his own family."

Jude pictured him shooting himself in the foot as he tried to come to grips with his .45 ACP. "If you think of anything, please call us," she said, getting to her feet. "We really appreciate your time."

"Are you saying we can go?" Calloway bounded up.

"We have your contact details," Koertig said.

They walked the Calloways out into the entrance foyer where Griffin Mahanes was still on the phone. He ended the call and said, "I take it my clients are free to return back East."

Pippa murmured under her breath, "The sooner the better."

Everyone shook hands and Koertig said, "Good luck with your swing."

As Calloway herded his wife and daughter out the doors into the late-afternoon sun, he yelled back over his shoulder, "Hey, I'll send you a postcard of me and Tiger."

"Wonderful." Koertig waved.

Jude said, "Nice people skills."

"Just tell me one thing," her colleague gloomily responded. "Am I like him?"

Straight-faced, Jude nodded. "Talk about charisma."

"Yeah, I was hoping you'd say that."

❖

Jude couldn't sleep. The air-conditioning in her hotel room was noisy and Debbie hadn't called. Jude reasoned that no news was good news. If she was in any trouble she would have sent a text message even if she couldn't talk.

At least Sandy would be distracted for the next day or so. If she'd invited Debbie to her lair, she must be serious about keeping their relationship alive. Hopefully she would see the potluck as something simple she could do to make Debby happy, and Jude would gain access to her cabin in Rico on Thursday morning.

Once she'd ascertained Sandy's status, she would turn the problem over to Arbiter. Her masters were paid to deal with interagency politics. She didn't want to find herself tangled up in a turf war, or worse, in the middle of an incident everyone would officially deny. A disturbing thought crossed her mind. When she found out who Sandy was and what she was doing, and fed back the data, Arbiter would go up the chain of command and word would reach Sandy's brass that she was blown. What then? Would they simply extract her and continue with their plans? Would she become a zombie, an agent who "dies" and is set up with a whole new identity? Or would she be seen as disposable?

Jude considered the ramifications. If Sandy was a deniable person in a covert military unit involved in a black op on U.S. soil, she would be looking at a 9mm pension plan, not a transfer. Did Jude want that on her conscience? Sweating suddenly, she shoved her covers aside and reached for the lamp. She could see why Arbiter hadn't pushed her for results sooner. He obviously hadn't wanted her to stumble into a sensitive situation when he was in the dark himself.

No wonder the Bureau couldn't get a fix on her. The Pentagon would have made most of her records vanish, and Sandy had done the rest herself, making sure she cast no shadow. Her secrecy about Canada suddenly made sense. Maybe she knew exactly how this could play out and had arranged her own disappearance in advance. If Arbiter's worst suspicions were a reality, the government wouldn't want anyone left alive to tell the story. Sandy had probably covered every base. New identity and legend. Offshore back account. The works.

Her one weak spot was Debbie. She had not expected to fall in love, Jude concluded, and doing so had driven her out in the open more than she'd intended. Now that her lover was suspicious, what would Sandy do—cash in her chips and disappear before completing her mission?

Jude got out of bed and pulled on a T-shirt. Several options took shape in her mind. She could tip Sandy off. Let her know she was about to be blown. Or she could delay her search, find some reason why she couldn't gain access to Sandy's house. Or she could carry out the search and tell Arbiter they were wrong and Sandy was just another veteran with mental health issues. Maybe that's exactly what she would discover, anyway. It seemed like a leap to assume Sandy was involved in this NORTHCOM scenario, even if they were recruiting commandos for a domestic operation. Jude had already concluded Arbiter had to have a basis for his suspicions. He just wasn't sharing it with her, especially not over the phone. But still, he could be wrong.

She splashed some water on her face. She had to switch her train of thought or her mind would circle endlessly around the maddening unknowns. Without knowing who Sandy really was, she could make no decisions, so there was no point in futile speculation. Jude rested her face in a towel, unable to shake a strange feeling that there was something missing from her mental calculations, something she wasn't seeing. She supposed a part of her just didn't buy that Sandy would sign up for a crazy operation like the one Arbiter was hinting at.

If there was one thing she'd noticed about her taciturn subject over the past year, it was her mistrust of the government. She didn't mouth off, and she avoided political discussions, but Jude had picked up on the little things. Sandy was deeply patriotic. She despised politicians. She thought everything on the news media was propaganda. Once, at Debbie's place, Jude had overheard her call the White House and the Pentagon "evil." Would she really work for them?

Jude made herself a cup of herb tea because it was crazy to drink coffee at 2:00 a.m. and she needed to get some sleep tonight. She and Koertig were meeting early tomorrow to search Fabian Maulle's house again. She sat on the sofa and opened her laptop. Her e-mail included one from Mercy. As usual, Jude selected it and hit Delete. She scanned the others. None deserved an intelligent reply at this time of night.

For want of anything better to do, she picked up her cassette recorder and wound it back to the Oscar interview. She hadn't found the time to listen to it again since she wrote up the transcript, and she wondered if she'd missed any other clues about the Russian suspects. She played the parrot's Russian chatter and Pippa's comments a few times, then let the tape run. At the quotation from Browning's poem she rewound and played the passage again.

Oscar, when asked where "the box" was, had answered unhelpfully, "God's in his heaven. All's right with the world."

Pippa said her uncle used to recite that verse to her as a child.

Jude entered the text in Google and up came the title: *Pippa Passes*. The coincidence of the name was too stark and too obvious to be unintentional. Jude jumped up and located the inventory of books Koertig had prepared. The Browning title wasn't listed. She read down the page more slowly, looking for general poetry collections. Nothing. She paused as another detail struck her. The self-help book she'd seen Maulle's living room wasn't there either. Koertig had only listed the titles thrown around Fabian's ransacked office.

She reached for her cell phone, then changed her mind and plopped back down on the sofa. What was she going to do—wake up the primary in the middle of the night and ask him if he saw a book of poems at the house? Jude sipped the musty-tasting tea and resigned herself to reading the complete verse on her computer. There was no accounting for taste, she thought, as she digested line after line of what appeared to be a play in which a girl called "Pippa" sang awful songs, got dressed, and went for a stroll. Jude doubted this had been a bestseller, even when the author was alive.

Yawning, she persevered and located the line Oscar had quoted. It appeared in the middle of a scene in which a woman and her lover were talking, having murdered the woman's husband. The language was so murky and confusing, Jude gave up trying to find a clue and skimmed the rest of the story. Thoroughly sedated by the time she reached the unsatisfying conclusion, she closed her computer and stumbled back to bed.

Killing the lamp, she closed her eyes and repeated, "God's in His heaven. All's right with the world." Did anybody really believe that?

CHAPTER FOURTEEN

Jude found *Pippa Passes* in one of the spare bedrooms. She could see from the lush decor that Maulle had probably intended this to be his niece's room.

"Bring in a team," she told Koertig, forgetting who was in charge, "and tear this space apart. Walls, ceiling, floorboards. Everything."

"What are we looking for?"

"A box. That's all I can tell you."

They'd spent an hour searching the house and Jude was certain if anything was here they would find it where Maulle had placed the book. She opened the slim leather volume, a first edition, and froze at the inscription inside the cover:

> *To Fabian,*
>
> *For saving my life.*
>
> *Yitzhak*
> *September, 1995*

Jude flipped through the pages until she found the strange murder scene. "Jesus," she said.

"What have you got."

"Some basic encryption." The kind a technophobe could cope with. Maulle, she assumed, had underlined words through the Ottima and Sebald scene.

She handed the book to Koertig, who pulled out his notebook and sat down on the bed.

"He didn't even scramble the words," he reported after a few seconds.

Jude read over his shoulder. "'Under noisy washing garments foul proof. A lie that walks, and eats, and drinks! Discovery of the truth will be frightful. Break the secret, little girl.'"

"Under noisy washing garments," Koertig repeated.

"Okay, so we tear the laundry room apart, too," Jude said. "First, let's go lift that washing machine."

❖

"What are you saying?" Pippa stared down at the paper the family attorney slid across the table. The legalese made as little sense as the information she'd just heard.

"He's saying your uncle couldn't resist stabbing this family in the back," her mother replied. "Maulle Mansion is to become, of all things, an art school for disadvantaged young people who—"

"For punks who think 'motherfucker' is a normal form of address," her father completed.

"Everything else goes to you except the London house, which comes to me." It was hard to tell if her mother was pleased that Uncle Fabian's loot would remain in the family, or aggravated that Pippa was the one getting most of it.

"Minus the fifty million endowment for the Maulle school of art," the attorney pointed out. "And miscellaneous bequests to charity, individuals, and so forth. Mr. Maulle was very generous with several long-term staff."

"What in the world was he thinking?" her father mourned.

"I don't want his money," Pippa said.

"Then you can sign it over to us," her mother snapped.

The attorney glanced at her as if assessing whether she was serious. Returning his even gaze to Pippa, he said. "I would recommend you retain independent counsel, Ms. Calloway."

"And she has done so," Griffin Mahanes announced. "My client would like to see a rough estimate of the estate's value if one is available at this time."

"I'm not your client," Pippa said. "My parents hired you."

"No money has changed hands, and let me say this, if ever there was a client more in need of representation than yourself, I haven't met one."

For the first time since they'd met, Pippa thought he was probably telling the truth. "Don't I have to give you a dollar or something?"

He stroked his gray and pink silk tie. "Yet again I owe that hack a debt of gratitude."

"Who, John Grisham?" Delia Calloway looked askance. "I adored *The Client*."

"You're a criminal defense counsel, Griffin," Pippa's father said. "Isn't this a matter for an estate attorney?"

"Probate's the least of your daughter's problems," came the silky reply. "She still hasn't been cleared of suspicion in a homicide." A pair of hazel-gold eyes sought Pippa's. "What do you think, Ms. Calloway? Me or the lapdog your folks will choose for you?"

Pippa took a one dollar note from her pocket and slid it across the table. Someone had defaced it with a marker, giving Washington big pink lips. "You're officially hired, Mr. Mahanes. Does this mean I can go to Uncle Fabian's house and unpack my stuff?"

"Absolutely. I understand the sheriff intends to release the house for occupancy on Friday."

Her mother fidgeted with the pearls at her throat. "You can't possibly intend to stay in that house. Be sensible, darling. Come back to Boston with me."

"Why?"

"You can't stay all alone in the home where Fabian was *murdered*," her mother replied. "What if the killer comes back? Did you think about that?"

"I hope he does. I'd like to blow his brains out."

"You've never even held a gun," her father said.

"Neither have you," Pippa flung back. She felt immature bickering with her parents, but she still couldn't keep her mouth shut.

"Any moron can learn how to shoot." Griffin Mahanes glanced through some papers the other attorney passed to him. "I should know. I defend them all the time."

"I told you I was going to live out here," Pippa said.

Her parents shared perplexed frowns, as though they hadn't been present during the row when she told them she wasn't going to be a dentist. They also seemed to have forgotten telling her she couldn't expect a cent of financial support from them if she embarked on an art career.

"You can turn the conservatory into a studio for your sculpting," her mother said. "We never use it."

"I know." Pippa had been begging to convert that space since she was fifteen.

She glanced down at a note Griffin Mahanes held in front of her. It read, *You are disgustingly wealthy. Rough guess $250 million after tax and my fees. And that's only what this sap knows about.* She lowered her head to rest in one hand. For a few seconds she thought she was going to faint.

"Are you all right?" her mother asked. "You're very pale."

"Is there anything I need to sign or can I go now?" Pippa stood.

Griffin Mahanes stood with her, sliding his papers into a briefcase. "Ms. Calloway is tired. We can continue this discussion at a later date."

"You can't just leave," her mother said indignantly.

"What else is there to talk about?" Pippa dropped a kiss on her father's cheek. "Watch your putting."

He beamed happily. All she had to do was mention his first love and he forgot to be angry with her. Ignoring her mother's cold stare, she gave Griffin Mahanes a quick nod and he accompanied her from the room.

As they reached the lobby, he said, "Well done, and remember something—you no longer ask, you tell."

A giggle curdled with the heartburn rising in Pippa's throat. "I wasn't joking, you know. I don't want all that money. I wouldn't know what to do with it."

"Spoken like a true child of privilege."

Pippa gave him a look.

"You're paying handsomely for my advice, so let me give you some," her new attorney said. "Spend the next year trying to make it on your own without touching that cash, then tell me you don't care."

With mild embarrassment, Pippa reflected on all she took for granted. The need to earn her own living hadn't factored into her decisions about her life. Her parents had paid for her education and

Uncle Fabian had promised to support her while she discovered if she could make it as an artist. Most people didn't have her choices.

"You're right," Pippa acknowledged. "I've never had to think about it."

"It's not a crime to be rich," Mahanes said. "I make no apologies for earning more than anyone should. The crime is when money is wasted on morons. Maybe your uncle thought you were better than that."

Pippa was silent, remembering conversations when her uncle had asked her what she would do about various problems if she had the power to make change. She'd always felt that her opinions mattered to him. None of the other adults in her life had ever bothered to find out what she really believed in.

"Let's face it," Mahanes said. "If he wanted to leave his money to a bimbo fashionista, he made a big mistake."

Pippa laughed. "You're not as creepy and amoral as I thought."

Griffin Mahanes lowered his sunglasses and regarded her with mock dejection. "Don't tell anyone."

❖

"Where are you?" Jude asked, sandwiching her phone between ear and shoulder as she lugged a floorboard out into Maulle's backyard.

"I'm still at Lone's. I can't talk for long."

"How's it going?"

"Wonderful." Debbie sounded elated. "I feel like she's really listening to me. She apologized for being secretive. The thing is, she's been going to the house she and Madeline lived in, just taking care of it. But she thought I'd be upset if I knew, so she didn't tell me."

Christ. She had a second property, no doubt in her deceased partner's name. Jude felt like an idiot. "Where's the house?"

"In Utah," Debbie said vaguely. "She's going to take me to see it, so I know she's telling me the truth."

"That's wonderful," Jude said. "When are you going?"

"Probably on Sunday." Debbie sighed. "I'm so relieved. You've got no idea."

"Me, too," Jude said. If she couldn't get to Rico on Thursday, she would have the place to herself on the weekend. Thank God.

Koertig staggered out of the house with a stack of planks. Jude helped him prop them against the fence.

"There's a false floor," he panted. "I'm going round to the garage to check out the tools."

Jude covered the mouthpiece. "Take a break. I'll be with you in a few."

"I've got a better idea." Koertig said, wiping his face. "I'm calling in a team. Why should we break our backs?"

"You're the man," Jude said. As he vanished back into the laundry room, she said, "Sorry about that, Debbie."

"It's okay, I have to go anyway. I'm out back in the privy. It's not exactly pleasant."

"Holy shit, no wonder she likes staying at your place."

Debbie laughed. "This place is definitely primitive. Although the views are amazing."

"Is it just the one cabin or is there actually a whole ghost town?"

"She's got a couple of sheds," Debbie said. "But there's nothing else up here except trees."

"That's a shame. I thought it might be fun to explore."

"I don't think hikers make it up here very often."

"The access sounds like a pain," Jude said, like she'd just lost interest. "Hey, are you coming back to Paradox tomorrow for the potluck?"

"Yes!" Debbie squealed softly. "I told her friends are important to me and they should be important to her, too."

Amazed that Sandy wasn't putting up more opposition, Jude said, "Great, so I'll see you then. Don't fall down a mine shaft or anything."

Debbie giggled softly, then said, "Jude. Thanks. This means a lot to me."

"I'm happy for you," Jude said, thinking, *Jerk*.

They said good-bye and she poked the cell phone into her back pocket. Sticking her head in the back door, she surveyed the damage. They'd shifted the washing machine into the kitchen, and the laundry room no longer had a floor. Jude picked her way across the joist framing to the kitchen. Koertig was right. She couldn't see girders, just another floor about eight inches below.

She found her colleague on the front verandah talking to a couple of the rookie detectives assigned to the case.

"They were on their way out here already," Koertig said, handing her a document. "The necropsy report came in. You want to read it while we lift the rest of that floor?"

"Knock yourself out."

The men collected up various tools Koertig must have found in the garage and traipsed into the house. A few minutes later, Jude heard the sounds of sawing and torn timber. She took her time reading the report. Coco had died instantly from a single shot to the head. Time of death was estimated at 4:00 p.m., which ruled Pippa out completely. Her tire was still being repaired at 3:36 p.m. She could not have made it from Towaoc to her uncle's home in under half an hour.

Maulle's killers had spent almost forty minutes at the property. The bloody footprints suggested only one of them was upstairs with the victim. Was one man responsible for the hit while the other waited in the car, keeping a lookout? Oscar the parrot had recited what could have been a cell phone conversation in Russian.

"Detective?" One of the rookies interrupted her. "You might want to see this."

Jude followed him to the laundry room, where Koertig was poised over a recess in the floor taking photographs. Blinking against the flash pops, Jude stared down at a dust-covered stainless steel box the size of a small file drawer. It was padlocked. She handed her car keys to the detective she'd followed inside.

"You'll find bolt cutters in the back of my Dakota."

Koertig and the other rookie hauled the box out and carried it into the living room.

"This had better be good," Jude said.

She needed to return to Paradox by this evening. It was time she visited Harrison Hawke for an update, and she wanted to help Agatha get organized for the potluck tomorrow. On her way out of town, she needed to drag her deputy away from dog training and send him to Telluride. SAC Hill wanted someone who knew the festival present at the first meeting with the organizers.

"Go ahead," Koertig told the young detective who'd returned with the bolt cutters.

The lock fell to the floor a few seconds later and everyone stared at the box. Koertig, enjoying the prerogative of the primary, lifted the lid. A cloudbust of white Styrofoam packing peanuts floated out. Jude picked up a stack of evidence bags from a coffee table and pulled on a pair of fresh latex gloves. The young detectives fished around their pockets. Koertig referred them to a stack of gloves the forensic team had helpfully left on the dining room sideboard. A few pairs he'd split lay nearby along with a pile of spilled fingerprint powder. The crime scene cleanup crew would be in on Thursday to return the house to its pristine pre-murder condition, a service paid for by Maulle's insurance company.

Jude scooped the peanuts from the box, pausing to enable Koertig to photograph the contents as she lifted them out. "Looks like our vic backed up his computer after all."

She pulled out a couple of zip drives and a storage box of CDs, all labeled with dates.

"Floppy discs," one of the detectives marveled. "You don't see these anymore."

"Old home movies." Jude bagged several Super 8mm reels, then dug down to a set of notebooks. She held them up for Koertig, scooped away the last of the peanuts, and lifted out a heavy stack of large yellow business envelopes.

She opened the first and withdrew a set of glossy photographs. They had the heavily saturated hues of 1980s Kodacolor. She only had to glance at the subjects and poses to know why Maulle had hidden this stash away.

"Child pornography," she said, sliding the pictures back into their envelope.

"Jesus," Koertig said. "Why would he want his niece to find this shit?"

"I'll leave you to figure that out," Jude said. "I need to get going."

Koertig walked out to the pickup with her. She could see he'd picked up on her mood. "You okay?"

"When I left Crimes Against Children, I hoped I'd never see that stuff again."

"I'll take care of it," Koertig said.

"Record everything," Jude told him. "Copy all the images and send them to CVIP for analysis and victim identification."

Koertig shoved his hands in his pockets as though he wasn't sure what to do with them. "I thought Maulle was an okay guy."

"So did his family," Jude said. "Let's hold off breaking the news for a few days. They have enough to deal with, and we need to process all the evidence before we leap to conclusions. There's a lot more to this case than porn."

"You got it."

"I'll check in later." She had a thought. "You might want to start with the notebooks. They could help put everything else in context."

"Great," said Koertig. "Diaries of a sicko."

❖

Jude walked around the side of Deputy Sherman's house and crossed the long back yard to the wire mesh fence that surrounded the dog-training area. As she'd expected, Tulley was there living his dream, hanging upside down on a climbing frame while Smoke'm licked his face. Gavin Sherman had his K-9 poised on a teeter-totter. Jude had the impression the Belgian Malinois thought the exercise was child's play and only tolerated these puerile games to indulge his human.

Sherman gave Jude a proud wave and called, "Afternoon, Detective. Beer's in the fridge. Help yourself."

Tulley lost his balance and fell off the frame trying to greet her. Yelling, "Watch this, ma'am," he flailed a padded arm and encouraged Smoke'm to attack.

The hound sat down next to him and yawned. Jude could not foresee them bringing home a $10,000 prize. She followed the concrete path to the back door and located the kitchen. The Shermans were remodeling. Drawers were stacked on the kitchen counter next to a belt sander, and various tools were strewn around.

As Jude hunted for a bottle opener, she realized she wasn't alone in the house. At first she thought the sounds she could hear were coming from a TV, then she listened more carefully and froze. Small shrill moans were punctuated with thuds, as if a woman in the back of the house was tied up and struggling to free herself.

For a split second, Jude considered rushing outside to get help, but the sounds were getting louder and she couldn't take the risk. She unholstered her weapon, flipped the safety, and crept rapidly along the hallway toward the back of the house. Her mind raced through possible scenarios. Sherman had a wife. Had she been accosted in her own home while her husband was out back teaching his dog to climb ladders?

"Oh, God. Stop. Please. I can't take any more." Frantic female cries came from behind the door a few feet away.

Jude closed the distance, soft-checked the handle, then kicked the door open and stepped back, yelling, "County Sheriff. Show me your hands."

She advanced into the room in a semicircle, checking over her shoulder to make sure there were no other assailants. Two adults occupied the bed. Both had their backs to her, the male kneeling over the female.

He raised his hands and said, "Oh, man."

The "victim" he was having sex with craned around to demand, "Who are you? What are you doing in my home?" She was red-faced and panting.

Jude stalked over to the bed to get a better look at the "offender." She lowered her weapon. "Bobby Lee?"

"Do you two know each other?" The victim pulled a sheet around her breasts.

"Tell her," Jude invited.

"This is Tulley's boss," Bobby Lee said.

"Oh, crap. Please don't say anything," the blonde begged.

"Are you Mrs. Sherman?"

"Yes, I'm Crystal." A panicky whine. "Where's Gavin?"

Jude was incredulous. "You two are fucking while her husband is out in the yard?"

Crystal gave her a sulky look. "If he didn't live out there, this wouldn't be happening."

"Don't you have a day job?" Jude asked.

"I sell male enhancement products on eBay."

Bobby Lee asked, "Do those work?"

"You don't need any help in that department, sugar," Crystal said, placing a purposeful paw beneath the sheets.

Jude groaned. "What were you thinking?" she asked Bobby Lee.

Before he could reply, the thud of footsteps in the hallway was followed by a shrill bleat of dismay. Tulley stepped into the bedroom, his ears cranberry red. In disbelief, he stared at Jude, then at the gun she still held loosely at her side.

"Don't shoot," he squeaked. "It's all my fault."

"You two, get dressed, for Chrissakes." She holstered the Glock, took Tulley's arm, and escorted him out into the living room. "You knew this was going on?"

"Bobby said it wouldn't matter none to you," Tulley whined. "If I would have known—"

"*I'm* not the problem." Jude marched him to the kitchen and pointed out the window. "*That's* the problem."

Even as she said the words, she realized she was looking at an opportunity. Being "cheated on" by Bobby Lee meant she could terminate their "relationship" and receive sympathy. Her hetero credentials would remain intact but she could get rid of the "boyfriend" who legitimized them. She and Bobby Lee had been trying to find a way to close down their "beard" operation, mostly because it cramped his style. But Jude also disliked the deception. It was one thing to leave assumptions uncorrected, another to have to lie blatantly to the few people she felt close to.

Backtracking slightly, she said, "What I'm saying is, *of course* I'm upset, but I'm not going to go crazy and risk my career over a no-good, cheating boyfriend. But out there is a husband who's a law officer."

"I told Bobby Lee this was a darn fool idea."

"Well, he's not a big listener when it comes to chasing skirt."

"Ain't that the truth?" Tulley gave her a sickly grin. "I mean—"

"It's a bit late to spare my feelings," Jude said.

"You have to understand something." Tulley's tone took on a frantic quality. Predictably, he tried to paint his best friend in a rosier light. "That Crystal, she's a man chaser. She can't keep her hands to herself. Bobby Lee said she's processing something and acting out inappropriately."

"Please tell me you're not sleeping with her, too."

"No, she laid off of me soon as she saw Bobby Lee."

"Well, that's lovely."

Tulley studied the floor. "Sorry."

"It was bound to happen sooner or later." Jude gave his shoulder a poke. "Now, listen carefully. You can't tell anyone about this. If Sherman found out, well, I'd hate to think what he might do. You don't want a colleague ruining his career over a cheating wife, do you?"

"No, ma'am."

"This unfortunate situation calls for a creative approach. Obviously, I'm going to dump Bobby Lee's ass."

Loyally, her deputy said, "He's sure asking for it."

"So, we have an opportunity."

Tulley squinted. "How's that?"

"You're going to circulate the story that I came around here all riled up and tore him a new one because I found out he's been seeing a woman in Durango."

"That'll work. Everyone already knows about her."

Jude produced a shocked expression. "Do you mean to tell me Mrs. Sherman isn't the only one?"

Tulley gulped. "I thought you knew."

"Apparently I'm the last person to find out my boyfriend's still up to his old tricks." Jude heaved a loud, self-pitying sigh. "How embarrassing."

"I know for a fact those women don't mean a thing to him," Tulley blurted.

Jude treated this thin consolation with the contempt it deserved. "I've had about all I can take. I'm going back in there."

Tulley hurried to stand in her path, his dark amber eyes flashing in panic. "Don't do something you'll regret. He's not worth it, boss."

"Get out of my way," Jude said. "It's time he learned his lesson." She shoved Tulley aside, noting, "You've packed on some muscle, Deputy."

As he beamed into the mirror at the end of the hall, she threw open the door to the master bedroom and pointed at Crystal Sherman. "You, get out of here and go make nice to your husband before he finds out he married a slut. As for you"—while Crystal looked on in horror, she spun Bobbie Lee around and handcuffed him—"you're coming with me."

"What are you going to do to him?" Crystal whined.

"Want to find out?" Jude produced a spare set of handcuffs and waved them in front of the nympho wife's startled face. "These are for you if you're not out of my sight in five seconds."

As Crystal scuttled from the room, Bobbie Lee said, "I guess this is gonna be all over town and I'll be a hunted man."

"Relax," Jude told him. "We can leave Crystal out of this. It's that woman in Durango I'm pissed about."

He craned around at her, his blond cowlick falling across his eyes. "The waitress or the teacher?"

From the doorway, Tulley said, "There's this program at the United Church. Sexaholics Anonymous."

"How would you know?" Bobby Lee asked, not unreasonably.

Tulley chose to ignore the question, instead negotiating on his friend's behalf, asking Jude, "If he promises to join the program, will you let him loose?"

"No." She hustled Bobby Lee out into the living room and through the front door.

As they reached the Dakota, Gavin Sherman strode out from behind the house, Crystal hanging off his arm. Her breasts heaving beneath her snugly fitting crop-top, she planted her hands on her hips and shrilly informed Bobby Lee, "I bet you're sorry now, asshole!"

Before Bobby Lee could utter a bemused word, Sherman's fist connected with his jaw and he sagged against Jude.

"That's for trying to grope my wife," the deputy said. With a respectful nod at Jude, he added, "You can consider that a blow in defense of your honor, too, Detective. If there's one thing I can't tolerate, that's a cheat."

"Fair enough." Jude signaled Tulley. "Wrap up whatever you're doing with that hound and meet me at headquarters in an hour. You're wanted in Telluride."

"Me? Why?"

"Because none of the FBI agents are handsome enough to charm the organizers."

Tulley studied her face uncertainly.

Jude said, "That was a joke, Deputy."

Fidgeting, he asked, "Where are you taking Bobby Lee?"

"Somewhere I can beat him up without witnesses."

Sherman clapped Tulley across the shoulder. "Hell hath no fury" was his cheerful verdict. "Come on, buddy. Let's go work that A-frame before you head back."

As soon as they were out of sight, Jude removed the handcuffs from Bobby Lee and helped him up. "Are you okay?"

He cradled his face. "I'm ruined."

Jude lifted his hand away to inspect the damage. "You'll live. Apart from the bloody nose, you'll just have puffiness and bruising."

"Oh, that's just perfect. Did you plan this?" he asked suspiciously.

"No. Did you?"

He shook his head. "Tulley couldn't handle her, so I intervened."

"I appreciate that. Sorry about your face."

"It's not the first time." Bobby Lee held out his hand. "Friends?"

"Absolutely." Jude dropped a quick kiss on his undamaged cheek after the handshake. She'd grown fond of her phony boyfriend in the two years of their fictional relationship. "Stay away from Crystal."

"You bet your ass I will." He tried to flash his teeth but winced in pain. "Stay away from Dr. Westmoreland."

"I'm working on it. Are you going to that goddamned soirée?"

"Yeah, Agatha sweet-talked me into it. Are you?"

"Uh-huh." Jude had arrived at a brilliant plan. She was going to invite Hill on the pretext that they would be seeing various Telluride Film Festival luminaries and could gather intelligence. In reality, she planned to flaunt Hill in front of Mercy to prove that she'd moved on.

Bobby Lee said, "Unbelievable. I'm going to have a black eye when I meet the beautiful people."

"You'll look like a bad boy."

He grinned crookedly. "Aren't you tempted by that, my darling?"

Jude laughed. "Get out of here before I blacken the other one."

CHAPTER FIFTEEN

Jude pulled into the CRAP compound slightly after 8:00 a.m. For a Wednesday morning, the place buzzed with frenetic activity. Weary from the past several days, she leaned against her pickup and fought off a yawn. She needed coffee.

"My Valkyrie." Harrison Hawke strode toward her from amidst a group of fellow fanatics, all in black uniform. They stared as he applied his dry lips delicately to her hand. "I wasn't expecting to see you."

"I hope this isn't a bad time."

His response came creepily close to a simper. "I am entirely at your disposal, *Fräulein*, regardless of the hour."

He escorted her toward his barricaded dwelling, acknowledging heel clicks and salutes with sharp nods.

"Are you holding a training day?" Jude asked as soon as they were alone in front of the surveillance monitors in the Nazified living room.

"In a manner of speaking." Hawke removed his black visor cap and dropped to his knees in of her.

Staring down at his shiny bullet head, Jude thought, *Oh, shit. Here it comes*.

"Actions speak louder than words," her suitor intoned. "The pages of the pan-Aryan struggle will be stained in blood and anointed with the honor and courage of those who sacrificed all. Among the names of those who founded the new White Homeland, yours will be emblazoned directly below mine."

Jude said, "Harrison, what about your knee surgery? We could sit down."

He gave a sharp, grateful nod and got to his feet with a grunt. They sat in the club chairs opposite the stone fireplace. As though to draw inspiration, Hawke gazed up his painting of Adolf Hitler for several revitalizing seconds. He then clutched Jude's hand.

"Crucial decisions have been made since we last spoke. A new banner has been erected. The bell tolls and an initiative is underway to eliminate the false obstacles that divide us. We must shake loose the Manchurian candidates draining the lifeblood from our movement."

So far, the strangest marriage proposal Jude had ever heard.

"The gauntlet has been thrown down." His voice rose. "Petty dissent and ego-politics must be crushed if we are to usher in a new era. The cop-out of leaderless resistance must be strangled at birth."

"You're going to meet with the ASS," Jude deduced.

Hawke's fingers poked between hers. They felt like lukewarm breakfast links. He said, "This Sunday. On neutral territory."

"Where?"

"They proposed Ghost Canyon. I haven't sent my response yet."

Jude shook her head. "No, you're too far from help out there. Access is via a bottleneck. And cell phone signal drops out in the canyon. Sounds like a trap to me."

She knew the area well, spending at least half her time on calls relating to campsite thefts and missing cattle. The canyons had provided a haven for rustlers and outlaws for the past 150 years. If you wanted to disappear, or make someone else disappear, the opportunities were infinite.

"I have the greatest respect for your feminine instincts." Hawke finally released her hand so he could fondle the reproduction SS dagger at his side. "Do you have a suggestion?"

"Lone Burro, the old mining camp just outside of Bedrock."

"I'm not familiar with it."

"Secluded but accessible. You can Jeep in and out. Close to a main highway. Excellent sniper positions. You can own this venue, Harrison." She tossed the baited hook. "Perhaps there's some advice I can offer, since I know the location. I'm willing to accompany you and your men. In plain clothes, of course."

Hawke's head flushed pink along with his face. His voice filled with emotion. "*Fräulein*, how can I ask you to take such a risk?"

"There is too much at stake for me not to."

As she feared, this declaration spurred Hawke to pick up where he'd left off earlier. This time he stood to attention before her.

"Your noble idealism would be an inspiration to any man. For me, it fuels a flame that devours all doubt. In his darkest hours, der Führer reached out to the woman who shared his destiny throughout the greatest struggle of the century. He honored her sacrifice as I honor yours. *Geliebte Fräulein*, I—"

"Harrison, we serve a higher goal and must never lose sight of that," Jude interrupted. "The personal cannot be permitted to eclipse the political."

Hawke drew her to her feet. "And when the two coincide?"

With a sigh, Jude placed a firm hand to his cheek. "The time will come when we can indulge ourselves in dreams, but that time is still in the future." Allowing a catch to enter her voice, she said, "Sometimes I feel despair."

He covered her hand with his own. Rare softness infiltrated his watery gaze. "Why, *mein Schatz*? Tell me what's troubling you."

"It will take more than words to organize the movement. I know you have the backing of a wealthy donor, but it won't be enough. Even if you can change the mind of the ASS leader and the April unity meeting goes well, how will we finance growth?"

Hawke tucked her arm into his and steered her toward the front door. "Put your mind at ease. We're not alone. The vision of a White Homeland has mobilized many across the globe, and a network of supporters is now channeling funds to my organization."

Jude gave him an uncertain smile.

Hawke couldn't resist a boast. "The CRAP is going to enter a business arrangement with my contacts in Argentina. The profits we earn will support our growth and fund the CPA."

"Your new political party?"

"Yes, the Christian Patriots Alliance."

Jude asked no more questions. She didn't want to pressure Hawke into making disclosures. He had a suspicious turn of mind. As if she'd already lost interest, she said, "Well, it sounds like you have everything in hand. I should have known."

Preening, he said, "I built the best organization in the racialist movement from nothing. Imagine what I can do with fifty million dollars."

Jude wasn't faking her surprise. "Fifty million," she breathed. "Is a donation like that legal?"

"No, but that's the beauty of the arrangement," Hawke said. "The money is invisible. No IRS. No tax. No paper trail."

"Don't tell me anything." Jude covered her ears. "For your own protection."

Hawke flashed his small, pointy teeth. "I feel safe, my dear. Perfectly safe."

As they stepped out into the brilliant sunlight, his men rushed to form ranks, standing at stiff attention. Jude could feel their eyes on her. She wasn't close enough to read each facial expression but she could sense the distrust. Height, muscles, clean-shaved faces, and prevalence of blond dye jobs distinguished Hawke's fighting force. They were also smarter than their kindred in the ASS.

The man of the hour, Hawke made a solemn announcement. "Brothers, we will soon be called upon to act. In the struggle for white self-determination, unity is essential, but our enemies are bent on dividing us. With its unlimited money and spying power, the government has infiltrated our movement, creating a cauldron of chaos where there should be order. As we stand here, they are fomenting a plot to discredit us.

"In the approaching days, I will call upon each man among you to join with me in crushing this threat." Hawke paused, seemingly weighed down all of a sudden. "Brothers, because of the sense of honor that is our genetic birthright, it is naturally repugnant to us to fight our own kindred. But make no mistake, a larger ideal is at stake here and every white patriot must make a choice. Unity or death."

In one voice, his men bellowed, "Unity or death."

Jude felt like she'd stumbled onto the set of a movie. Its title was *What the Fuck Am I Doing Here?*

❖

"Hello, stranger," Jude greeted Sandy Lane like they were old friends.

She had half expected a no-show at the last minute, but Sandy had apparently decided her relationship was important and she had to make an effort. Her eyes bored into Jude's. Debbie called them Windex blue. She was right.

Sandy indicated a steak. "That's overcooked."

Jude poked the guilty party with her fork. Yes, indeed, the perfect sirloin for the wimp who gagged on medium rare. She flipped it onto the platter next to the grill and remarked in a conversational tone, "Debbie tells me you've been on vacation."

Sandy was only five-eight, but she made Jude feel physically threatened. The sensation unsettled her. She rarely felt at a disadvantage, even with men taller and heavier than she was. But around Sandy, she was acutely aware of every vulnerability.

As if she could read Jude's mind, Sandy asked, "How's that ankle coming along?"

Jude produced a chagrined shrug. "Things heal a whole lot faster when you're twentysomething." It suited her if Sandy thought she was off her game.

"That shit about heating pads. Don't buy it," Sandy advised. "Long term, ice works better."

"Funny you should say that. I feel like the anti-inflammatories aren't helping."

"Is it still painful."

Wouldn't you like to know? Jude made a show of tough talk, as though she was covering the truth. "Not so much. Walking and driving are okay. I still can't ride a horse."

"That's a drag." Sandy tucked her thumb in her belt and propped herself against the pillar at their end of the stationhouse verandah. She took a slug of beer and ran the back of her hand across her lips.

Jude found herself fascinated by the corded muscles of her neck and the swell of her shoulders and biceps. Sandy hadn't slacked off over summer. If anything, she'd stepped up her physical conditioning. She was a little leaner, like she'd added some distance running, and her movements were more fluid, probably thanks to martial arts. Jude decided she'd also been pain training. She was combat ready and focused, her muscles not just for show. Jude had never seen her so calm. A scary composure supplanted the tense urgency she often exuded. Whatever she was planning, the transition phase was underway, Jude decided, and her lethal serenity was a sign of confidence in her mission.

"If you keep looking at me that way," Sandy drawled, "I'll think you want to fuck me."

Jude dropped the steak she was trying to transfer. Controlling her breathing, she glanced swiftly around the friends and locals who'd shown up for the potluck and barbecue. No one was paying any attention. The music and laughter had drowned out Sandy's voice. She and Jude were the only people standing near the grill. Everyone had gathered around Tulley and Smoke'm. He'd just arrived back from his Telluride assignment and wanted to show off.

"Is that your cute way of telling me I'm so sex-starved it shows?" Jude asked casually.

"Still striking out?"

Jude forced a self-effacing grin. "Just lucky, I guess."

Sandy swept her up and down, eyes glinting. "You're looking kind of soft, but you've still got the right stuff. If I were a ninety-pound weakling with a thing for women in uniform, I'd date you."

"Coming from you, that's a real lift." Jude slid a couple more steaks onto the plate. "So, enough with the foreplay. Where were you hunting?"

Sandy set her beer down on the table. "What makes you think I went hunting?"

"That fact that you won't tell Debbie where you've been." She watched Sandy register the reply. Like a co-conspirator, she said, "If I were you, I wouldn't tell her either. Killing Bambi? No, you'd have to be nuts."

Sandy gave a noncommittal shrug.

"Friends of mine just brought home an eight-hundred-pound bull elk." Jude pressed forward with the hunt narrative. "Debbie might change her mind about your vanishing acts if you showed up with enough meat to fill her freezer."

"Debbie doesn't want for anything." Sandy sounded a little stung.

"Don't tell me you just take the rack." Jude showed her distaste. "That's depraved."

Sandy moved away from the pillar. She took the fork from Jude and stabbed a steak. "You're not concentrating. This is beyond well done." She was so close, her skin brushed Jude's. As she rearranged everything on the grill, she said, "I don't kill for fun."

Jude caught her scent. Sharp, clean, just salty enough to suggest a trickle of sweat down her spine. "I had a feeling about that."

Sandy stayed close, asking softly, "What's with all the questions?"

"I told you, I'm the one your girlfriend talks to. She's been asking me if you're having an affair."

"What did you tell her?"

"The truth. I'm a detective. Frequent unexplained absences aren't a good sign."

"You never heard of minding your own business?"

"Maybe if you talked to your partner a bit more, she wouldn't drag other people into your domestic dramas."

Sandy stiffened. She oozed danger. "Debbie knows she can trust me."

Refusing to be intimidated, Jude reclaimed the fork and added the rest of the cooked meat to the plate. She decided to push. "Not so long ago, you asked me to take care of her if anything happened to you. I've been thinking about that."

"And?" Sandy reached past her for her beer.

Jude's stomach plummeted, and every sense quivered its awareness of the hard body close to hers. An ache spread through her. She felt weak for a moment as blood rushed to her extremities. Her heart was noisy in its work, pumping and pounding. The barbecue was ready. She should wave everyone over. Her arm refused to comply.

"Is there something I should know?" She looked Sandy in the eye. "If you're tangled up in a problem situation, you can tell me. I'm not a blabbermouth."

Sandy lowered her beer bottle to her side, suspending it casually from the neck. She stepped in even closer. Her breath warmed Jude's neck. One of her nipples rolled like a warm marble across Jude's arm. "What are you suggesting?"

That you're full of shit, Jude thought. She watched Sandy's pupils dilate and contract in a split second, inky droplets haloed in radiant blue. "I guess I'm asking if you're okay."

"You care? I'm touched." Sandy lifted the beer bottle, lightly moving the glass lip over Jude's hard nipples. "For me?"

"Don't flatter yourself." Jude took a step back, colliding with the table. The plates wobbled and a tall glass fell off.

As it smashed, Sandy said, "Loosen up, Detective. I'm just messing with you."

Shocked to find herself damp-skinned and breathing quickly, Jude said, "You didn't answer my question."

Sandy's mouth quirked, like she was laughing at a private joke. "Do I seem okay to you?"

"How the fuck would I know?"

"You wouldn't."

Aggravated by her placid unconcern, Jude turned off the grill. The more she thought about her conversation with Arbiter, the likely it seemed to her that Sandy was involved in something covert. If so, she would do whatever it took to complete her mission, including using the people around her. Jude wondered if the story about her lover and stepson was true, or whether Sandy had invented a convenient fiction to excuse her odd behavior.

"Hey, you two." Debbie approached with flushed cheeks and a large salad bowl. She looked delighted to see them in conversation. "Are the steaks ready?"

"Sure are," Jude said.

Debbie hollered to the guests to come eat. "Want me to fix you a plate?" she asked Sandy.

"Thanks, baby." Sandy kissed her lover's cheek as a friend might, respecting Debbie's desire not to broadcast her sexual orientation.

She met Jude's eyes. "I'm going to take Debbie back to my place for a couple of days after this. Could you feed the cats?"

Jude knew exactly what was going on. Sandy was going to play house with a happy hostage. She'd just raised the stakes, adopting countermeasures in anticipation of an external threat. With Debbie in her home, she would seem less suspicious and she could also use Debbie as a shield. Jude would have to find a way to get them both out of there.

"I'm driving down to Cortez again tomorrow, but I'll make arrangements for the cats," she said pleasantly.

"How's the case going?" Debbie asked. "You must be exhausted driving backward and forward."

"We have some good leads," Jude said.

"Is it someone from around here?"

"Between us, I don't think so."

"A tourist." Debbie's relief was tangible. "That makes sense."

Sandy chuckled. "No one's any safer because he's not from 'round here."

"Yes, we are. That's one less evildoer living among us."

"Who am I to argue with a beautiful woman?" Sandy handed Jude a beer and knocked her own bottle lightly against the side. "Good hunting."

Filled with unease, Jude echoed the genial toast. She had a feeling Sandy was laughing, and the joke was on her.

CHAPTER SIXTEEN

"Hugo Debroize of Counter Threat Group?" Jude asked.

The response came in a deep South African drawl, the vowels broad and flat. "I'm your man. How can I help you?"

"This is Detective Jude Devine with the Montezuma County Sheriff's Office in Colorado."

"Don't tell me. Fabian Maulle?" He added, "CTG notifies us when clients are hit. I was expecting this call."

"Hit?" Jude repeated. "You think Mr. Maulle was executed?"

"It's an assumption in our line of work. Most clients are at-risk individuals." Debroize spoke so rapidly Jude had to concentrate to follow his speech pattern. A faint rise on the final syllables reminded her of Tulley. When he was nervous, his voice took on an unusual sing-song lilt.

"I understand you were employed by Mr. Maulle last year," she said.

"Yes, for six months."

"Could you tell me about that assignment?"

"Why don't I save us both time and tell you who killed him?"

"Go ahead," Jude invited. "But I'll still need answers to my questions."

Debroize barked a brief, resigned laugh. "Anton Voronov had Mr. Maulle killed, but you won't pin anything on him. Even if you catch the *skebengas* who pulled the action, they won't give him up. He has special punishments for idiots who rat him out."

Not wanting to sound like she knew very little, Jude said, "We have information that Mr. Maulle and Mr. Voronov had a business relationship."

"Ah, so you know who I'm talking about."

"Of course," Jude lied smoothly. If Debroize thought the police already had the facts and he wasn't a sole source, he would speak more freely.

"Mr. Maulle hired CTG when Anton decided to blackmail him. He sent in a couple of goons to vandalize Mr. Maulle's property, then threatened a family member."

"Pippa Calloway?"

"You know the girl?"

"She found Mr. Maulle as he was dying."

"*Yissus*, that's rough. Nice young lady. Is she okay?"

"Yes, shaken up, of course. What was the blackmail about, Mr. Debroize?"

He became cagey with exact detail, testing to see how much she knew. "Mr. Maulle had class, but he did business with some real animals."

"I guess when you deal arms to the highest bidder, that's inevitable," Jude remarked. "Anton piloted for him, didn't he?"

"They both flew. But Mr. Maulle stopped when he didn't need to skivvy anymore. Anton gets a rush from playing the big man, so he's still running shipments himself."

"I heard they argued."

"Mutual loathing, but Anton went too far. Mr. Maulle said he was cleaning house before the New Orleans incident and told Anton he was out. The blackmail was retaliation, and Anton wanted back in, so he threatened to have Miss Calloway killed."

"The break-in at Maulle Mansion was a calling card?" Jude queried. "Proof that he could get to her."

"Yes, the warning shot."

"How did Mr. Maulle resolve the threat in the end?"

"He gave Anton what he wanted," Debroize said without emotion. "You have to understand something. Vermin like Anton Voronov don't let go. Mr. Maulle had no choice. He knew what they would do to his niece."

"So he believed he'd dealt with Anton."

"Strange, hey? Anton's busting his *knaters* to stay in the game, then he takes Maulle out anyway. Insane."

"Very weird," Jude agreed.

And why would Maulle have put up with an associate he hated for so long? She thought about the photographs. Maybe Anton knew about Maulle's "hobby" and had used it as a lever to keep their business connection alive. Then Maulle got fed up and tried to cut him off, so he had to raise the stakes.

"Is there anything else you can tell me?" Jude asked.

"I'll ask around. Give me your number." After Debroize had taken her contact details, he said, "Please tell Miss Calloway I'm sorry. Also, if she needs security, CTG can take care of everything. She can ask for me personally."

Jude felt a prickle at her nape. "Are you implying that Pippa's still at risk?"

"*Ek sê.* That's the problem. I don't know what I don't know."

"Well, I appreciate your help. One more thing, why did Anton want to stay in business with Maulle?"

"Mr. Maulle was the one with the government contacts, and he never included Anton in that side of the operation."

"So without those contacts, Anton would be frozen out?"

"Dead in the water. Scum would deal with him, but what's he going to sell? Small arms like everyone else." He was quiet for a few seconds, perhaps weighing how much to say. "Mr. Maulle was world class. Jet fighters. Submarines. Maybe even nukes."

Jude's heart raced. How did Debroize know all this? They'd googled Maulle and all they found was this or that charity awarding him medals. "Was his business common knowledge?"

Hugo Debroize chuckled. "No, strictly to insiders. But we have to know what we're contending with when we provide close protection. Most CTG clients provide a detailed profile."

"What was Maulle's beef with Anton before the threats to Pippa?"

"Can't help you there. Mr. Maulle never talked about it."

"Okay. Thanks for your time, Mr. Debroize."

Jude wasn't sure if she was happy they'd talked or depressed. The more she found out about Fabian Maulle, the more bizarre this case got. It was already way beyond the scope of a standard homicide investigation.

She was about to end the call when Debroize said, "Something you might want to know… The Solntsevo crime syndicate put a contract out on Anton about a month ago."

"They want him dead?" Jude scrawled down the name. "Why?"

"Your guess is as good as mine. But it's interesting, wouldn't you say?"

"Yes, very."

Jude ended the call and strolled to the window, her mind racing. As she watched whirls of dust rise from the ochre plain beyond the headquarters building, a motive for the crime took shape. Anton thought Maulle was going to have him hit as payback for the threat against Pippa, so he sent in a couple of thugs to scare him into canceling the contract. Only they took things too far and Maulle died. That explained Coco's murder and the bizarre attempt to clamp Maulle's wounds with the bulldog clips. They weren't supposed to kill him, Anton needed him alive.

To prove her theory, she needed to catch one of Anton's men. Even if he wouldn't cut a deal and give up his boss, maybe he would provide a few answers. So far there'd been no response to their composite drawings, although a couple of detectives in Miami said they had an angle on a Russian pimp and might get an ID.

As she left the undersheriff's office she'd borrowed for her overseas call, Jude wondered how much longer they could run the case without involving the feds.

Koertig raced up to her as soon as she showed her face. "This isn't what we thought."

"Yeah, no kidding." Her cell phone vibrated against her hip and she said, "Hang on, pal."

She stepped away to check an incoming text message, hoping for something from Debbie. At Wednesday night's potluck, she'd tried to get some time alone with her, but Sandy made sure that didn't happen. Jude had gone on to spend most of yesterday stuck in Telluride with a team of FBI agents trying not to draw attention to themselves. The first film festival arrivals were already in town and being greeted with open arms by those about to endure a long winter at the mercy of the hedge-fund crowd.

The people who worked for wages at the Mountain Village resort and local restaurants couldn't afford to live close to Telluride. Instead they commuted along suicidal snowbound roads throughout winter only to find they could work all day without a tip from jerks who expected their shoelaces to be tied for them. The general consensus was that the film festival crowd might not have lots of new money, but they did have some class.

Having heard the bad news, the festival organizers were frantic, trying to decide if they should call the whole thing off and look like pawns in a phony government terror alert or let it roll and discover, via a theater full of dead celebs, that the FBI was telling the truth. Their position could best be described as one of mordant pragmatism. Amidst dark rumblings about the McCarthy era and outbursts over police-state tactics, they had handed over their VIP lists, festival program, and the names of anyone Jewish or any film that might attract a Jewish audience. The Klaus Barbie feature was among them.

Jude had left Hill and the team poring over risk-reduction options last night so she could get to Cortez in time for dinner with Koertig and his wife and an early start on the Maulle case this morning. Between times, she'd had a conversation with Arbiter and they'd agreed that she would search Sandy's property first thing Monday and confirm whether she was a friendly or not. Arbiter had a heavy squad on stand-by in case the situation went south. The same applied to the ASS op on Sunday. Jude had her orders, and he'd even forwarded them in writing.

Having sown seeds of doubt in Hawke's mind about a mole in the ASS, she was now supposed to spin some bullshit to Aidan Hill at the soirée tomorrow, giving her a last minute heads-up about the meeting at Lone Burro. Jude's mission was to extract Hawke the moment the feds arrived. If they didn't arrive, she had to use her judgment. Arbiter didn't care if there was a body count so long as she didn't compromise long-term objectives.

No pressure.

Jude read the text on her cell phone a second time: *Won't be at soirée. Going Utah late Sat. Home Tues. XX Deb*

Jude keyed a quick reply: *Cats fine. Have fun. Keep in touch.*

As Debbie signed off, Jude looked up to find Koertig had migrated to a huddle at another detective's desk. She joined him and asked, "What's up?"

"It's Miami PD."

"I think you better take this." The detective passed the phone up to him.

Jude watched the excitement drain from Koertig's face as he listened. He was silent for a while, then said, "Yeah, we'll send someone. Thanks, Lieutenant." He replaced the receiver and took a few seconds before announcing, "Listen up, everyone. That was Special Investigations Section in Miami. There's two DBs in their morgue that fit the descriptions of our suspect males. Both died of gunshot wounds thought to be sustained during an altercation over a prostitute. No arrests have been made."

He glanced toward Jude. "Devine will brief you shortly on her conversation with the security guard. This could shed light on the motive for the homicide."

"Do you still want us working the Mercedes SUV trace?" someone asked.

"Yeah, it's business as usual," Koertig said. "We still have to prove these guys are the killers."

"We have DNA, a shell casing, and a bullet," Jude said. "If we get a match, or if the Miami PD find that Apple laptop or other property that ties the dead men to Maulle, we have our killers."

She told the team to assemble for the briefing in fifteen minutes, and drew Koertig aside. After filling him in on her conversation with Hugo Debroize, she said, "If these are our guys, this was an inside job. Probably Anton having his own troops murdered for screwing up." She gave him a beat or two to absorb the ramifications, then suggested, "Maybe take the waitress down to Miami with you and have her ID them in person."

"I'm pretty sure it's them," Koertig said. "They've got the tattoos, and the lieutenant says they're Russian and known to the Organized Crime Detail."

He sounded deflated. Jude knew the feeling. Adrenaline fueled a homicide investigation like this one, and when the primary would never get the chance to try for a confession or even interview the suspect, because he was deceased, the case suddenly became much more clinical and the drive faded away.

"If they're our guys, you've closed a major case," she reminded him. "It wasn't just good luck."

"What about everything else?"

"Maulle is dead," Jude said flatly. "If he was a pedophile, the FBI will eventually investigate him and determine whether or not to make the case public. I doubt they will. What's the advantage in humiliating his family?"

"I'm not convinced that he was," Koertig said. "I just got through the first notebook. It's not sex fantasies or anything like that. You should take a look."

"I don't need to," Jude said. "And neither do you. In another few days, this case will probably be history. Just have someone pack it all up and I'll see it gets to the right people. We can also pass on what we know about Anton Voronov to the FBI."

Koertig managed a glum nod. "I wanted the perp walk."

"You'll get to stand next to the sheriff at the press conference." Teasing him gently, Jude said, "If you're lucky he might even let you say something."

"First I have to squeeze him for the Miami trip."

Jude pointed toward Pratt's door. "Go break the good news. He'll be all over it."

❖

"Thanks for helping me with this," Pippa told the handsome deputy carrying her boxes into the log house.

Jude had said she would send someone, and Pippa was half expecting a stringy, middle-aged trooper who would spit in the shrubbery every time he came up the steps. She felt bad about checking out a hot guy in the house where her uncle was murdered not even a week ago, but it was hard not to notice six feet of gorgeous male standing right in front of her with a smile that made her heart pound in her chest.

Pippa wished she'd remembered to put on antiperspirant or bothered to wear a decent top. Instead she smelled of pizza and had a tomato stain in the center of her T-shirt where her cleavage was supposed to be. She also had greasy hair because the shampoo in her hotel room had run out and housekeeping had replaced it with conditioner by mistake.

"Where would you like this one, ma'am?" Again that old-fashioned sideways glance and shy flash of white teeth.

Pippa pointed anywhere, knowing she was blushing. She reminded herself that she was now a stupidly rich millionaire who could buy handsome men like she bought purses, and throw them away when she got bored. She wondered if her parents knew how much she was going to inherit. Was that why her mom had suddenly wanted her to come home and had even offered the conservatory for her sculpting?

She thought about Ryan and his bitch wife who always put her down. Pippa wanted to share the money with him, but not while he was married to *that*. Besides, Griffin Mahanes could say what he wanted, but she wasn't going to keep it for herself. There was so much good she could do with a fortune like that, Pippa got emotional thinking about it. She loved animals and the environment. If she was smart, she could put the money to work and help make the world a better place. In her heart she knew that was why Uncle Fabian had left his fortune to her. He knew she cared about the things that really mattered.

Pippa let herself look at the deputy again. Tulley. The name suited him. His coal black hair dropped over his forehead, tempting her to slide it back between her fingers. She wondered whether he would act differently toward her if he knew she was rich. Probably. The thought made her uncomfortable, and she was glad no one knew except her family and the attorneys. The detectives all thought she was just staying in the house temporarily. Pippa had let them make assumptions. She had the impression they thought her mother was in charge now. Naturally Delia had encouraged that idea.

Pippa decided if anyone asked, she would say what she'd said all along, that her uncle had left a lot of money to charity. It wasn't a lie. She would just leave out the other half of the story. If she was going to live here for a while, she wanted to make real friends who liked her for who she was.

"I never saw a log cabin like this one." Deputy Tulley stood in front of the windows gazing out at the splendor of the mountains.

Pippa could sense his awe. He wasn't just talking about the house but also the matchless perfection around it. She let her gaze slide over him again, taking in his long legs and slim hips. The gun rested on his right, a little lower than his waist. His torso was lean, rising to a chest and shoulders that filled out his shirt without making him look like a hulk.

If she had to find a word to describe him, it was "beautiful." He reminded her of the marble gods she'd seen in Italy one summer. She wished she could run her hands over him. Warm living flesh as smooth as cool stone. He would make the perfect model, supposing she could concentrate enough to sketch him. She caught her breath as he turned, and for an awful moment she thought her fascination must be obvious. His expression was almost skittish, his eyes screened by long black eyelashes.

"Are you going to be okay here, by yourself?" he asked.

"I'm not sure. I thought I'd just close up his rooms and try not to think about it. I guess I'll just see how it goes."

Tulley didn't look at her directly. Tucking a thumb in his belt, he said, "I was thinking, if you want I could fix you up with a dog. I'd let you borrow Smoke'm for a couple of nights, except that he's a duty animal and we have to be on call at all times."

"Don't worry." Pippa tried for a lighthearted tone. "I have Oscar, and I'm going to pick up the cats tomorrow morning, once I've finished unpacking."

She felt uneasy and a little confused for the second time that day. Earlier, when Jude had called her about moving her stuff into the house, she'd mentioned Hugo. They'd spoken and Jude said he'd offered to provide security if Pippa wished. Because they weren't face-to-face, Pippa wasn't sure if the concern in Jude's tone was just sympathy or if she was worried. Now, here was Deputy Tulley suggesting she got a dog.

"Deputy?" she asked. "Do you think I should get a security guard in case those men come back?"

Tulley rested his right hand on his holster. He seemed to be considering his next words carefully. "Talk at headquarters is that won't be a problem. There's a couple of dead bodies down in Florida that look a whole lot like those composite pictures you saw."

"Really? You caught them!" Pippa felt light-headed with relief. "Oh, my God. And they're *dead*?"

"We don't know for sure it's them, and don't tell anyone I said so. Okay?"

"That's fine. I won't say a word." Impulsively, Pippa asked, "Are you off-duty now, Deputy Tulley?"

He checked the solid stainless steel watch at his wrist. "Yes, ma'am."

"Want to have dinner with me?"

For several noisy heartbeats she thought he was going to say no, but a broad, slow smile creased the corners of his mouth. "I sure would like that, Ms. Calloway."

"That's Pippa," she said, not for the first time.

"My name's Virgil," he responded. "But I answer to Tulley…and darned near anything else a lady wants to call me."

The line would have been hokey from another guy, but from Tulley it seemed too sweet and sincere to be anything but the bald truth.

"Make yourself comfortable," Pippa said. "I'll go change and be back in a few."

As she climbed the stairs, a chill crept over her and she caught hold of the banister, suddenly overcome. Images danced before her eyes. Blood. Uncle Fabian's gray face. Her legs shook and sweat broke across her forehead. She took a step back and glanced behind her.

Before she could say a word, Tulley took the stairs two at a time. When he reached her, he said, "It's okay. Take a breath. Real easy."

He placed his arm behind her, barely brushing her waist, and walked her up the stairs like a partner in an old-fashioned dance. When they reached the top, Pippa let herself lean against him for a moment.

Tilting her head, she said, "Thank you."

Their eyes met and this time he didn't look away.

CHAPTER SEVENTEEN

"This house has an elevator," Tulley whispered in Jude's ear. They were just inside the doorway of a contemporary living room that opened onto a slate-paved terrace. People roamed the outdoor entertainment area, carrying cocktails and converging around the pool. Mercy's home on High Desert Road was what realtors would term a "luxury retreat." She and Elspeth had bought the place soon after their wedding. Jude had given the housewarming party a miss.

"That's Portia di Pazzesco." Tulley tilted his beer glass toward a conical-breasted blonde. "She's in the new Rupert Palmer-Forbes film. The one about the movie star whose girlfriends all look the same."

"In art as in life," Elspeth Harwood cooed from behind them. "Portia's real name is Mary Stubbs and she's a total slapper. Be warned."

Jude stepped sideways to avoid the kisses Elspeth was doling out to party arrivals. Tulley stayed where he was and went pink beneath his tan when Elspeth brushed her lips against each of his cheeks.

Jude had to admit Elspeth had pulled out the big guns tonight. Her incredible red hair cascaded in natural ringlets over her milk-white shoulders. The ivory dress she wore was a filmy, strappy thing that made her look naked underneath, which upon closer inspection, was possible. Her ingénue-pink lipstick probably matched her nipples. It would have been easy to find out since the front of her dress barely covered her breasts. On some women this look might have seemed slutty, but Elspeth looked like a wood nymph who'd strayed into the realm of mortals. It seemed pointless to hate her just because she was absurdly beautiful.

"What's a slapper?" Tulley asked, gazing at the actress in breathless adoration.

"That's British for a vulgar flirt who'll shag anyone if it will help her career. Or even if it won't. Which reminds me," Elspeth hooked her arm in Tulley's, "there's a favor I want from you, sweetie-darling."

Eager as a puppy, Tulley asked, "Do you want me to light the fire pit?"

"Not yet." Elspeth patted him indulgently. "See that woman, the one with the trout pout and the diamonds? She's executive producing my next movie and she wants to meet you."

"Me?" Tulley fidgeted with his belt buckle. He got anxious talking with strangers at social gatherings. That was one of the reasons he didn't have a girlfriend, at least that was a theory he'd shared with Jude. "Why?"

"She enjoys handsome young men and you're the handsomest in the room, silly boy."

"I don't want to be an actor," Tulley said.

"I know. But that won't matter to her, trust me." With a radiant smile at Jude, Elspeth said, "Do excuse us. Must go schmooze."

Jude couldn't resist watching as her deputy was fed to the she-wolf. Elspeth must have told him to say nothing and smile. He did his best but could not quite hide his alarm as the bejeweled fingers trailed down the front of his shirt. Jude ignored his "rescue me" stare. Her thought was *You wanted to come to this shindig, pal.*

She strolled to the bar and observed the activity out on the terrace while she waited her turn. This was clearly an upscale party. Instead of the usual potato salad, hot dogs, and scorched steaks off the grill, platters of sushi and froufrou finger food were being toted about by crisply dressed waiters who looked like models. Jude hadn't eaten since breakfast. She flagged down a pretty boy and scooped a handful of edibles onto a napkin. Everything tasted of spinach, a vegetable that had never inspired rapture in her.

The long-bodied brunette ahead of her in the line dropped a ten-dollar tip on the bar and sashayed away with a couple of cocktails. Jude asked the bartender if there was a decent Scotch to be had.

"Ms. Devine?" he replied.

"That's me." Jude gave him a sharp second glance, expecting to recognize a local parolee trying to make a go of it on the outside.

The man produced several of her favorite single malts. "Dr. Westmoreland got these in for you."

Instantly flustered, Jude picked up a bottle of twenty-four-year-old Caol Ila. Mercy had really gone the extra mile tracking down this rare dram. Jude enjoyed the delicacy of the younger Caol Ila bottlings when she could find one. They were almost like Lowland malts, except for the peat and brine character that was so distinctly Islay. She'd never expected to sample a twenty-four-year-old.

"Good choice," the bartender said. "Water?"

"Just a dash."

"If I'm not here when you want a refill, tell the other guy it's in the cabinet with your name on it."

Jude thanked him and carried her drink to a spot near the tiled main entrance. She wished Debbie had been able to make it. No doubt she thought it wouldn't be diplomatic to come now that she and Sandy were rediscovering their passion and were leaving shortly for Utah. Jude wasn't really expecting Aidan Hill to show, but she thought she'd wait where she could be seen, just in case.

"You came." A hand slipped into hers. An unmistakable perfume taunted her senses. L'Heure Bleue, Mercy's choice the last few times they made love.

In a bid to expel the scent, Jude exhaled sharply. It didn't help. Mercy's presence washed over her like acid rain. "Nice place," Jude said.

"Would you like the tour?"

"Maybe later. I don't want my date walking into a room full of strangers and wondering if she's crashed the wrong party."

Mercy's registered this information with a flicker of tension that made it as far as her eyes and froze in a slow blink. "I didn't realize you were planning to bring someone."

"The invitation was for two."

Mercy sipped her cocktail and cast gracious smiles around her guests. "Who is she?"

"No one you know. And she might not make it anyway. She's working a case."

"She's a cop?"

"An FBI agent."

"Are you sleeping with her?"

"What do you think?"

Mercy swept Jude with a faux-disinterested gaze. Jude returned the favor. Mercy wore a silky midnight blue shirt tucked into a black pencil skirt. Her waist looked smaller and her exquisite facial bones a little more pronounced than last time Jude saw her up close. She'd lost weight. Had she been pining, or was her hairdo to blame? Sculpted blond waves framed her face, but beyond the illusion of glamour, they lent an air of vulnerability that surprised Jude. She looked a little harder, and for a fleeting moment she thought Mercy was going to cry.

"You're full of shit," Mercy said. "You're not getting any. Or if you are, it's second rate."

"Well, you'd know, or have your lovely bride's bedroom skills improved?"

"Keep your voice down."

"Not denying it, I notice."

"Love is not just about sex," Mercy hissed.

Jude sipped her Scotch. "We've had this conversation."

Mercy's gaze darted toward Elspeth. "So change the subject. You're good at that."

"Jesus, what's your problem?" Jude was genuinely puzzled. "Look around. Don't you have *everything*? The big house. The hip crowd. The famous *wife*. Isn't this everything you wanted?"

Mercy was silent. Her plush lips moved a tight response to the greetings of guests who brushed by. Her chest rose and fell too quickly. She lowered her eyes to her empty glass.

Jude pried it from her fingers. "What are you drinking?"

Mercy's hand strayed to the front of Jude's shirt. "Jude, please. I can't bear that we're so—"

"There you are." SAC Aidan Hill squeezed Jude's shoulder like they were tough-girl sorority sisters. "You didn't tell me I needed night goggles to find this place."

Jude squeezed out the smile that was called for. "Aidan Hill, meet Mercy Westmoreland, one of our hosts and a forensic pathologist from the ME's office in Grand Junction."

They shook hands. Mercy's expression never shifted from socially appropriate, but Jude sensed something dark beneath the serenity. Hill's pupils dilated just a fraction. She'd picked up on it, too.

She looked good, Jude thought, still uptight, but she'd done something to her medium brown hair that made hints of copper shine through. Her khaki knit top flattered a body well worth a second glance, and her dark green pants hugged her nicely. She probably felt naked without her shoulder holster, although she was carrying all the same. Jude could relate. She never set foot out of the house without a collection of weaponry concealed on her person. She got distracted for a moment thinking about the two of them stripping down, dropping their guns, knives, wrist restraints, Tasers. She'd seen something like that in a movie, when two assassins were trying to get naked and have sex.

Did she want to have sex with Aidan Hill? As she asked herself that question, her eyes locked with Mercy's and after several long, hot seconds she knew the dismaying answer.

Hill said, "You have a beautiful home, Mercy."

As they exchanged a few meaningless comments, Jude pretended to be caught up watching sparks fly from the fire pit. She forced her jaw and eye muscles to relax, wiping her face clean of pining and frustration.

"Oh, look at the time," Mercy said. "We have a video hookup to Lars von Trier starting any minute. Excuse me."

"Who's Lars von Trier?" Hill asked as they watched Mercy cut a path toward her seminaked wife.

"He directs animal movies." Jude tried to remember the film Tulley and Agatha had talked about. "*Dogville?*"

Hill grimaced. "I can't stand when cartoon animals talk like they're just as moronic as people." She pointed to a reddish blond head bobbing between designer styles like an old tennis ball in a barrel of well-polished apples. "Is that Philip Seymour Hoffman?"

"I don't know. Is he related to Dustin Hoffman?"

Hill wasn't sure about that. "Let's get some food and sit outside. I want to talk about tomorrow."

"What about tomorrow?" Again Jude noticed that the SAC was attractive. Not stunning. Not beautiful. Just a good body and plenty of confidence. Nothing wrong with that. She didn't seem straight, but Jude had been wrong before. Lately she was wrong about women most of the time. She made eye contact. Hill dropped her gaze.

"Cocktail sauce," she said and wiped something from Jude's lapel.

Awareness stirred between them, proving Jude could lust after Mercy relentlessly but still sustain nipple tension for another woman. Surely that was a good sign.

Watching Elspeth sashay in front of a large video screen, she nudged Hill and said, "Let's get out of here."

Agatha scurried past them, making a determined bid to nail one of the remaining chairs. Tulley hurried after her carrying a crocheted shawl decorated with red satin roses.

"Isn't that your deputy?" Hill asked.

"Yes, Virgil Tulley. He's also a K-9 handler."

"He's cute."

"And single," Jude felt obliged to report, just in case Hill was straight and shopping for a boytoy. According to Bobby Lee, Tulley would benefit from a few uncomplicated romantic encounters with experienced women other than those married to deputies. He would also save the money he planned to spend on a prostitute in Denver.

"I'll keep his availability in mind," Hill said blandly.

Jude wasn't sure if she was kidding. She found a couple of plates and loaded them up with more tiny food. "We could grab a burger somewhere after this," she said once they'd found a place to sit.

"Now you're talking," Hill said.

"Is there anyone here you need to speak with?" Jude asked. "About Telluride?"

"No, we've got it covered. The organizers are on board. Actually, that's an understatement. They're our slaves, mostly thanks to your deputy."

Pratt must be eating it up. In his fantasies, he probably imagined overpaid celebrities clinging to one another in a panic when they smelled chemical during the screening of a movie about Romanian goatherds. Reality was another matter. Everyone wanted a happy ending. The Four Corners needed Telluride.

Trying not to be obvious about cruising Hill as she slid snack food into her mouth, Jude tuned in to a conversation a few feet from their picnic table.

"An ACME pass?" the woman said. "No way. You'll be stuck at the Chuck Jones theater all weekend. Get an upgrade." When her companion grumbled about the cost, she said, "Obviously we have different priorities. I want to experience everything, everywhere. You want to wear a neon sign announcing that you're cheap."

"I'm broke," the guy protested.

The woman picked up her purse. "I'm *so* not seeing that line in the script of my life."

Hill choked on an oyster. Jude reached over and thumped her gently between the shoulders. They both burst out laughing.

"Are you single?" Hill asked.

"Everyone has a talent," Jude replied like a flirtation pro. "Mine is for avoiding domestic bliss."

This disclosure was met with a discreet smile that made Aidan Hill seem much more human. "Want to buy me a drink?"

"Sure." If this was a proposition, Jude wished she could feel excited.

Hill must have read something into her hesitance. "You're right. It's improper and professionally reprehensible for us to have a one-night stand. Interested?"

Jude prevented her gaze from wandering into the next room. Injecting some enthusiasm into her tone, she answered, "Yes."

The drought had to break some time. She wondered what had warmed Hill to her. Perhaps the prospect of that burger.

"That drink you're going to buy me," Hill prompted, "piña colada."

Jude thought, *I'm going to sleep with a fed who drinks fluffy cocktails*. Waiting in vain for her heart to beat faster, she retreated to the bar.

While she killed time in the short line, she let herself watch Mercy chatting and laughing with plastic ease. Finally, taking in the phony scene in front of her, she understood something she'd refused to see all along. Mercy hadn't chosen Elspeth because she loved her more. Or felt closer to her than to Jude. She'd simply married the lover who could offer her a different world.

❖

Hill rested her chin on Jude's stomach. "Is there something else you want?"

Jude thought her fake orgasm was right up there with one you'd see on television, but apparently Hill knew an unresponsive clitoris when she sucked on it. Jude had let the stimulation go on far too long and now she was numb. She scrambled around, trying to think of something hot that would get her interested in trying again. A quick flash of Sandy Lane caught her off guard. Dismayed that she couldn't stop thinking about work, she reached down for Hill and drew her alongside.

"You don't have to explain," Hill said. "It's just one of those nights. I have them, too."

"I guess I'm more distracted than I thought, working this homicide as well as being on the task force." Very plausible.

"How long were you with Mercy Westmoreland?"

"Jesus, is it that obvious?"

"I recognize the symptoms. I was in love with another agent for three years. Unrequited."

"That's serious self-torture."

Hill rolled onto her back and fell against the pillows with a small defeated huff. "I was an idiot."

"What happened?" Jude tugged the sheets up and covered them both.

"It's strange." Hill sounded sad and disillusioned. "For a while I thought she felt the same way I did. We kept dancing around each other, getting close, then pulling away. In the end nothing happened. We both let go and the connection died."

"Do you still work with her?" That would have to be awkward.

"No. She switched to another division."

"I didn't know if you were gay or straight," Jude confessed.

"That's good. I knew you were queer the minute I saw you."

"Also good. Why did you decide to sleep with me?" Jude asked.

"You're hot."

"Albeit a disappointment."

"It's okay." Hill laughed. "I know you can do better."

"Yep." Jude stared at the ceiling. An uneasy certainty gripped her. "Did you fake it, too?"

"Uh-huh."

"Shit." Jude propped herself on one elbow and traced a hand over Hill's pleasantly full breasts. "It may not seem that way, but I'm technically proficient. Tell me what gets you off, and this time you won't have to pretend."

"Tempting offer, but I'm not wet thinking about it."

"We're talking too much," Jude said. "Getting into our heads."

"Maybe that's it," Hill conceded.

Jude glanced around. The lighting wasn't right. She should have burned candles instead of leaving the night-light on. And the room was chilly. Then there was Yiska. It was hard not to be aware of a cat sitting on the ottoman a few feet away, eyes glazed with disgust.

"I have a lot on my mind." Jude almost talked herself into self-pity. But what was she thinking? Finally she had a woman in her bed and they were navel-gazing.

"The Maulle homicide?"

Jude nodded. "We're waiting on DNA results, but it looks like our killers could be in the morgue in Miami. Meantime the case has split wide open. Arms dealing. Child pornography. The Russian mafia."

"You've got the guys who killed him. Your job's done. Hand the loose ends on to the Bureau."

"Good advice." Jude refrained from mentioning that she'd already come to the same conclusion. "There's something I need to run by you, another reason I've underperformed."

"Wow, you're really on a roll."

"Harrison Hawke has a meeting planned with the ASS."

"Really?" Hill put a little more space between them, her stare intent. "When were you going to tell me about this?"

"I wasn't."

"So Hawke's involved?"

"No, not in the plot."

"And you know this how?'

"We're acquainted." Jude played the local law enforcement card. "He holds these so-called Aryan Defense Days at his compound and I got stuck with the liaison job, dealing with him and the protesters. For some reason that convinced him I'm a secret sympathizer."

"Are you?"

"Jesus, was my oral sex technique *that* bad?"

"I'm not crazy about racists. Blame it on my African American grandma." Hill narrowed her eyes. "Are you saying Hawke told you about the meeting?"

"No," Jude lied earnestly. "I was at his compound discussing his request for increased protection for an event in a few months' time. I overheard him talking to one of his men."

"What's the deal? Is he trying to muscle in on the attack for kudos?"

"No, he's trying to stop them from going ahead with it. He thinks it'll set the white power movement back fifty years."

"Like they're not living in 1950." Hill was silent for a few seconds, her fingers drumming an impatient beat against the bedcover. "When is this happening?"

"Tomorrow," Jude said. Arbiter wanted last minute. It didn't get any better than this.

Hill bolted out of bed. "Jesus, why didn't you tell me?"

"We were otherwise engaged."

"Sex? That's your reason?" Hill started getting dressed.

"What are you doing?" Jude asked.

"My job," Hill replied scornfully. "You were right about Moon, by the way. I think one of his people has ties with the ASS. It seems possible that they're behind this plot."

"You're kidding me?"

"You should have more confidence in your analysis." Hill combed her hair. "You could kick ass in counterintelligence."

Jude spluttered a laugh that made Hill look at her twice.

As the unsatisfied agent left the bedroom, she called over her shoulder, "If this operation goes well, I'll be sure to mention your contribution."

"Thanks," Jude replied. "You could leave out the flunk grade for the orgasm detail."

She heard Hill laugh. Seconds later the front door slammed shut.

CHAPTER EIGHTEEN

The bed dipped with the weight of another person. Lured from her snug morning doze, Debbie drifted toward full awakening as Lone's hard body moved against hers. A husky murmur warmed her ear. "I have a surprise for you."

Debbie rolled over and opened her eyes.

"I'm not sure if I can handle too many more of those."

"Sore?" Lone chuckled.

"I'm fine so long as I'm not walking or sitting down."

"That doesn't leave many options. Are you saying you'll have to spend the next two days laying flat on your back?"

Debbie gazed into Lone's remarkable blue eyes. Running a finger over her no-nonsense mouth, she said, "Gee, now that you mention it, isn't that how I got into this state? Not that I'm complaining."

Far from it. In fact, Debbie couldn't believe how wonderful this week had been. From the moment she'd set foot in Lone's cabin on Monday, she'd gotten to know her lover on a whole new level. The discoveries were amazing. Lone had talked about her childhood and shown Debbie photographs of her family and her comrades in the 82nd Airborne. She'd answered questions and listened to Debbie's opinions. They'd discussed the future, even the possibility of having a baby one day.

Debbie had always seen the tender side of Lone, but she'd also been aware of a constant tension in her. She understood that Lone's moodiness probably came from stress and anxiety related to her experiences in combat. She'd grown so accustomed to the way things were, she didn't realize how many allowances and compromises she made, and how often she felt hurt and excluded. Until now.

Like magic, something had lifted the weight of the past from Lone. The hair-trigger anger had gone and she was calm and happy. Debbie had to believe the change in their relationship was the key factor in this transformation. Lone had finally let her in, and now that she didn't keep so much hidden the strain between them had disappeared. They were connected as never before.

Planting a contented kiss on Lone's lips, Debbie said, "I love you."

"I love you, too, Debbie doll. Very much. Do you believe me?"

"With all my heart."

Lone kissed her deeply. "There's something I want to share with you."

"You can tell me anything."

"I know." Lone's expression was full of trust and devotion. "You have no idea what it means to hear you say that."

Debbie melted. "Is this the surprise? That you really love me?"

"No, there's a little more to it than that." Lone held a photograph in front of her. She ran her fingers in a loop across the image. "All this land is ours. I've put your name on the title."

Debbie gasped. "You didn't need to do that."

"You're my partner. Everything I have is yours."

The place was beautiful. A partially built cabin stood on a rise overlooking a sapphire blue lake. There was also a luxury trailer home parked nearby.

"It's amazing," Debbie said. She wondered if there was a supermarket nearby. The property looked to be in the middle of nowhere, with no other houses in sight.

Lone stroked her hair and kissed her softly on the forehead. "I know you're worried about moving, so I have a plan." She unfolded a sheet of paper, a printed-out e-ticket. "We're flying up there today."

"But we just drove here."

"Baby, this is the house I lived in with Madeline. I want to take you to a place that's only ours, yours and mine. I promise you, if you don't like it up there, that's fine. We'll stay in Colorado."

"Really? You really mean that?"

Debbie was assailed with guilt. She knew Lone wanted to move permanently, and having seen the glorified shack in Pariah, she wasn't surprised. The fabulous setup in Canada was infinitely more appealing. Debbie studied the picture again. The least she could do was make the trip up there and keep an open mind. Even if they didn't move there, it would probably be a lovely place to take a vacation.

"I should have packed warmer clothes," she said. "If I'd known—"

Lone looked embarrassed. "I'm sorry. I just decided on the spur of the moment."

"Whoa. You made a spur-of-the-moment decision?" Debbie giggled.

"I know." Lone laughed with her. "I guess we better get used to it. With everything so…different between us now, I kind of lost my mind. I'm sorry."

"You have nothing to be sorry for."

Debbie felt close to tears. She'd been so afraid everything would slip away that she'd behaved like a coward in their relationship. Her fear of being alone in the world had almost created the very reality she dreaded. She was so clingy Lone had to find space and had excluded her. Now that she was acting like a real partner, things had changed. Debbie promised herself she wasn't going to let baggage from the past rule her again.

"So, what do you think?" There was a hint of nervousness in Lone's voice, proof that she wasn't taking Debbie's agreement for granted.

"I'd love to go," Debbie said wholeheartedly. "Thank you for inviting me."

❖

Harrison Hawke deactivated his elaborate alarm system and led Jude into a secure room at the back of the house. The space had been expanded recently and was fitted out as a weapons room.

Jude scanned the shelves and storage racks, amazed by the huge cache of special forces weaponry. An array of MP5 submachine guns occupied a lockable cabinet. Numerous M4 carbines were ranked along one wall, with various optics and accessories like M203 grenade launchers. Arranged next to these were Heckler & Koch G3s, AK-47s, and a sniper rifle collection that included a heavy-duty Barrett M107 .50-caliber, several SR25s, and a short-range G3 SG1. Jude noticed specialized tear-gas rounds next to a bunch of Remington 870 pump-action shotguns.

"Wow, I've never seen one of these." She picked up an XM8 assault rifle, a lightweight modular weapon barely out of the experimental phase.

"It was a gift from my friends in Buenos Ares," Hawke said. "Don't be deceived because it looks like a toy."

Jude picked up a handgun. Beretta M9s were standard issue for Hawke's men, and in addition to these, he kept a range of other sidearms including the SIG Sauer P226 and the Kimber Custom. Magazines and boxes of ammunition were stored along the top shelves above various mortars, fuses, primers, detonator cords, standard and flash-bang grenades. She assumed Hawke stored his explosive compounds somewhere other then the house he slept in.

"How many men do you have here?" she asked.

"Twenty present today."

"And the ASS?"

"No more than six." Hawke opened a security door that led to a concrete entry hall. Beyond this lay an armored exterior exit. He opened this, inviting, "*Fräulein*."

A Hakenkreuz Commando unit stood to stiff attention in the dusty yard. One of them saluted and snapped forward. Jude could feel the sneaky appraisal from the ranks but sensed a more respectful reception than usual, perhaps in response to her attire. In deference to Hawke, she'd chosen black pants and top and a black ballcap, and she wasn't carrying her usual Glock. Instead she wore her favorite six-gun on a low-slung belt, a neat line of .38 ammo gleaming from the cartridge loops.

The Model 19 was a gleaming nickel-plated tribute to days gone by. It had been her father's revolver, passed to her when she graduated from the FBI Academy. Jude loved its the elegant lines and custom wood grips. The Smith & Wesson also had wonderful balance and a smooth, classic action. Shooting from the hip wasn't exactly a guarantee of accuracy, but she could blow a few tin cans off a fence, playing gunfighter. This being the twenty-first century, her shootout chic was spoiled by sunglasses, hiking boots, and a cell phone, but Jude could still daydream.

"We'll need a reconnaissance team and a tactical assault group," Hawke commanded the troops, rudely interrupting her nostalgic contemplation of Old West traditions.

While the neo-Nazis busied themselves preparing for their version of a showdown, Jude strolled around the compound perimeter, stopping occasionally to practice her draw. She would be glad when today's unfolding drama was over and she could clear another objective from the clutter of her mind. Returning the 19 to its holster, she glanced back at Hawke, who was demonstrating the MP5.

Whatever happened at Lone Burro, Jude hoped she would be firmly cemented in Hawke's trust and affection and could extract the information her masters sought. They would want her to keep stringing him along, but the day was approaching when he would expect bedroom perks. Jude was only willing to take the "personal sacrifice" ethos so far. If making a graceful exit meant leaving the Bureau, she would.

Sheriff Pratt would offer her a real job if she asked, and life would be a lot less complicated. She could buy herself a little house on a few acres, get a horse, adopt one of the shelter mutts Bobby Lee's mom was always hinting about, and find a real girlfriend. She wasn't getting any younger. It was time to stop obsessing over Mercy and accept that some things weren't meant to be.

Jude blinked as a needle of intense light pierced her peripheral vision. In the same split second a sharp, distinctive whiz carved the air a few feet ahead of her and a bullet careened into the yellow earth.

She hit the deck, yelling, "Get down!"

A couple more shots ricocheted off a storage shed about twenty feet away. Jesus. Had Aidan Hill summoned the big boys to take Hawke out so no one could stand in the way of the ASS attack? If so, she was taking career advancement way too seriously.

Jude stared around. She was hopelessly exposed on flat terrain with no place to duck for cover. The men at the rear of the compound were taking positions. Most had stampeded into the house. There was no sign of Hawke. So much for gallantry.

Cursing beneath her breath, she belly-crawled toward the shed. The way things were going, it was probably the explosives repository.

Several more bullets skittered around her. Jude spotted one of them and scraped it into her hand. It was a .243. FBI snipers typically fired .308 Winchester rounds.

She made it behind the shed and hunkered there, trying to get a sense of the situation. The shots only seemed to be coming from one area. Jude got to her feet and brushed herself off. She drew her pistol, although there didn't seem to be much point. She couldn't see who was shooting at her. Wiping dust off the barrel, she thought about calling the sheriff for assistance, but her presence on the compound would take some explaining.

She peered around the corner of the shed. At that moment, she heard someone running and Hawke fell in next to her carrying a Kevlar vest.

"Thank God you're alright." He was pale. "Here, put this on, *Fräulein*."

"Do you have some binoculars?" she asked.

"Inside the house. We can't stay here. This shed has a gasoline storage tank in it."

"Wonderful."

"My men are ready to cover us."

He flicked a hand around and Jude realized he knew how to defend his compound. Shooters were in position in most of the rooms inside the house. None made easy targets.

"You first," he said. "I'll cover you from behind."

Jude nodded. "Ready when you are."

Seconds later she was running toward the front of the house in a deafening storm of gunfire. It occurred to her that if Hawke wanted to take her out, this was his opportunity. The fact that she made it in the door alive spoke highly of her undercover skills. Evidently he trusted her.

Catching her breath, she holstered the 19 and said, "Who in hell is attacking us?"

One of the men checking assembling weapons and ammunition in Hawke's living room answered, "The ASS, *Fräulein*."

Hawke waved his cell phone. "Another text message from those traitors. They're demanding we submit to their leadership."

"Or they're going to shoot everyone?" Jude was incredulous.

"They want this compound," Hawke said. "Preemptive strike"

A young Hakenkreuzer scurried in. "There's a Hummer approaching, *Herr Oberst.*"

Hawke continued to study his phone. "They want a meeting."

"And the negotiations begin with gunfire?"

Hawke paused to gaze up at the Führer portrait, probably wondering, *What would Hitler do?* He made his decision and announced, "I'll speak to them, but a leader doesn't allow compromises that harm the movement."

He sent a text message, summoned a handful of men, and moved to the door. To Jude, he said, "Stay in the house, *Fräulein.*"

With that he stepped outside and a couple of the men opened the gates. A Hummer swept into the compound and disgorged the ASS leadership. Jude felt deeply uneasy as she watched the discussion from a viewing shaft in the front windows. The Hakenkreuzer standing next to her had his M4 trained on the men.

"We're meant to be fighting for the same thing," he said grimly. "But these chickenshits don't know the meaning of loyalty."

Their voices were raised and every man had his hands on his sidearm. Jude checked her watch. By now Hill was probably staking out Lone Burro. It was time to let her know that the situation was fluid.

No sooner had the thought crossed her mind when a shot rang out and the scene in front of her devolved into chaos. Hawke was down. Men ran in all directions, trading gunfire. The Hakenkreuzers in the house started yelling and shooting. A man tried to drag Hawke to cover, but he was hit.

Jude thought, *Christ, Arbiter's going to fucking kill me.*

Resigned to the inevitable, she grabbed an MP5 submachine gun, shouldered it, and charged out the front door. Firing continuously, she ran to Hawke, hooked her free hand in the shoulder of his vest, and dragged him back toward the house. The distinctive thwack-thwack-thwack of the MP5 resounded in her ears along with volleys from Hawke's men. A couple of Hakenkreuzers emerged from the doorway and hauled their leader the final few feet inside. She backed up after them, spraying the Hummer with fire.

As the front door slammed closed, she dropped to her knees next to Hawke, took his pulse, and ripped away his vest.

"We're calling 911," she said to gasps of consternation. "Second thought, the ambulance won't find this place."

Hawke said weakly, "You have my absolute devotion and—"

"Not now, Harrison," she interrupted, throwing her car keys to one of the faithful. "Bring my Dakota around to the back door. The rest of you, provide cover until I get Mr. Hawke out of here. Then it's time for all of you to vanish. I'm calling the feds."

❖

"Well, this is just lovely." Aidan Hill marched back and forth in the hospital waiting area. "I have four bodies. No ricin. And the Telluride Film Festival will probably sue us."

"On the bright side, you look really hot in your SWAT gear," Jude said.

"What were you doing out there?" Hill regarded her with narrow-eyed suspicion.

"I told you. MCSO liaison."

"Dressed for the gunfight at the OK Corral?" Hill threw up her hands. "Please. Don't insult my intelligence."

"You'll find the ricin," Jude said wearily. "I think it's in a storage pod at one of their houses."

"Something else you overheard?"

"Yes."

Hill dragged her hand dramatically through her hair. "Something smells bad."

"What's the problem?" Jude asked. "You've arrested all the ASS who weren't dead. The Bureau didn't kill anyone. The film festival is safe from terror. You can go public with an announcement about foiling the plot. Everyone gets what they want."

"This situation went completely out of control," Hill said.

"The glass half empty," Jude mumbled.

"I expected more of you."

"Well, we both know what a disappointment that can be," Jude said.

Hill stomped around some more, and Jude considered the idea of sleeping with her again. Maybe there was enough anger to make for passion.

"Don't even think about it." Hill glowered at her.

"I can't help myself. You have a very attractive ass."

"God, I wish I could arrest you."

Jude turned on the charm. "That might be fun."

"Do you think this is some kind of joke?"

"If you must know—"

"Don't try me. I'm not a patient woman." Hill fell silent as a doctor approached.

He said, "I'm Dr. Samuel Bettelheim."

A coughing fit overcame Hill. Bright red, she apologized.

Jude managed an expression of polite interest. She did not ask *So, how's your neo-Nazi patient doing?*

"Mr. Hawke is in stable condition," the doctor informed them. "He's asking for Ms. Devine."

"Thanks, Doctor. I'll ask one of the nurses to show me in." With a sweet smile at Hill, Jude said, "I guess you'll be packing up and heading home soon."

Still brooding, Hill promised, "This is not over. I'm looking into your story, Devine."

"Whatever. I have to go now." Jude took the agent by both hands, jerked her forward, and kissed her on the mouth. "Take care of yourself."

As she walked away, Hill came after her.

"Jude?" She hesitated. "Whatever you're doing out here, be careful."

CHAPTER NINETEEN

Jude forced open her eyes. At first nothing came into focus. Her disorganized senses relayed pain. A pounding, leaden headache, sharp bolts of agony when her neck moved an inch. Plastic restraints bit into her wrists. As she tried to elbow herself into a sitting position, a hand was planted solidly on her chest.

"Not so fast."

Jude groaned as her head reconnected with the floor. She stared up at Sandy Lane's face. Her mouth hurt when she spoke. "I thought you were in Utah."

"We were until I checked Debbie's cell phone. Text messages, for God's sake."

Jude watched her load a hypodermic. "Sandy, we need to talk."

"We will, once I shoot you full of babble juice."

"You don't need that shit," Jude said. "I'll tell you what you want to know."

Sandy laughed. "Okay, surprise me."

"I'm FBI undercover."

"I said surprise me. I made you the first time we met." She set the syringe aside and sat down in the sole armchair in her one-room cabin. Her brilliant blue eyes bored into Jude. "What's your assignment?"

"White supremacists and other domestic terror cells." Jude shuffled around until she reached the table. Using the leg for support, she pulled herself upright. Everything ached. Her jaw. Her shoulders. Her gut.

Sandy had been waiting for her. They'd fought hand to hand for a half hour or more before she was knocked out. Jude still had no idea how that had happened. She'd arrived late in Rico, held up by the aftermath of yesterday's incident. The Montrose sheriff wanted a meeting since Hawke's compound was in his jurisdiction. True to her word, Hill had made Jude a special focus. She would be answering stupid questions from paper pushers for the next six months. Arbiter had told her to sit tight and wait for the heat to die down.

It was dusk when she reached Pariah, negotiating her way between booby traps and dead-end hiking trails. She'd gained access to the house without too much difficulty. The reason was obvious as soon as she dropped down from the window.

"Your turn," Jude ventured. "Are you CIA?"

Sandy give her an odd look. "Why would you ask that?"

"You don't exactly blend in."

"I'm not CIA and you've entered my home illegally," Sandy said. "Why?"

"Because you purchased a few hundred pounds of plastic explosive in Debbie's name."

"That was a mistake," Sandy acknowledged.

"Where's Debbie now?" Jude asked.

"In Canada." Reading something into Jude's reaction, she seemed to take offense. "Do you really believe I would hurt her?"

"You already have. She has no idea who you are."

Sandy lit a cigar. Contemplating the glowing tip, she said, "She knows all that's worth knowing."

"Do you love her?"

"Yes." Her face softened. Something philosophical and sad entered her tone. "Whatever you think, don't ever doubt that. Or let her doubt it."

"Be there for her." Jude worked at the plastic around her wrists. "Then she won't have a reason to doubt."

"If I can, I will." Sandy puffed on the cigar. "You looked in my personal files on Debbie's computer, didn't you?"

"Yeah, riveting stuff," Jude said dryly. "My favorite was your galley of mullet hairdos."

Sandy offered a cynical bow. "Did you enjoy aphid control or the stuff about the best boy bands?"

"Come on, Sandy." Jude wasn't getting anywhere with the restraints, which was the general idea. "I don't care who you work for. Just give me a name so my boss can verify your status, and we're done."

"I can't do that."

"What's the explosive for?"

"If I told you, I'd have to kill you," Sandy said pleasantly.

"You're right. That's a deal breaker."

Sandy lapsed into silence for a few minutes. With a note of regret, she said, "It's a problem that you're here."

"I'd be happy to leave. All I need is a couple of answers and we're good."

"It's not that simple."

"Let's make it that simple," Jude wished she could stop the deafening pounding of her heart in her ears. It was making her headache even worse. "We're two adults. We work for the same government."

Sandy puffed slowly on her cigar. Seemingly to herself, she quoted, "*Quis custodiet ipsos custodies?*"

Jude translated, "Who guards the guards?"

With a tight smile, Sandy stood. "I have stuff to do before I leave. Who else knows you're here?"

"Just my handler."

"Get up." She reached down and hitched Jude by one elbow.

"You could cut me loose."

"Not a bondage fan?" Sandy jerked her toward the bed.

Jude didn't resist this curious turn of events. She felt groggy and nauseous. Sandy arranged her so that she was as comfortable as possible with her arms secured behind her.

"What do you know about my mission?" she asked.

"Nothing."

Sandy slid her fingers into Jude's hair and angled her aching head so she could look into her eyes. "Sodium Pentothal?"

"I'm telling you the truth."

"What does the Bureau think I'm involved in?"

"NORTHCOM," Jude said.

Sandy's face showed no emotion. "Which project?"

"We're not sure. All we've heard is rumor about a special op on U.S. soil."

"Could have seen that coming," Sandy said.

She released Jude's head, then padded around the room, stuffing items into a duffel bag. For a while, she was out of sight, and Jude heard soft noises. When she approached the bed again, she had a needle.

"Don't fight me," she said. "If I wanted to kill you, you'd already be dead."

"What are you giving me?"

"A sedative. You'll wake up fresh as a daisy."

"Sandy," Jude pleaded, "don't do this. There's no need."

She watched the plunger move down the glass tube. Her mind began to fog almost immediately and her limbs flopped. Sandy cut the restraints from her wrists and rubbed her flesh to get the circulation going.

Jude wanted to speak but her voice drifted away from her. The last thing she remembered was Sandy bending over her, kissing her on the lips and saying good-bye.

❖

Lone had parked her white Ford E150 van into the rear section of the parking lot nearest the Qwest Building in downtown Denver. It joined several others, all with the same cleaning company logo on the sides. Hers had a different logo, but on her trial run the only people who noticed that fact were employees of the cleaning company who almost mistook the van for one of their own. They knew better now.

From the top of the Qwest Building, the view along Stout Street and Eighteenth was sweeping, so the Secret Service had the building staked out well ahead of time. The MCI Building and the Marriott, where Cheney would be pressing the flesh for money, also offered desirable rooftops. These formed part of the Vice Presidential Security Zone, real estate occupied by sharpshooters who would report in to their command center constantly.

Various rooms in the surrounding buildings also formed part of the protective web. In one of these, in the former office of a recently bankrupted corporation, Lone had hidden the equipment she would need. Her MK-153 SMAW rocket launcher and Confined Space rockets, and her submachine gun. The leasing agent had been very helpful, mentioning that she could probably take her time making a decision since there was plenty of space available downtown and the owners were asking more than the market would bear.

Lone was pleased that she wasn't going to be hiding in plain sight on a rooftop. She'd planned for either contingency, but this office suite only freed up two weeks ago, a long while after her first advance assessment. She'd expected a Denver fund-raiser sometime soon. Marilyn Musgrave's shameful record had made her a shaky candidate for reelection, and she was an eager recipient of GOP largesse. She was also proud to be seen with the president and with Cheney, unlike most candidates worried for their political survival.

She entered the offices of the defunct Verminax Corporation the easy way, by sliding a credit card in the door. From the window she watched police and Secret Service coming and going as they planned for tomorrow. First thing in the morning, buildings would be cleared and roads blocked off. Her space had already been cleared, but they would send someone back, just in case.

The protestors would assemble on the corner of Welton Street and Eighteenth at 10:00 a.m.. Lone had been interested to hear that a Disabled Persons organization intended to participate. Sidewalks jammed with wheelchairs would add something to the flavor of the chaos.

She rolled out her sleeping bag and removed a layer of clothing. She had eighteen hours to kill. Hopefully she would sleep through the night. She called Debbie and told her she loved her and that everything was under control. Then she thought about Jude Devine, drugged into inertia on her bed in Pariah. The detective-*cum*-FBI agent was probably awake by now. She have no idea what was going on. Lone hadn't left a paper trail.

Lone chuckled to think that she'd probably been given a pass for a long time because they mistook her for a friendly. That was the great thing about Homeland Security. The left hand didn't know what the right hand was doing.

❖

"Where the hell have you been?" Arbiter demanded. "Jesus, I thought you were burned."

"She's in the wind," Jude said. "And she's not a friendly. I need that team in here ASAP."

"You're rock solid on her status."

"She left me a note. But if someone in the alphabet soup thinks an assassination would be the perfect fake flag operation, she could be their shooter. Who the hell knows?"

"Okay, who's her target?"

"That's why I need the team," Jude said. "It'll take me days to make a thorough search here."

"Where is she?"

"I called her girlfriend. She hasn't seen her since first thing Monday morning. I was attacked Monday night."

"Any injuries?"

"Nothing I want to discuss." She'd found some Motrin in a first aid kit and her headache had abated a little.

"Nice work in the Hawke business, by the way."

"Thanks." Jude wasn't going to run with the ball. "Call me when the team's due."

She climbed back down into Sandy's bunker. In front of her, taunting her from the message board above the worktable, was the note Sandy had left for her.

Jude,

I don't work for NORTHCOM. You'll hear about my mission in a couple of days. Thanks for being a friend.

Lonewolf

❖

When the van exploded, there was panic on the streets below. The protestors rushed the police lines, tearing through the yellow tape. Cops fired warning shots and tried to keep the crowd back from the Marriott. Lone could picture the scene inside the banquet room, Cheney in the middle of another salute to the heroes in uniform, hustled out and raced down the stairs to await his car. A quick escape from a side exit.

Lone removed the glass she'd cut, rested the rocket launcher on the window sill, and waited for the motorcade. She didn't care which car she hit. If she got lucky, it would be his. If not, there was still enough time to get down onto the street. In her uniform, carrying a gun and looking like she was in an official capacity, who would stop her?

Like long black bullets, the armored limos glided along the artery below. They halted to a crawl as protestors poured into the security zone. City, county, and state police pounded down the streets, trying to drag people out of the melee. But they were far outnumbered and the situation went crazily out of control.

Lone checked her earplugs and took aim. She heard the whoosh and thunder as she fired. She scored a direct hit. Not waiting around to watch, she crammed her gear in a trash bag and headed for the fire exit. She took the stairs at a fierce run, making it out onto the street in less than ninety seconds. She dropped the trash bag and joined everyone else rushing toward the cars.

Members of the security detail had converged on one limo alone, their brief to guard the man inside. Lone lifted her MP5, but people scrambled in front of her, pounding the windows and yelling abuse. She ran to the front of the car and lifted the submachine gun again. But her arms were jolted and her aim went wild. Bullets sprayed. People shrieked.

Something hit her with tremendous force and she was down. Blood fountained from her neck. She felt no pain. She heard sirens. She tried to move but couldn't. Debbie's face passed across her mind, then everything collapsed into a dark spiraling abyss. She felt a hand stroke her cheek like a farewell caress. She sensed Madeline and Brandon close to her, talking to her. The noise and smells receded. The light behind her eyelids faded. And she surrendered to a stillness so blissfully peaceful she smiled.

❖

Debbie stared at CNN. Breaking news. There had been an assassination attempt on the vice president's life in Denver where he was at a fund-raising dinner for Marilyn Musgrave. Just looking at the screen, it was hard to tell what was going on, except that he'd survived. Thank God for that, Debbie thought.

The reporter was standing on the street with lights flashing all around him. Protestors with placards were milling round noisily. He described how the Secret Service had to chase the shooter across rooftops before

They switched to Wolf Blitzer in the Situation Room and he announced the story all over again. Her cell phone rang and Debbie snatched it up, expecting another update from Lone about the movers and the cats. She still couldn't believe Lone had just deposited her by the lake and left almost immediately, promising to return in a few days.

"Debbie?"

"Jude, did you get my message?"

"No, I lost my cell phone." Jude sounded tightly wound.

"Is everything okay?" Debbie asked.

"Are you watching TV?"

"Yes, isn't it terrible?"

Jude was quiet for a long time, then she said, "Debbie, I'm sorry to have to tell you this. There's been a serious incident involving Lone."

Debbie sat very still, her blood pumping like ice in her veins. "Is she all right?"

"No." Jude was having trouble speaking. "I'm so sorry. She's dead."

Debbie got up. She dropped the phone and staggered to the bathroom, cold sweat running off her face and down her back. She threw up into the toilet, then sat down on the cold tile floor, shaking violently. She had no idea how long she stayed there. When she crawled back into the living room on her hands and knees and picked up the phone, Jude had hung up and a text message was waiting.

It read *You're not alone. Come back to Paradox.*

CHAPTER TWENTY

W hat are you doing here?" Jude asked.

Mercy's expression was one Jude couldn't remember seeing before, a mixture of naked desire, tender amusement, and sadness so profound it silenced her.

"I've been waiting for you. I heard about your hairdresser's girlfriend."

Jude's head pounded. Words floated just out of reach, tantalizing her with their potential. If she could just summon the right sentence, she would be completely in control. Staunch. Stoic in her sense of duty. Untroubled by doubt.

"Invite me in," Mercy said.

Jude released her hold on the door and marveled that she could stand upright without its support. She stepped to one side. Mercy walked past her, smelling of damp mountain air and beautiful skin.

"Where's Elspeth?" Jude asked.

"Don't." Mercy slid her jacket off and dropped it over the back of a chair. "Pour me a Scotch, Jude."

"You could have just left me a note." Jude took two glasses from the sideboard and poured a shot of Talisker and a dash of water into each.

"A note. Yes, very appropriate," Mercy said with cool irony.

Jude tapped their glasses. "Here's looking at you."

They both drank. Mercy sat down at one end of the sofa and crossed her long slender legs. She was dressed for work in a plain coffee-colored shirt and dark brown tailored pants.

"Did you come straight from the office?" Jude asked inanely, like this was just another day and they were going to chat politely for a few minutes, then Mercy would leave.

"When I heard the name announced, I had a feeling you might need me.."

Jude finished her drink and set the glass down on the sideboard. "Thanks for coming." She pretended to be preoccupied, putting the bottle away. "I don't want to seem rude, but I'd rather be alone."

"Liar," Mercy said softly.

"Let me rephrase. I'd rather not be with a married woman."

Mercy placed her glass on the coffee table on front of the sofa and said, "What if it was over?"

"You looked very married the last time I saw you."

"Appearances can be deceptive. We both know that."

Too drained to stay standing, Jude sank down at the other end of the sofa. "I don't have the energy for this. Please, just go."

Mercy removed the bobby pins from her hair and shook it out of its tight chignon. She sagged back against the deep cushions, eyes closed. "Here's what I'm thinking. When Elspeth gets back from Poland, I'll tell her things have to change."

"She's in Poland?" The pieces fell into place.

"They needed to capture the pathos of an Eastern European village for her new film, but they didn't want to be too far from a decent hotel."

Jude propped her head in her hands. "Pathos? I could show her pathos, right here in Colorado." Her shoulders shook. She started laughing and couldn't stop. "What do you think? Too real?"

"Jude." Mercy reached out, then let her hand fall.

Jude gazed down at the curl of her fingers, the soft hollow of her palm. Anger dragged at her heart like an anchor.

"Is that what you saw in her?" she demanded. "The safety of illusion? Is that what you need—an exile from death and ugliness?"

Jude could almost understand. Like her, Mercy needed to escape. For a while they'd escaped together, into one another. But Jude had always wanted something more real. Was that why Mercy rejected her?

Jude lifted her gaze at the sound of a strangled breath.

"Stop." Tears shimmered in Mercy's eyes. "You win, okay?"

"It's not a competition." Jude stood up. She didn't know what to do with herself. Pacing to the window, she said, "You really hurt me."

"I know." Mercy got up and joined her.

They stared out into the black oblivion for a while.

"I wish it was snowing," Jude said.

"Yes. Everything is new. Starting over clean." Mercy slipped her hand into Jude's. "I'm sorry." She drew closer, insistently lifting Jude's hand to the home between her gossamer breasts. "I love you."

She seemed vulnerable. Younger. Her eyes were bright with emotion. Her mouth parted and the wet pink line beyond her faded lipstick emerged just enough to draw Jude closer.

"I love you, too," Jude murmured. Their lips brushed with each word.

Mercy's heart accelerated beneath her hand. She said, "I missed you so much I thought I would die."

Jude slid her tongue delicately beneath Mercy's upper lip. As their mouths flirted, she said, "Stay with me."

"That's why I'm here."

Jude walked her backward across the living room and into the hallway, helplessly kissing her. Tugging at her clothes. Aching for her with a burning, gut-wrenching hunger like nothing she'd ever known. A wild creature strained inside her, the darker self Mercy had always invited.

As they stumbled toward the bedroom, they knocked over the file box she'd brought home from headquarters, spilling Fabian Maulle's secrets all over the floor. Jude kicked the papers aside and carried Mercy the rest of the way. When she banged into the side of the bed, she dropped Mercy down onto the mattress and fumbled messily with her clothes, pushing her hands away when she tried to help. It wasn't right to destroy a perfectly good shirt, but Jude ripped it open and pulled it away. The bra came with it. Jude dropped them on the floor.

"Leave her," she said as she unzipped Mercy's trousers and dragged them off, along with her panties. "She can't touch you ever again."

Mercy caught Jude's face between her hands. Sweetly, she insisted, "No rules."

A fiery thrill ran from Jude's mouth to her groin. She knew that tone. "You don't make the rules anymore," she said, stepping back to remove her T-shirt.

With shaking hands, she unfastened her belt and jeans. The room was very dark.

When she reached for the light, Mercy said, "No. I don't want to see anything. I just want to feel you."

Which was perfect, Jude thought, because she wanted Mercy to feel her as she never had. She wanted to cradle Mercy's heart and soul, not just her body. A tiny doubt gnawed at her, and she cupped Mercy between the thighs and squeezed.

"Are you with me now?" she asked. "Only me."

"Yes." Mercy gasped.

"Tell me again."

"I'm with you. Only you."

Mercy opened to her, and Jude sank her fingers deep inside. They rolled onto their sides, facing each other, legs scissored. For a long while, they lay still, lost in a kiss. Then Mercy whispered in Jude's ear, "Make me come."

"I will," Jude promised.

"I love you," Mercy told her again.

"Okay, now I'll make you come."

❖

Hours later, as Mercy slept, Jude got tired of staring up at the ceiling wondering if she'd done the right thing. Mercy was *married* and Jude had steadfastly resisted her overtures for months. Now, in a moment of weakness, she'd broken the rule she made to protect her own heart. She desperately wanted to believe that Mercy meant what she said and her marriage was over, but she would believe it when she saw it.

Jude slipped out of bed, pausing for a moment to stare at the woman she'd made love with all night. Her heart quaked in her chest. What if Mercy left her again? She couldn't stand to think about that possiblity.

Silently, she closed the door behind her and started along the hallway. She promptly fell over the file box. She shuddered as her bare feet connected with the contents. The thought of these photos and notebooks in her house, especially now, made her flesh crawl. The sooner she dispatched the evidence to the FBI, the better. Distracted, she hadn't done her job. In the half-light of dawn, she gathered up every item and created stacks on the dining table. As she arranged the photographs according to size, something puzzled her and she turned on the light in her dining area so she could see more clearly.

In successive photographs one boy after the next sat on the same bed, in the same pose, in the same room, with the same vapid yellow décor. The back of each photograph bore a year and a classification number that linked the set together.

Jude lifted a different set from another envelope and found photographs once again taken in the same setting, this time a room with different features from the yellow one. Once more, boys of similar appearance were grouped together. Each envelope had an index of the contents on its front. The name Yitzhak Eshkol jumped out from one envelope.

Jude hastily tipped its contents onto the table and found several photographs of boys with dark hair. Among these was Yitzhak. His wrists were bound in front of him and he sat on a bed wearing only his briefs. Jude thought about the inscription he'd written to Fabian in *Pippa Passes*. "For saving my life." Were those the words of a grown man to a pedophile who'd abused him as a boy?

She turned Yitzhak's photo over and stared at the date. 1982. A cold fist gripped her gut and her body was instantly clammy. She sat down at the table, her breathing shallow. Frantically, she worked her way though the envelopes, fishing out the photos for 1982. Four bundles, around forty pictures. It was crazy to think she would find anything, but she looked anyway, at one face after the next. She felt physically ill as she struck a sequence of blond boys.

Her heart pounded. Yitzhak was in Maulle's files and he was still alive. She put the photos down, afraid of what she wouldn't find. She'd been down so many dead ends she expected nothing else, yet she still hoped.

Her mind was playing tricks on her, she thought, as one photo called her attention from the rest. Jude turned on extra lights and held the image up to the glare, doubting everything. Her eyes. Her memory. Her sanity. A fair, slightly built boy gazed out at her through time, beckoning her from the darkness and silence at the edges of her nightmares. For twenty-five years she had waited for this moment.

Jude burst into tears.

Ben.

Author's Note

Like any work of fiction set against a backdrop of real political events, *Place of Exile* names real people and mixes fictional events with real ones. To serve the timeline of the novel, I've occasionally taken license with the timing of a real event, such as the anti-war protest at Jackson Hole. That event takes place in my text a week later than it did in real life. A real Marilyn Musgrave fund-raiser in which Dick Cheney's motorcade was disrupted by protestors occurred in 2004; the similar event depicted in the novel is entirely fictional.

We live in a time when fear and paranoia play an increasing role in the national psyche, and moral dilemmas abound over where lines should be drawn between individual liberties and privacy versus the collective interests of society. To a small extent this terrain is explored in *Place of Exile*. Moral ambiguities offer authors interesting opportunities for plot and character, while simplistic black-and-white portrayals of heroes and villains can be less intriguing to write (and, possibly, to read). I hope readers will indulge my forays into the gray areas.

A subplot in this novel involves a fictional assassination attempt on the vice president. This subplot forms part of a broader theme of the work, that of the threat faced when extreme views give rise to acts of violence. This theme also finds reflection in a fictional bio-attack plot against the Telluride Film Festival. It should go without saying that the inclusion of such content per se is not an endorsement of the actions of the fictional characters depicted; neither should the opinions of these characters be mistaken for the author's personal views.

As always, I write to entertain and I make the assumption that I'm writing for intelligent readers who know they are reading a work of fiction. I hope you enjoy my latest effort.

About the Author

New Zealand born, Jennifer Fulton resides out West with her partner and daughter and a menagerie of animals. Her vice of choice is writing; however, she is also devoted to her wonderful daughter, Sophie, and her hobbies—fly fishing, cinema, and fine cooking.

Jennifer started writing stories almost as soon as she could read them, and never stopped. Under pen names Grace Lennox, Jennifer Fulton, and Rose Beecham, she has published seventeen novels and a handful of short stories. She received a 2006 Alice B. award for her body of work and is a multiple GCLS "Goldie" Award recipient and Lambda Literary Award finalist.

When she is not writing or reading, she loves to explore the mountains and prairies near her home, a landscape eternally and wonderfully foreign to her.

Rose can be contacted at: jennifer@jenniferfulton.com

Books Available From Bold Strokes Books

Place of Exile by Rose Beecham. Sheriff's detective Jude Devine struggles with ghosts of her past and an ex-lover who still haunts her dreams. (978-1-933110-98-1)

Fully Involved by Erin Dutton. A love that has smoldered for years ignites when two women and one little boy come together in the aftermath of tragedy. (978-1-933110-99-8)

Heart 2 Heart by Julie Cannon. Suffering from a devastating personal loss, Kyle Bain meets Lane Connor, and the chance for happiness suddenly seems possible. (978-1-60282-000-5)

Queens of Tristaine by Cate Culpepper. When a deadly plague stalks the Amazons of Tristaine, two warrior lovers must return to the place of their nightmares to find a cure. (978-1-933110-97-4)

The Crown of Valencia by Catherine Friend. Ex-lovers can really mess up your life…even, as Kate discovers, if they've traveled back to the eleventh century! (978-1-933110-96-7)

Mine by Georgia Beers. What happens when you've already given your heart and love finds you again? Courtney McAllister is about to find out. (978-1-933110-95-0)

House of Clouds by KI Thompson. A sweeping saga of an impassioned romance between a Northern spy and a Southern sympathizer, set amidst the upheaval of a nation under siege. (978-1-933110-94-3)

Winds of Fortune by Radclyffe. Provincetown local Deo Camara agrees to rehab Dr. Bonita Burgoyne's historic home, but she never said anything about mending her heart. (978-1-933110-93-6)

Focus of Desire by Kim Baldwin. Isabel Sterling is surprised when she wins a photography contest, but no more than photographer Natasha Kashnikova. Their promo tour becomes a ticket to romance. (978-1-933110-92-9)

Blind Leap by Diane and Jacob Anderson-Minshall. A Golden Gate Bridge suicide becomes suspect when a filmmaker's camera shows a different story. Yoshi Yakamota and the Blind Eye Detective Agency uncover evidence that could be worth killing for. (978-1-933110-91-2)

Wall of Silence, 2nd ed. by Gabrielle Goldsby. Life takes a dangerous turn when jaded police detective Foster Everett meets Riley Medeiros, a woman who isn't afraid to discover the truth no matter the cost. (978-1-933110-90-5)

Mistress of the Runes by Andrews & Austin. Passion ignites between two women with ties to ancient secrets, contemporary mysteries, and a shared quest for the meaning of life. (978-1-933110-89-9)

Sheridan's Fate by Gun Brooke. A dynamic, erotic romance between physiotherapist Lark Mitchell and businesswoman Sheridan Ward set in the scorching hot days and humid, steamy nights of San Antonio. (978-1-933110-88-2)

Vulture's Kiss by Justine Saracen. Archeologist Valerie Foret, heir to a terrifying task, returns in a powerful desert adventure set in Egypt and Jerusalem. (978-1-933110-87-5)

Rising Storm by JLee Meyer. The sequel to *First Instinct* takes our heroines on a dangerous journey instead of the honeymoon they'd planned. (978-1-933110-86-8)

Not Single Enough by Grace Lennox. A funny, sexy modern romance about two lonely women who bond over the unexpected and fall in love along the way. (978-1-933110-85-1)

Such a Pretty Face by Gabrielle Goldsby. A sexy, sometimes humorous, sometimes biting contemporary romance that gently exposes the damage to heart and soul when we fail to look beneath the surface for what truly matters. (978-1-933110-84-4)

Second Season by Ali Vali. A romance set in New Orleans amidst betrayal, Hurricane Katrina, and the new beginnings hardship and heartbreak sometimes make possible. (978-1-933110-83-7)

Hearts Aflame by Ronica Black. A poignant, erotic romance between a hard-driving businesswoman and a solitary vet. Packed with adventure and set in the harsh beauty of the Arizona countryside. (978-1-933110-82-0)

Red Light by JD Glass. Tori forges her path as an EMT in the New York City 911 system while discovering what matters most to herself and the woman she loves. (978-1-933110-81-3)

Honor Under Siege by Radclyffe. Secret Service agent Cameron Roberts struggles to protect her lover while searching for a traitor who just may be another woman with a claim on her heart. (978-1-933110-80-6)

Dark Valentine by Jennifer Fulton. Danger and desire fuel a high-stakes cat-and-mouse game when an attorney and an endangered witness team up to thwart a killer. (978-1-933110-79-0)

Sequestered Hearts by Erin Dutton. A popular artist suddenly goes into seclusion, a reluctant reporter wants to know why, and a heart locked away yearns to be set free. (978-1-933110-78-3)

Erotic Interludes 5: Road Games, ed. by Radclyffe and Stacia Seaman. Adventure, "sport," and sex on the road—hot stories of travel adventures and games of seduction. (978-1-933110-77-6)

The Spanish Pearl by Catherine Friend. On a trip to Spain, Kate Vincent is accidentally transported back in time—an epic saga spiced with humor, lust, and danger. (978-1-933110-76-9)

Lady Knight by L-J Baker. Loyalty and honor clash with love and ambition in a medieval world of magic when female knight Riannon meets Lady Eleanor. (978-1-933110-75-2)

Dark Dreamer by Jennifer Fulton. Best-selling horror author Rowe Devlin falls under the spell of psychic Phoebe Temple. A Dark Vista romance. (978-1-933110-74-5)

Come and Get Me by Julie Cannon. Elliott Foster isn't used to pursuing women, but alluring attorney Lauren Collier makes her change her mind. (978-1-933110-73-8)

Blind Curves by Diane and Jacob Anderson-Minshall. Private eye Yoshi Yakamota comes to the aid of her ex-lover Velvet Erickson in the first Blind Eye mystery. (978-1-933110-72-1)

Dynasty of Rogues by Jane Fletcher. It's hate at first sight for Ranger Riki Sadiq and her new patrol corporal, Tanya Coppelli—except for their undeniable attraction. (978-1-933110-71-4)

Running With the Wind by Nell Stark. Sailing instructor Corrie Marsten has signed off on love until she meets Quinn Davies—one woman she can't ignore. (978-1-933110-70-7)

More Than Paradise by Jennifer Fulton. Two women battle danger, risk all, and find in each other an unexpected ally and an unforgettable love. (978-1-933110-69-1)

Flight Risk by Kim Baldwin. For Blayne Keller, being in the wrong place at the wrong time just might turn out to be the best thing that ever happened to her. (978-1-933110-68-4)

Rebel's Quest: Supreme Constellations Book Two by Gun Brooke. On a world torn by war, two women discover a love that defies all boundaries. (978-1-933110-67-7)

Punk and Zen by JD Glass. Angst, sex, love, rock. Trace, Candace, Francesca…Samantha. Losing control—and finding the truth within. BSB Victory Editions. (1-933110-66-X)

When Dreams Tremble by Radclyffe. Two women whose lives turned out far differently than they'd once imagined discover that sometimes the shape of the future can only be found in the past. (1-933110-64-3)

Stellium in Scorpio by Andrews & Austin. The passionate reunion of two powerful women on the glitzy Las Vegas Strip, where everything is an illusion and love is a gamble. (1-933110-65-1)